PRAISE FOR
THE SUMMER KNOWS

"*The Summer Knows* is a delightful and exhilarating novel that will remind you of why you started reading in the first place—to be enchanted, to be carried away from your world and dropped into a world more vivid and redemptive than the one you're living in. Sarah E. Pearsall knows that every story is many stories, and one of those stories is 'You can go home again.' She writes with intelligence, grace, and tenderness. She breathes life into Adrienne, Kali, and Quinn, and they will breathe life into you."

—JOHN DUFRESNE, author of *My Darling Boy*

"As sensual as the touch of a beach breeze, *The Summer Knows* immerses readers in the sights, sounds, and scents of a summer at the shore. Heroine Adrienne takes us with her as she fishes, cooks, and falls in love with the rich boy next door. All the emotions are here: the headiness of first love, the invincibility of youth, the burn of salt water and rejection. Author Sarah E. Pearsall hits a home run with her debut, crafting a novel that is perfect for fans of Elin Hilderbrand and the *Gilmore Girls*."

—JAMI DENISON, reviewer, *Chick Lit Central*

"*The Summer Knows* is a masterful exploration of memory, identity, and the ties that bind us to people and places, even when we try to outrun them. Yet for all its nostalgia and melancholy, *The Summer Knows* is ultimately a story about healing and hope. A beautifully written, emotionally resonant novel that lingers long after the last page. Sarah E. Pearsall is a storyteller of rare depth and compassion."

—LAURA MCDERMOTT, author of *Visions on Alligator Alley*

"*The Summer Knows* is a tour de force of a novel. In Sarah Pearsall's expertly created world of the imagination, the reader is drawn into a haunting story that is both captivating and believable. She weaves memories flawlessly into the story of a single mother at a crossroads who must confront a painful past. This is the quintessential beach read and will have you sitting at the edge of your beach towel, turning pages furiously to get to the next chapter. I highly recommend this book."

—**JAN BECKER**, author of *The Sunshine Chronicles*

"*The Summer Knows* by Sarah E. Pearsall immerses you in a thoughtfully crafted world, where haunting and romantic past stories collide with the current grim reality for lead character Adrienne Harris. The novel is a true page-turner that makes you want to just give up on all other activities and read the whole thing cover to cover. A delightful read."

—**KRISTA MARTINELLI**, founder and editor of AroundWellington.com, the online publication for good news!

"Sarah E. Pearsall's debut novel dives deeply into the sometimes desperate need for redemption, self-discovery, forgiveness, and place. Alternating between intensity, deep reflection, and tenderness, *The Summer Knows* shares the complexities of family, community, and the pasts we all possess but occasionally seek to ignore. There's a commonality in this, a mosaic of the inevitable tension between the present, the past, and the potential to reauthor what might lie ahead. This is a splendid read, and one that promises the beginning of a literary journey by an author worth following."

—**GREG FIELDS**, author of *The Bright Freight of Memory*, American Writing Award–winner for Literary Fiction

THE SUMMMER KNOWS

The Summer Knows
by Sarah E. Pearsall

© Copyright 2025 Sarah E. Pearsall

ISBN 979-8-88824-745-7

All rights reserved. No part of this publication may be reproduced, stored in a retrieval system, or transmitted in any form or by any means—electronic, mechanical, photocopy, recording, or any other—except for brief quotations in printed reviews, without the prior written permission of the author.

This is a work of fiction. All the characters in this book are fictitious, and any resemblance to actual persons, living or dead, is purely coincidental. The names, incidents, dialogue, and opinions expressed are products of the author's imagination and are not to be construed as real.

Cover art and design by Lauren Sheldon

Published by
◤ köehlerbooks™

3705 Shore Drive
Virginia Beach, VA 23455
800-435-4811
www.koehlerbooks.com

THE SUMMER KNOWS

SARAH E. PEARSALL

VIRGINIA BEACH
CAPE CHARLES

For Mike and Randy. If we are never sure of anything else, know this to be true: In the kingdom of childhood, where summer is eternal, love never dies.
That is where we live.

CHAPTER ONE

The tips of Adrienne Harris's fingers got cold and tingly whenever trouble was coming. She was like a finely tuned divining fork, often sniffing out impending hurricanes before the TV meteorologist. But it wasn't a storm brewing when the winds shifted and the birds fell silent on the walk to her evening shift at the Clam Bucket. No, this was different.

Adrienne's stomach churned as she donned her white apron. And it wasn't just her. The line cooks and dishwashers engaged in hushed conversations, exchanging glances between the sinks and stoves. Nonetheless, Adrienne tried to focus on her hands as they deftly transformed rubbery lobsters and overcooked shrimp into something palatable for the babbling tourists in the dining room.

"Get to work," Adrienne barked. Her crew sprang into action, filling the tiny kitchen with movement.

The owner stepped into the midst of this activity, the harsh light casting deep shadows into the creases of his weathered face. His hands, pristine, dangled limply at his sides. Adrienne set down her pan and regarded her boss with narrow eyes.

"Are you really going to drop this bombshell on us when we have customers to feed?" Her words sliced through the kitchen noise, and her crew froze.

At first, the owner scrunched his brow into quizzical slants. But he seemed to realize Adrienne could see through his facade and let his face go lax.

"Regrettably, I've decided to close the Clam Bucket. I apologize for surprising all of you, but we've run out of money. Rest assured, you will get your final check," he announced, his hands lifted as if being held at gunpoint, before hastily retreating through the double doors.

One glance through the doors as they flapped shut revealed the sea of empty tables and the place settings spread thinly throughout the cavernous dining room. A pall settled over the few patrons like a stagnate summer day.

"Coward," Adrienne muttered, flipping a piece of cod in her pan.

Around her, the clatter of pots and pans resumed as the line cooks and dishwashers plunged back into their work.

"Boss, what you going to do?" Patrice, Adrienne's sous chef, whispered as they stood on the line. "A bunch of us are heading up north for the summer tomorrow. Come with us. You can make good money. There's always a spot. We can come back next winter, and there will be something new. There's always something new."

"It's not that easy for me. I got my kid." Adrienne wiped the sweat from her forehead with the back of her hand. "I don't have time to think about this right now." She nodded toward the ticket machine spewing out the early-bird specials. "And it's not like I haven't been through this before."

"Ever noticed how the new joints have a sparkle? Attracting tourists like bees to honey." Patrice's face hardened, his voice dropping to a murmur. "But as the glitter fades, so do the people. And we keep moving. Nothing else to do for us. But you don't belong here, boss. We are here because we got no choice. But this place, this life ain't for you. You are better than chewy lobster and dried-up shrimp."

He sucked on his teeth as he shook the fryer basket loaded with golden squid nuggets.

Adrienne's spatula clattered to the counter, her hand reaching out to rest on Patrice's shoulder, their silent agreement cutting through the chaos of the kitchen. "You're better than this too."

"Cha!" Patrice grunted and gestured at Adrienne's pan. "Your sauce is going to burn."

EMERGING FROM THE restaurant, Adrienne was surrounded by searing heat and the scent of low tide tinged with the promise of decay. She tried to ignore her queasiness as she headed home. Her skin prickled, sweat sliding down her back in rivulets. Each breath was like inhaling embers.

In Seaside, summer had brought hardship to them all. Streets that once bustled with tourists and playful children now lay deserted. Adrienne gazed too at the empty beach. Some lovers, dreamers, and a few homeless people enjoyed the midnight hour with a water view in the moonlight. She was tempted to take a night swim but resisted and headed home along Main Street, to her daughter.

The empty windows in the shopping quarter's former tourist traps and cafés further reflected the summer's grim reality. Three blocks later, she turned onto Palm Way, lined with small bungalows hastily constructed during the last boom. The large shore house sectioned into three small apartments, loomed at the end of the street. Home.

Unbuttoning her greasy chef's jacket, Adrienne let down her long, sweaty tangle of dark curls and huffed up the three flights of stairs to the top floor. She recited her evening mantra as she climbed: *The higher I go, the cheaper the rent.*

She quietly slipped into the dark apartment to avoid waking her daughter, Kali, and placed a brown bag of leftovers from the restaurant on the counter. Shedding her work clothes, Adrienne left them on the cramped living room floor. She grabbed a beer from the fridge.

The climb to the crow's nest made her knees ache, but she was rewarded with a spectacular view of the Gulf. Over the rooftops, the water loomed dark and pulsing as she drank a beer, clad in only a flimsy tank top and underwear. The knotted muscles in her shoulders started to ease. Yet an element of tension remained, humming beneath her skin like an insistent bee.

A lump formed in her throat. The impending gloom, the weight of poverty—Patrice's words rang in her head. A tear collected at the crook of her eye, almost too timid to slink down her cheek.

She examined her life as it was. A spinning top always teetering on the edge, always making do. *Is this it?* she pondered. *Is my life like that dead-end street down there?*

Her grandfather's old fish market came to mind. The heady aroma of the stock they made from the bones of their fresh catch lingered like a dreamy sea haze over the simmering pot of her memory. Gramps was there, standing on the porch and singing to the crabs in the live wells.

No. She let out a bitter laugh, pushing the images aside. *Why didn't I bring another beer up to the roof?*

Kali might find her passed out in the crow's nest in the morning. But that humiliating fate did nothing to stop Adrienne from returning to the apartment for the rest of the six-pack.

I'll have to chase down my mother and ask for more money.

The thought rose like bile in her throat.

Adrienne's cell rang just as she stepped back outside with the six-pack, the trill making her jump. An unknown number flashed on display. *Who calls at one in the morning on a weeknight? Only someone with bad news, that's who.* The "561" area code began to register.

The end of the world.

Her stomach twisted as if a dark abyss had yawned open beneath her, the pull of its gravity insistent and hungry.

Don't answer.

"Adrienne?"

She wanted to hang up as soon as that familiar British accent floated through the speaker.

"Christopher?" she whispered into the phone. Though she was

outside, the old house walls were thin, and the last thing she wanted was to disturb her daughter's sleep.

"Yes." A sigh, a pause to gather air. "I wasn't sure if you'd know who I was. It's been a long time."

The strange premonitions that had plagued her all night, the unease, now made sense. *Was the universe warming me up for this call?* A shiver rippled through her.

"I'm psychic," she quipped.

"Uh, okay," Christopher replied, his tone telling her that the joke had missed its mark.

"Is she dead?" Adrienne's tone hardened as she pressed back against the wall and sank to the wood planks of the landing.

"No." He paused again, then let out a long sigh, something he did when trying to find the right words, his voice a perfect time machine.

Come home, Adrienne, a familiar tug in her gut told her. Words fixed in the stars since the day she ran away. Words waiting for her to let her guard down and invite them in. She wished she hadn't answered the call. She wished she could find the resolve to throw the phone over the rail. Her gaze strayed to the six-pack left unfinished, its call drowned out by the pull of Christopher's voice, irresistible.

Her skin went clammy with sweat as she closed her eyes and tried to slow her heartbeat.

"Adrienne, you need to come home," he finally said. Each of his words sounded weighed, rehearsed. They'd likely been turning in his mind for at least a day.

"Christopher, there is no way in hell I am stepping foot in that town," Adrienne said through gritted teeth. Heat flared, her hands trembling at his audacity. *Doesn't he know better?*

"The kitchen, it's in ruins. She left a bloody tea towel unattended on the stove. Firefighters got there fast, but the damage . . . She's . . . she's shaken, Adrienne."

"Gran does not get *shaken*, Christopher. Why are you calling me? It sounds like everything can be taken care of without me."

"Elizabeth cannot live alone any longer. She may burn the whole place down next time. At eighty-five, is living on her own the best option?"

"She will outlive us all." She used the tone she wielded in the steam-filled chaos of the kitchen, commanding line cooks and sending out plates of food under pressure. Christopher might as well have asked her to march into the pits of hell.

"I'm not asking you to stay forever," he added cautiously. "But I'm not family. There is only so much I can do to help her."

Adrienne laughed, cold and sarcastically. "I am the last person in this world she wants help from, Christopher, family or not."

"You are the only person, Adrienne. You know your mother will never come. I wouldn't know how to contact her. Do you even know?" His words shot out in clipped, sharp fragments, reminding her of a parent scolding a child. "Besides, she asked for you to come."

He'd never spoken to her that way before, not in all the years they had worked side by side, though she had deserved his anger and frustration on many occasions. But Christopher asked for the moon, and she didn't have the moon to give. Harbor Point was a wound, gaping and raw, that she would spend an eternity fruitlessly stitching closed. Her grandmother summoning her was the last thing she thought could happen.

"God, Christopher, why are you doing this to me?" Adrienne's voice hitched in a whine she hadn't heard since childhood.

"I had no choice. I'm sorry."

A rustle at the other end of the line, a scratchy sound like fabric against a microphone, then his voice returned.

"If it helps, the Merritts are gone. I heard that Bob died about five years ago. Heart attack while scuba diving off the Dry Tortugas. But I don't think anyone has been in the house since . . . you left." Christopher cleared his throat. "It's up for auction next month."

The mention of the Merritts conjured up a new ache.

"Nothing helps, Christopher."

WITH A PROMISE to consider Christopher's plea, Adrienne slid her phone across the deck as if it were tainted. Once she found the will, she returned to her perch on the roof. The sea undulated in black currents.

Christopher's call was a hand reshaping her life, twisting it. She could never return to the blissful ignorance of Seaside now, mundane and weary though it had been. The past demanded acknowledgment. *Pandora must be laughing now.*

It seemed fitting that the Fates would call her home on the cusp of summer. Adrienne's whole life could be mapped out in summers. As a girl, she held her breath between September and June, waiting for Quinn to return.

"Quinn." His name came out rusty and laced with bittersweet longing.

She shuddered and clutched the weathered railing, then trudged down the steps to her apartment. She cracked the bedroom door to check on her daughter, hoping to slip into the bed and bury her face in the delicate strands of Kali's hair.

But at two in the morning, Kali's bed was ominously empty. Adrienne's mind struggled to reconcile an absent child with the image of the obedient daughter who always returned home after school. She went to find her phone, cursing in the dark apartment, remembering she left it on the landing. Retrieving the contraption, she dialed Kali's number.

Adrienne pinched the bridge of her nose, her breath escaping in a frustrated huff.

Of all nights . . .

Kali's disgruntled voice slunk through the earpiece. "Don't freak. I'm almost home."

The line went dead. She was safe.

There was a cold shift. Their relationship, their story, seemed dark with uncertainty. Adrienne had played out this scenario in her head for years, always with a tinge of inevitability, despite her faint hope that they might be the exception—that Kali might glide through her teen years unscathed.

Adrienne straightened, her mind bracing for the battles ahead.

Christopher's words taunted. *Come home, Adrienne.*

The tide was heading out on the Gulf. The waters churned restlessly.

CHAPTER TWO

It's just a terrible dream. Adrienne blinked hard at the unfamiliar landscape.

Two weeks after Christopher's call, she and Kali sailed by the Harbor Point welcome sign in their old Chevy Malibu. Adrienne's great-grandfather had helped build the massive shell-and-coral landmark when Harbor Point was an enormous pineapple plantation owned by a Civil War general. Many gravitated to the area after the abolition of slavery, seeking paid work tilling the fields. Robert himself crossed the ocean from Hungary, the American dream whispering promises in his ear, and that dream left his pockets heavy with wealth, the source of which Adrienne could only speculate about. Even more mysterious was how he had lost it all.

The ghost of Adrienne's seventeen-year-old self recoiled in confusion at her changed surroundings. The old false-front stores were extinct, replaced by newer stucco strips of small shops along A1A. All that remained of Twyla Pushcart's Flower Heaven, with its tropical plant mural, was an empty lot guarded by a chain-link fence, a ragged chunk of painted concrete jutting up from the middle like a page torn from a child's coloring book. The Sunshine Self-Serve car wash, where Adrienne had spent hours each week helping the locals wash their boats, was now a tiny Audi dealership. The shiny, expensive cars glistened in the June heat. The few people out on the sidewalks were well dressed and wearing designer sunglasses. She passed by two women in Lilly Pulitzer capris and walking dogs the size of giant rats, each animal wearing a rhinestone-crusted fuchsia collar.

Where is the button to change the channel? To rewind? But there was no going back. All Adrienne could do was ogle the landscape like a rubbernecker passing a gruesome wreck.

In the passenger seat, Kali's fingers danced on her phone screen. A grimace pulled at the corners of her mouth. Adrienne wished she could admit to Kali that she didn't want to be in Harbor Point either, but she had to be mature and stay the course. There was no other option. She rummaged through her purse, her fingers tracing over the lonely fifty-dollar bill. No map, no itinerary, just a destination.

We will regroup.

It will only be for the summer.

She would figure it all out by then. She had to. And then they would be on their way, somewhere far from Harbor Point.

The light ahead changed to red. Preoccupied with her town inspection, Adrienne had to slam on the brakes to avoid hitting the car in front of her.

"Mom," Kali said, her eyes glued to her phone and her voice dripping with disdain. "I'd like to live a little longer. You know, get to high school at least."

Adrienne shrugged. "I didn't see the light change." Undeterred by her near miss, she gazed out at two condo buildings towering about the mangrove swamp like alien monoliths, casting the car in shadow. The new complex wiped out a whole block of her childhood haunts in one fell swoop.

Next door, Two Tom's Marina was equally unrecognizable. Adrienne and her grandfather had spent their mornings at the marina, bringing in fresh-caught fish, shrimp, and crabs for their market. The fish scales would glitter like jewels in the sun. Now the weathered wooden docks were bleak concrete structures. The rows of shabby open fishermen's boats had been evicted by enormous sleek powerboats.

Adrienne sighed, pulling her hand through her hair. "You're going to like Gran's house. You can roll out of bed and fall into the ocean."

"We are never going home, are we?" Kali finally looked up from her phone with a defiant scowl. "You're doing this to me because I stayed out all night. You think you can finally be a mom by stashing me in this Podunk town, and you think I will be okay with it all."

"No, we are here because your great-grandmother is getting old and needs help. The house caught fire, and we must take care of it." Adrienne tucked her hands into her lap like a penitent child. The red light lingered stubbornly in the abandoned intersection.

"Admit you lied to me. Admit that part of why we're here is because of me." Kali's voice hitched in her throat, filled with emotions Adrienne could only guess at. "I didn't even know I had a great-grandmother until a few days ago."

"Okay." Adrienne put her hands back on the wheel. "It was a wake-up call. I know I've been a distracted parent."

Her daughter grunted, her face twisting into a mirthless smile.

Adrienne softened her tone, a wistful smile touching her lips. "I've done my best. And having a smart kid like you, it's something to be thankful for." She put a hand on Kali's knee, hot from the triangle of sun coming through the window. "We will regroup and make a plan while we're here. It's a place where we can figure out our next step. Maybe we'll head back to Seaside when work picks up in the fall. Let's take it one day at a time for now."

"Whatever." Kali turned away, her glare burning holes outside the car window as she withdrew her knee from her mother's touch. Thunder rumbled far out on the water. Adrienne gripped the steering wheel.

The light turned green. She darted through the intersection.

"There's the market." She pointed out the window. "I used to work there with Gramps. I used to cook in that kitchen."

"Yeah, great," Kali said automatically, back to punching the keys on her phone.

Adrienne's muscles relaxed at the sight of the market, its fresh coat of blue paint and cheerful awning standing as a bulwark against time's relentless march. She felt the tug of nostalgia, recalling how the older men used to swap fishing lore while the ladies bought their Friday-night fish.

Is Christopher there right now? Adrienne drove by, unsure what she would say to him. Though she was curious about his life over the past fourteen years, Gran awaited them.

As they neared South Road, Adrienne's heart pounded against her ribcage. Of course she knew where she was going, yet a small part of her disbelieved that she was going home—that she would be facing Elizabeth Harris, her grandmother.

Adrienne drove over the Back Bay bridge onto the lonely thumb of sand where Gran had lived her whole life. Jutting out into the Atlantic Ocean from the mainland, home teetered at the end of the world. She coasted to a stop and parked her old white Chevy at the end of Gran's driveway.

As she stepped out of the car, a profound silence hummed in her ears. Even the cicadas hushed for their arrival. The atmosphere was thick with humidity and salt. Kali joined her in the empty street.

A new estate had replaced the small cottage at the end of the road. A white stucco wall ran the length of South Road, stopping at Gran's property. Adrienne let out a rough chuckle, vividly remembering Gran's vehement objections to this wall years ago. She had lost the battle, and the beauty of the sea was now kept prisoner on the other side of the stark white barrier.

At the very end of the street stood the familiar black-and-white barricade with its two dim flashing yellow lights, like eyes. It protected the end of the road, letting you know not to go further.

Gran's cottage was the last original house on South Road. Adrienne saw only the tip of the rusted tin roof from the street. The dense mini tropical rainforest of plants Gran had cultivated over the decades cloaked the rest from sight. This fortress of foliage was Gran's answer to the stucco walls of her neighbors.

Adrienne's feet remained anchored as a silent war between longing and fear played out within her.

"Mom, this is dumb standing out here." Kali jabbed her elbow into her mother's side but kept her eyes on the phone screen.

"We're alone. No one is watching us." Adrienne spread her hands wide, the emptiness wrapping around her like a shroud.

"Whatever. I'm hot," Kali said.

A biting rejoinder perched on Adrienne's tongue, but her daughter had already moved off. Adrienne turned to find Kali in the field on the west side of the road, battling thigh-high grass as she headed for the row of mangroves cloaking the Back Bay.

"Kali, no!" Adrenaline rocketed through her. She ran to the edge of the road but stopped at the line of tall grass: her personal Rubicon that she couldn't bring herself to cross, her fears and regrets stacked high and impregnable. She averted her eyes from the thickets, bending her head toward her feet, not wanting to face the shadows the trees made.

"What?" Kali demanded.

"D-don't go in there. It's not safe," Adrienne said. Kali had halted midfield with a quizzical look. "The dock might be rotted. You could fall in."

Shoulders slumped, the girl reluctantly returned. Her compliance caught Adrienne off guard.

"Can we go now? I'm dying out here." Kali popped a big bubble of gum.

"Alright, but promise me you won't go in the mangroves or near the Back Bay. You could get hurt." Adrienne touched her shoulder. "Please promise me. I'm not kidding."

"God, Mom, I get it. You don't have to get all serious about it. I won't go there."

Biting words again hovered, but as Adrienne took in her daughter standing there, dark hair floating around her face from the wind of the coming storm, she froze. Kali had the same eyes as Lucas. They were clear, pale blue, nearly the color of the sea in the early-morning light. It was wrong for a child to have a dead man's eyes. Yet Lucas was always there, peering out.

If Adrienne were brave, she would have told Kali that Lucas had died beyond the mangroves, in the dark, moving waters of the Back Bay, steps from where they stood.

This was never supposed to happen. Kali was never supposed to be in Harbor Point.

"Thank you," Adrienne said, unsettled. She turned to the house and sighed. "Okay, let's do this."

"I'm not a scaredy-cat like you." Kali poked her in the shoulder, a cocky grin on her face. An ever-spinning wheel of teenage emotion, her sudden shifts were dizzying.

"You should be." Adrienne raised her brow, playing along, knowing this light mood was a fleeting thing.

Kali rolled her eyes and started for the house, disappearing under the natural arch formed by two pink oleanders. Now that the spell had been broken, Adrienne could do little but follow her.

They followed the narrow rock path through an untamed mosaic of fruit trees that grew into one another, their footsteps releasing the smells of rotting fruit and fallen flowers. There were grapefruit, lemon, tangerine, and key limes. Coconuts and ancient bits of seashells littered the terrain like tiny bones.

The house sat in a small clearing, defended by a thin line of overgrown grass. They climbed the steps to the shade of the porch. Two canvas paddle fans hanging from the beadboard ceiling rotated lazily, bringing no relief. Angry waves broke onshore behind the house.

A curious collection of old coffee cans and ceramic vases filled with sea glass and driftwood lined the railings. Clippings from various plants sat rooted in water-filled mason jars on the old wicker table by the front door. Mosquito larvae wiggled around the sheer, hairlike taproots. It was a mad botanist's laboratory. Gran seemed to be up to her old tricks, tinkering with her plants. When Adrienne tapped the glass, the larvae went into a frenzy.

"Knock already," Kali said, nudging her toward the door. "I've got to pee." She examined the congested landscape warily. "And it smells like dead bodies out here."

"Nice thought," Adrienne said. Her hand seemed to rise of its own accord to rap against the door, and she released the breath she'd been unconsciously holding.

The silence stretched out, every second punctuated by the distant rhythm of the waves.

Maybe she's dead?

The screech of the deadbolt put her concerns to rest. The door cracked open. Gran peeked out from the dark slit and made no move to open the door, as if waiting for a secret password.

"Well, it's about time you showed up." Her voice was a gravelly husk of its former self as it clawed past the mucus in her throat.

"Traffic was awful on Ninety-Five." Adrienne mustered as much cheerfulness as she could, her words coming out brighter than expected. Anything to keep Kali's spirits up.

"I thought maybe you were taking your time. Hoping I died and saved you some trouble, eh?"

"You'll outlive all of us," Adrienne said through a sickly-sweet smile.

"Wouldn't that be something, eh?" Gran said, a strange cough-laugh gusting from her mouth. "Maybe I'd finally get some peace."

Adrienne eyed the path of escape behind her. "No, Gran," she said.

A subtle change swept over Gran's face, and the grip on the door eased, letting it creak open. She wore an old pink terry cloth bathrobe covered in dark stains.

When did Gran last wash her clothes?

The great Elizabeth Harris had been a fiercely vain woman. She was seventy-three when Adrienne left town but didn't look a day over sixty—a young sixty to boot—with nary a wrinkle to be found and an impeccable, if eccentric, wardrobe. Now in her late eighties, time was catching up with her. She had never been a tall woman, but now she was a miniature figurine you might put on a bookcase. Her face was still smooth and hardly wrinkled, but it was worn. Haggard was a good word. And Gran's jet-black coif had been reduced to a gray, wispy halo.

The sight tugged a gasp from Adrienne. Gran had never gone more than six weeks without a dye job. Adrienne assumed that Gran would keep up the facade to her last breath, leaving the world with her "face on" and a fabulous "do."

"I told Christopher not to call you. I don't need any help, you know. I don't need anything. But I know you are out of work. So I said, okay, you can come and stay with your little girl."

"How did you know I don't have a job?" Adrienne said. She flipped on the switch in the hallway, and the old yellow damask wallpaper appeared. In the yellow glow, the two women stood, hands stiff by their sides.

Kali's eyes widened, the indignation evident as she scoffed, "I am *not* a little girl."

Gran sized Kali up in the narrow hallway. "You know nothing of this world. You are a child."

"Whatever." Kali rolled her eyes. The stubborn tilt of her chin mirrored Gran's. *Good Lord.*

The older woman raised her brow. "She seems to have inherited the Harris tongue."

Kali rolled her eyes once again. "Your house smells like old peanut butter."

"I guess I shouldn't be surprised you're a brat," Gran practically growled.

"How did you know I don't have a job?" Adrienne said again, this time with more agitation.

"I know what I need to know." She shrugged as if the information had simply fallen into her lap, like manna from above. Then she shuffled past the two younger women and went into the kitchen.

"This place is creepy," Kali said rather loudly from behind Adrienne as she poked at a spiderweb in the corner of the hall mirror.

"How did you stand it?"

Adrienne peeked into the study, where the heavy curtains were closed. The only light came from the kitchen window. Mildew, smoke, and mothballs permeated the humid air.

"It wasn't like this," she said.

"Ugh," her daughter groaned as she headed for the dark living room. "Where's my room?"

Adrienne eased into the kitchen, where Gran stood at the sink. Char marks darkened the cabinets around the warped, blackened range. Gran kept her back to them, her attention apparently absorbed by dirty dishes. They were on their own to settle in.

"I guess you'll sleep in my old room. It has a bathroom and gets good light in the mornings for painting. I'll take the guest room upstairs next to Gran." Adrienne took Kali's hand and led her into the darkness, flipping the switch on the wall and bringing the "great room" to life. Kali inspected the relics. The plank floor creaked under their weight. White sheets draped all the furniture except Gran's wingback chair and a small side table that held a reading lamp. A large bouquet of petrified flowers sat in a dry vase on the center table. Kali stopped at the back door and pulled the shutter open on the window. A fat shaft of light burst in, making a square of sunshine on the dark floor.

Maybe it won't rain after all.

"I swear someone's going to jump out and kill me," Kali said. "This house is full of ghosts."

Adrienne chuckled at the comment. "Gran hasn't had use for much of it in a long time. It's a lovely house; she can't keep it up anymore. We'll get the kitchen fixed and blow the cobwebs out." She put her hands on the sheet covering the couch and, with great flourish, pulled the linen off, producing a cloud of dust. "A little elbow grease, and it will be great."

Adrienne couldn't shake the feeling of sounding like a programmed Stepford wife.

"Yeah, right." Kali peered at her suspiciously as she batted dust clots from her face. "This place should be bulldozed."

Adrienne's old room was by the stairs at the other end of the great room. It was the only bedroom on the first floor, and Adrienne wondered what changes Gran might have made. She had to push hard on the old door to loosen wood swollen with seawater.

Inside, she found her answer. The room was a time capsule. The windows were closed, and the drapes were drawn as in the rest of the house, but her shirt still lay on the wood floor in the exact spot she had dropped it while packing her things years ago. A puka shell necklace hung on the knob of her headboard. A palm hat, once green and now brown, rested on the lampshade. Her bed was unmade, and the sheets were covered in the same pale-yellow daisies she had slept on for years. *Odd.* Adrienne thought Gran would have jumped at the chance to erase her from the house.

The photos and sketches around the dresser mirror's frame drew Kali in. A sharp phantom pain shot through Adrienne's arms as Kali reached for the photo of a lone boy, plucking it from between the frame and the glass.

She turned to Adrienne, holding the picture, her face full of speculation. "Who is this?"

Adrienne's heartbeat pounded in her ears as Kali inspected the image. Quinn stood shirtless, tan, and carefree in the photo under the summer sun, holding on to the outrigger of his father's boat. A summer's worth of sunny days had whitewashed streaks of light into his dark hair. Her breath grew rapid with a remembered exhilaration, as if standing on the brink of a world about to unfurl.

"Is it my father?"

Adrienne nodded, her throat tightening, a lump of unspoken words threatening to betray her.

"I wonder where he is now."

"I wish I knew." She avoided Kali's gaze.

"If you only knew his last name, I could look for him."

"Hindsight, you know." Adrienne fixed her line of sight out the bedroom window, the evasion second nature.

Of course she knew the boy's last name. Though years had passed, she recalled the placement of each freckle on his beautiful face. Quinn Merritt had lived right next door in the big white house. Adrienne flinched at the thought. Each lie she told was a ticking time bomb. Her only consolation was that the mansion was a tomb, and Quinn Merritt had been lost to time and space.

"I look like him." Kali brought the photo in closer for inspection.

"You do—so beautiful," Adrienne said, the room spinning slightly around her. Kali was the perfect mixture of the two brothers, Lucas and Quinn, bearing the unmistakable Merritt stamp: the same deep-set eyes and sharp jawline. Harbor Point's old-timers would take one look at Kali, and the rumors would stir and snake like tendrils of smoke through the town.

Kali sighed and tossed the photo on the dresser. "I wonder what he's like."

Adrienne bit her lip and followed Kali around the room for a few more minutes. "I'm going to take a shower," the teenager finally said with a finality that meant she wanted to be alone.

"I'll get you some towels."

Before leaving the room, Adrienne took Lucas's sketches, once cherished gifts, from the mirror. She folded them into a packet and stuffed them into her pocket. When Adrienne returned, the door was shut and locked. She put the clean towels on the floor and knocked hard.

She had long told herself that being close in age to her daughter was a good thing. It helped her understand Kali's moodiness and know when to leave her daughter alone. But the cold, hard truth had been unavoidable since the night Kali came home late. Each missed recital, each unread bedtime story added to the tally of Adrienne's neglect. A voice within screamed at her to spill the truth, to repair the rift.

Adrienne sighed and went to the kitchen. The draped furniture lurked like spectral figures in the semidarkness, the white sheets rippling as if reaching for her.

Gran sat at the long kitchen table Adrienne's grandfather had made from giant driftwood logs. Adrienne leaned against the doorjamb, words caught in her throat as Gran drank her steaming cup of coffee. The rich, acrid scent of the mixture pervaded the kitchen, causing a slight tickle in Adrienne's throat as she inhaled. Gran's father had concocted the rich black brew to resemble the drink he enjoyed as a young man in Hungary.

Adrienne reluctantly took the seat across from the old lady. Gran's eyes slid past her as if she were an apparition, fixing instead on the big picture window, the front yard jungle past the glass panes.

Besides the fire damage, the kitchen was untouched by time. The gold linoleum, the gold Formica countertops, the dark wood cabinets, and the avocado-green appliances formed a snapshot of the American home circa 1970. The poor avocado stove was toast from the fire. Adrienne would have to get it replaced so they wouldn't starve.

She removed her shoes under the table, feeling the grit that could never entirely be erased in a house by the ocean.

"We'll need a repairman," Adrienne murmured.

"Christopher has called a man," Gran said flippantly.

"Good." Adrienne took a deep breath and rubbed the painful spot between her eyebrows.

"There is no hiding it. That child is absolutely a Merritt. As soon as anyone in town sees her, they will put two and two together," Gran adjusted herself in her chair, smugly exposing Adrienne's fears. "Ah, but which brother is the question. Shame it's too late to make them pay. What's the use of having a child with a rich father when no one is left to make it worthwhile?"

"Despite what you think, I wasn't a whore." Underneath the table, Adrienne's hands twisted into knots. "She is Quinn's. There is zero doubt. And I never wanted anything from any of them. I never wanted their money."

"What a terrible mess." The shallow creases on Gran's forehead deepened. "That poor child—what a weight to bear."

"She doesn't know anything about it. I'd appreciate it if you kept it to yourself."

"So what does she think? Was she born out of thin air? And you bring her here and think she won't find out? I don't care that the Merritts disappeared. This town has a nasty habit of remembering. And if you forgot that, you are a more stupid girl than I thought." A scoff of a laugh followed. "Don't get any ideas about leaving her and running off. I'm too old to go through that again."

"Your track record raising kids isn't so good either."

"I gave you every opportunity, tried to make a respectable girl out of you. Those Merritts"—Gran brandished her fork, thrusting it toward the specter of the big white house beyond the window—"bewitched you. Always throwing around their money, showing off." The fork clattered onto the table, the echoes of her outburst fading as she slouched back in her chair, visibly drained.

"Well, I'm not here for a visit. I came to figure out what to do with you. We must make sure you have dependable care. You cannot live alone any longer." Adrienne retreated into the pitch Christopher had given her over the phone only two weeks before.

"I am fine. I don't need any help. I told Christopher the fire was a fluke. It could have happened to anyone. I didn't die, did I?"

Adrienne folded her arms across her chest. "Christopher said you asked me to come."

"Ah, he exaggerates."

"I think we should tour some retirement places. It will be like living at a resort for you. You can play bridge all day and not worry about a thing. It's too isolated out here on South Road. You never leave the house. You need Christopher to run errands for you. He tells me you never visit friends anymore. What if you fell and broke your hip? No one would know."

"I will die in this house." Gran's fist came down like a gavel, rattling the sugar bowl and jolting Adrienne. "My father built this house with his bare hands. He built this town, though no one seems to care anymore. This family never needed anyone. Even when my father died and left us penniless, stripped of our fortune, we Harris women rose to the challenge and survived. This house is the last testament to our history. I will never let you sell it."

Adrienne kneaded her temples. "Okay, we'll find someone to come in and help. An aide who can help with the cooking and cleaning."

But that alternative wasn't promising either. The mere thought of hunting for someone patient enough to endure Gran amplified Adrienne's brewing headache. Christopher was an outlier in his invulnerability to Gran's high-handed antics and oddities. While others retreated from her stubborn will and volatile temper, Christopher found an odd delight in Gran's idiosyncrasies.

"I don't need some stranger in my house stealing my jewels."

"You're not eating," Adrienne said as she got up from the table and inspected the food supply. "And as expected, there is hardly any food in the house." She opened and motioned into the refrigerator to highlight two rotten bananas and a jar of blue mayo, which she tossed into the trash before continuing her inspection. In the pantry she found a box of egg noodles with an actual spiderweb inside the cellophane. "The pantry is no better."

"Don't throw out good food." Gran hoisted herself from her chair, a scowl etching lines on her face, when Adrienne dropped the noodles on top of the bananas and mayo. "Those noodles haven't even been opened yet."

"They're bad, Gran." Adrienne shook her head. "You can't eat food like this. It will make you sick. What have you been feeding yourself? Toast? Coffee? That's no way to live." She returned to the pantry.

"I'm not Ava Gabor." Gran's hands rested defiantly on her hips. "When your mother abandoned her duty, I drained my last cent raising you."

"We'll go talk to your financial planner and work it out. People do this every day. It's a natural progression many people go through as they age."

Adrienne emerged with two cans of tomato soup, the only safe choice she could find to feed Kali for dinner. Finding Gran rummaging through the trash stirred a sigh from deep within her. Adrienne retreated. Only throwing the rotten food out in the dumpster at the market tomorrow would ensure the old woman couldn't sneak the stuff back into the house.

"I fired that dimwit ages ago," Gran said once she was satisfied she had removed everything Adrienne had thrown away. She shuffled to her seat, easing down as gently as possible. "There's no money. It's all gone."

Adrienne stopped opening the soup. "What do you mean there's no money?"

"I closed my bank account last year. They were scamming me; I know it. I kept the money here, and now there's no more. It's all gone. I use the little check the government sends each month. I get by."

Adrienne was frozen, unmoving. Thunder boomed low and sleepy over the ocean. "Well, you have the income from the market and Gramps's pension money."

"The pension went bust five years ago during the recession." Gran busied herself with a bit square of crochet she was working on, her eyes fastened to the needles. "And if you think the market will help you with this scheme of yours, you'll have to talk with Christopher about that."

"Why the hell would I have to talk to Christopher about the market?"

"I sold the place to him a while back. He was always so in love with it. I hated that godforsaken place since the day your grandfather bought it. We were supposed to retire and travel the world, not buy a fish market. I wasn't supposed to have to work my fingers to the bone. I didn't want to be a parent all over again. Your grandfather wasn't supposed to have to work to keep food on this table to feed you."

Gran's expression was one of utter innocence. "I made a good deal of money off it too."

"You sold the market . . . to Christopher?" The words escaped her lips as a broken whisper, her chest gripped with dread.

"And the boat."

A gasp snagged in Adrienne's throat.

"And think again before you think of using the money to pay some stranger to babysit me like I'm some child. All of that money is gone too."

Adrienne slammed her hands on the table and cast a hulking shadow over the old woman, blocking the overhead light like a cop interrogating a witness. "How, Gran? What earthly way did you find to bleed out every cent?"

"I'm not stupid. I know I'm getting old. I know I don't have much time left on this planet. I wanted to make sure this town remembers the name Elizabeth Harris. My father built this town, and they will all remember the Harris family name when I am gone. They will have no choice." Gran's hands, nimble and determined, continued to work at the crochet project, the shapeless beginnings of a potholder forming under her fingers.

"Christ." Adrienne had to sit. "And how did you secure the legacy of the Harris name?"

"I donated the money to various charities around town. But I was smart and only gave money to those who would give me something good in return, like a brass plaque or a commemorative bench." Gran paused her work and faced Adrienne with a twinkle in her eye. It was the most life Adrienne had seen in her since they arrived. "You can't walk around town without knowing my name."

Overwhelmed, Adrienne's world tilted. She rested her head heavily on the table.

"They all thought they'd be done with me once I died. Boy, were they wrong. They'll never get rid of me. I'm like my tree, eh?" A chuckle rumbled in the old woman's throat, laced with eerie satisfaction. Her gaze strayed toward her cherished banyacado tree.

In true fashion, Gran took the last word. Adrienne had no energy to continue. Tomorrow, she would go to the market, have it out with Christopher Crane, and try to salvage her plan to make her stay in Harbor Point as short as possible.

Adrienne heated the soup for Kali and added to the plate a small package of saltine crackers from their road trip. With the mournful meal in her grip, she drifted out of the kitchen, leaving Gran under a cloud of silence.

The towels were gone when Adrienne arrived with dinner. She pressed her ear to the door. Kali hummed an unfamiliar tune, probably listening to her MP3 player. The faint scratch of her brush against a canvas was just detectable.

Good. Adrienne closed her eyes and rested her forehead on Kali's door. The image of Lucas with his head buried in a sketch pad, furiously outlining a new picture, shimmered in her mind—the brim of that old sun hat of his always resting on the lip of the paper, hiding his face. He would have loved Kali. They would have been inseparable. Uncle and niece. Adrienne's heart burned to think of impossible worlds where the two existed together. She missed him, maybe even more than Quinn. Lucas had been her safe harbor, and she had been his muse. The sheets of sketch paper still in her pocket were heavy. Her thumb caressed the worn folds, her mind contemplating the tranquility that death promised.

What was death like for Lucas when the world slipped away from him? Is this rock bottom?

Adrienne set the tray on the floor and knocked, calling softly to Kali that dinner was waiting. She waited a full minute, but the door stayed shut. Sighing, she went upstairs.

She slipped into the vacant guest bedroom and went to the window without turning on the light. Opening the window did nothing to clear the stuffiness. The storm had been a fleeting menace, its departure marked by the hot, lingering breath of the sea. The sun sank to the horizon. She wasn't sure what to do with herself. She could empty the car, but the last thing she wanted was to see Gran again, even if it meant sleeping in her clothes.

Adrienne leaned out the window and beheld a world so familiar yet removed. The view from the window was a faded snapshot from an old album. Gran's controversial banyacado tree stood in defiant prosperity, the scars of its past still visible amid the lush foliage. The crop of avocados was peaking. The green orbs, some newly fallen, some half rotted, littered the ground below her window.

The big white house next door demanded her attention, though she tried to avoid its pull. She had spent countless nights gazing at the Merritts' estate, waiting for Quinn's bedroom light to turn on. Summers belonged to Quinn.

How she had once revered the house, its majesty feeding her dreams of another life, the marrow of her bones pulsating with a profound love—not a childish fantasy of love but one as enduring and vast as the sea itself. Those dreams now seemed cloaked in absurdity.

"Stupid girl," Adrienne said aloud, mimicking Gran's husky voice, tinged with the slight nuance of her Hungarian upbringing.

The sea was unkind to things left untended. The dreamlike house, once full of summer and desire, was crumbling. The roof was missing shingles. Kudzu crept along the front entryway, and a stack of rusted patio chairs rested by the side door. The estate's disrepair bore a peculiar flavor, one part bitter reality, another part sweet liberation. The Merritts had been erased from the pages of Harbor Point.

As the sun faded, a sliver of moon crept out of the ocean, and the windows of the white house became dark eyes beckoning her to return to the place that once held her whole world. Adrienne rested her chin in her hands, listening to the cicadas. A crisp vegetal scent rose as the chill of the distant storm trickled in and cooled the wild fauna.

The chill roused her from her trance. Darkness had come. *Minutes? Hours?* The passage of time had become a stranger to her. Yawning, she backed away from the window.

As she went to pull the shade, a light came on in Quinn's old bedroom. A warm, yellow, flickering glow. She stood still, blinking, demanding the light evaporate and return Quinn's window to sensible darkness. But the light persisted. Her mind buzzed, doubts gnawing at the edges of her sanity. A gray shape moved across the shade.

Am I imagining this? Is someone there?

Adrienne stood in the gloom of the guest room, fixed on the square of brightness, unmoving, until the light turned off again.

CHAPTER THREE

Adrienne was up early the following day after a largely sleepless night. The house, once a haven, now felt alien and unwelcoming. The drone of the waves, a sound that used to lull her to sleep, was driving her batty, and the old cottage shifted and groaned in forgotten ways. Adrienne found herself at the landing throughout the night, craning her neck, listening for any indication that Kali was in distress.

Then she would hover at her window, waiting for the light in Quinn's old room. The light never returned.

"There's no one living at the Merritts' house, right?" Adrienne asked Gran brusquely as she hurried into the kitchen and straight to the pantry. She wanted to spend as little time with the woman as possible. Her to-do list for the day was long: visit Christopher and have it out with him, buy real food for the house, and check if Gran had truly closed all her accounts at the bank. It would have to be a quick excursion. Adrienne didn't want to leave Kali alone with Gran longer than necessary.

"I haven't seen anyone in that house for years." Gran seemed to choose her words carefully.

"Strange, I was sure I saw a light last night."

The old lady's face was unreadable. "Maybe bad wires?"

"The eyesore is finally going to auction next month. Though I don't know who would want to buy it." Gran frowned. "The salt is eating away at it bit by bit. Whoever buys it, I hope they knock it down."

The grand old clock in the living room ticked off the weighted silence following her declaration. Adrienne gave up on finding food in the pantry. Kali would have to wait for her to return from the grocery store.

"Good riddance," Gran added between sips. "That house should never have been built in the first place."

ADRIENNE PULLED UP to the market and parked in the lot behind the building, shell rock crunching under her tires. The faint smell of salt and fish permeated the breeze from the live wells bubbling under the porch's tin roof.

She headed for the back door, almost rushing right in, a habit ingrained in her DNA. But the market wasn't hers. She would have to use the front door like the other shoppers. But at the front door, her hand stubbornly refused to move toward the handle.

The bright-blue stucco gleamed under the late-morning sun. The sign her grandfather had hand-carved above the big picture window boasted a fresh coat of paint. A row of cone-shaped rosemary bushes lined the walk, each a perfect triangle under the new striped awning. Two small tables sat in its shade. *It's a fine place to sit on a nice day.* All Christopher's work, she guessed.

The glare on the window made it impossible to peer inside. The bell above the door jingled, and she startled. Without thinking, she caught the door before it closed and went inside.

A small group of well-dressed and meticulously groomed women crowded around the high counter of fresh fish and seafood. She glimpsed Christopher past the sea of ladies. His smile emerged, then retreated, playing hide-and-seek among the waves of their styled hairdos. Their voices clambered over each other, a cacophony of chatter reminiscent of geese. It was Sunday, and Adrienne knew they had come from church seeking something for the sacramental dinner, which explained the parade of color and glitter, the updos, the rouge, and lipstick.

"No, you want to take the bones out before cooking the fish, Ms. Mallory," Christopher said. His deep voice made the last fourteen years melt away. God, she felt like a blushing teenager again. "Don't forget your quart of stock. I made it last night. It will make magic out of this gorgeous piece of fish."

"Oh, yes, now I remember. You told me that before, didn't you, Christopher?" The woman Adrienne assumed was Ms. Mallory laughed and picked up her paper sack with a deliberate coyness.

Adrienne slipped into the crowd, trying to get closer to the counter. The women were not going to move for her. They followed Christopher's every move with eyes wide and shining. One of the older ladies licked her lips as Christopher recited the best method for poaching salmon.

After some wrestling, Adrienne made it to the front of the brood. The woman she had to push aside gave an exasperated groan, but Adrienne ignored her. When the swarm of ladies thinned by the counter, Christopher noticed her, and his charming smile widened. As their eyes locked, an unfamiliar warmth in her chest softened the edges of her anger. The rest faded into background noise.

"Well, look who it is," Christopher said, leaning against the counter. Every gesture, every word laced with that British accent exuded a charisma as natural as breathing. Understanding why Harbor Point's housewives frequented the market took no detective work. "A pleasant surprise indeed."

A cleared throat marked the crowd's growing impatience. Adrienne again became aware of the bodies pressed against her, their cool inspection. She swallowed hard.

"It can't be surprising." Her words trembled on her lips under the scrutiny of the crowd.

"No, but it's been a long time." Christopher wiped his hands on his apron and punched numbers into the cash register for the fish he'd wrapped up.

If possible, he was even more handsome than when she was a girl. Now into his mid-thirties, he had a professorial air, his thick black hair splattered with early grays and his green eyes magnified by black-rimmed eyeglasses. His bottom lip was still a bit fatter than his top; he always seemed to be pouting when he was thinking hard about something.

His tan arms rested casually on the counter, the defined muscle of his bicep peeking out of his rolled-up shirt sleeves. Adrienne knew his hands would be rough from days spent hauling fish. He would have the scent of the sea on him.

Christ, what am I thinking?

The sting of loss pricked her heart, replacing the nostalgia as she took in the market. Her market. She wanted to turn and run, but recognition spread through the group of ladies. Blocking her escape route, they leaned forward slightly, eyes wide like lionesses eyeing their unsuspecting prey.

Despite the taste of tears threatening at the back of her mouth, Adriene had to hold back a laugh.

"Adrienne Harris? Is that you?" Tessa Parker squinted at Adrienne. "Oh, we heard you were coming home."

I'm sure you did.

Tessa had gone to school with Adrienne. They were the same age and in the same grade, though never close friends. Tessa's mother shared the chair position for the Junior League with Gran, so Tessa and Adrienne were forced together at many functions. Tessa was always polite to her in a formal way. She was still tall, blond, and beautiful, as Adrienne would expect.

Janet Miller, one of the two older ladies Adrienne recognized from the golden era of clubs and organizations Gran had reigned over, put her hands to her cheeks in a comical expression of surprise. "You absolutely look the same." Her voice rose. "I would know you anywhere. After all these years, it must be something to be back in Harbor Point."

"Yes, it's something, alright." Adrienne's eyes crinkled with forced cheer as she watched Christopher at the counter, the hint of a smirk tugging at his lips.

"How is your grandmother? We haven't seen her in quite a while. She's really become a hermit the last few years." Tessa's voice was restrained.

Adrienne stiffened, her mind piecing together the signs. Something had happened. Gran must have committed the proverbial straw that broke the camel's back. Adrienne wondered what could have finally gotten her ousted from Harbor Point Society. Court trials, petitions, and even food tampering had not been enough in the past.

"We all heard about the fire," Tessa went on to say.

Adrienne tried to brush it off. "She's doing okay. You know her. The fire was no match for Gran."

"Well, at least the house is still standing." Janet touched Adrienne's arm. "It's good you've come to take care of things. I know it must be hard for you to be here, dear."

A familiar weight dropped into the pit of her stomach. Sure, they all knew exactly how hard it was for her to be here, and she was so happy they had pointed it out.

"Yes, we never expected you'd come back here. I should round up all our old classmates. We can catch up." Tessa's smile seemed vicious. "I swear you were all we talked about our senior year."

"No wedding ring?" Adrienne hadn't meant to say it aloud, matching Tessa's nasty tone.

Tessa recoiled at the remark. "My husband passed away last year."

"Too young. Too soon," Tessa's mother said, cupping Tessa's elbow in comfort.

"Will you be staying long?" Janet piped up.

"For a bit. Only to get Gran squared away." Adrienne's eyes shot toward Christopher in a silent cry for rescue.

Tessa's shoulders eased, and her voice held more certainty than curiosity. "So, you are not staying for good?" As she spoke, Tessa sent

Christopher her own glance, which Adrienne found odd. *Why is Tessa so eager to know my time frame? What does it matter to her?*

Adrienne answered anyway to make sure they understood. "No, I have no plans to move back."

Christopher raised the section of the counter that acted as a gate, the screech of the mechanism drawing the ladies' focus back to him. He motioned for Adrienne to come through. "Why don't you go in the back while I finish up with these ladies? Have a look around the old place. See if it passes inspection."

"Okay," Adrienne said, glad to flee.

"Well, we hope you stay at least until the summer gala. It's always such a wonderful event," Janet called out as Adrienne slipped away.

The back room welcomed her. Adrienne leaned against the cool wall and drew in a deep breath, dampening the anxiety. The familiar walls of Harbor Point were closing in.

Once she gained some composure, Adrienne took stock of the changes in the kitchen. Christopher had morphed the old, fishy, haphazard space into a real kitchen with a top-end range, a giant Sub-Zero french door fridge, and beautiful butcher-block counters smoothed from wear. The window held a planter box brimming with thyme and basil, their scent seeping into the room on the sultry breeze off the Back Bay.

The soft rustle and chatter of the ladies filtered through the kitchen as they collected their purchases and left the market one by one. Tessa and her mother were the last to leave. Adrienne leaned into the doorway, eavesdropping without shame.

"So, we will see you for dinner?" Tessa purred.

Christopher's voice carried an uncharacteristic stiffness. "I'll be there at six."

When the front doorbell jingled a final time, Christopher appeared. He brushed fish scales from his hands with a bar towel. The silence was loud with buried history as Christopher moved to the large fridge and pulled out two beers. He flicked the caps off and handed her one. Her heartbeat quickened, drumming against her ribs. *Why did I come?* There was really nothing she could do about the situation.

"I saw you got in yesterday. I was going to come by, but I thought I'd give you time to settle," Christopher said, taking the stool opposite her. They faced off across the island.

"How could you buy this place from Gran? Why didn't you tell me?" She had planned to warm up to the subject, but it came out as soon as she opened her mouth.

Christopher leaned against the counter and sighed. "I wanted to, but I knew you would be furious and decide not to come home." He bowed his head, inspecting some nonexistent mark on the butcher block. "I only bought it to help your grandmother and preserve the market."

Adrienne downed the full beer. "Gran says all the money is gone, so it didn't really help her, now, did it?"

A silent apology danced in the creases on Christopher's forehead and around his eyes.

"You said this wouldn't be permanent, you know." Adrienne choked out a laugh. "But what am I going to do with her? I don't believe she spent all the money. I bet she hid it somewhere in the house. Heck, it could be buried in the backyard."

"We'll figure it all out." Christopher placed his hand on top of hers. As she pulled away, an uneasy stillness quickly filled the space between them.

Adrienne finally said, "I didn't mean to pull back. I'm stressed. I haven't been here twenty-four hours, and I'm already on the gossips' radar. I've got a teenager I barely know who wants nothing more than to go home to her friends. And now I have to figure out how to deal with Gran."

"Why don't I come over tomorrow night and make dinner?" Christopher rose and went to the sink to rinse their bottles. "I have a magic effect on your grandmother." He turned and winked at her. "I need to come by and meet the contractor anyway. He'll be over to inspect the kitchen damage."

"You won't be having dinner with Tessa tomorrow night?" Adrienne was shocked by her boldness. Maybe in the past they had been on terms that allowed such banter, but Adrienne wasn't a bratty teen now.

Christopher turned from the sink. "It's new. Started a few weeks ago. Nothing serious. Just two lonely people enjoying each other's company."

"I'm sorry I said that. It's none of my business."

"It's okay." He approached the table, flattening his palms on the counter. "Hungry?"

His kindness prickled her conscience. "Don't go to any trouble."

"No trouble. I promise."

He puttered at the counter by the range, and she took a seat. The strain ebbed from her shoulders, leaving a sense of peace that was foreign yet soothing. The kitchen was cozy and filled with memories of her grandfather busying himself with the day's tasks—prepping the lunches before heading out to their old fishing boat, *The Dolly*, named for Adrienne.

There was always a soft glint in his eyes, as if each moment of Adrienne's childhood were a treasure. Vernon Harris's face was a calm sea, his emotions concealed beneath the surface. The boat was the declaration of his affection. But it had a different meaning for Adrienne's grandmother. Every mention of the boat drew her face taut. The market and the boat were constant reminders of the dashed dreams of Gran's golden years.

"I put in the new kitchen over a year ago. The place feeds my need to cook," Christopher said after a long pause, but it had been a comfortable silence. The rhythm of their conversation was like that of a favorite song.

Adrienne chuckled. "I didn't know you liked to cook."

"I guess you were too busy being mad at me for some reason or another to notice I was cooking with you the whole time," Christopher teased.

He was right. He had been there, helping with all the events and suppers, galas, and festivals as Gran stood tall in her culinary kingdom, a spatula as her scepter, with Adrienne, her constant shadow, expected to follow her every stir and sauté. Christopher had slipped into Harbor Point market like a fish to water soon after his arrival and helped to hold them together when Gramps fell ill.

She smiled, thinking of the epic arguments they'd had.

"Come help," he suggested. "For old time's sake?"

He conjured a seafood salad, his hands deftly combining scallops, shrimp, sea urchins, and mussels. She lit up at the sight. All her favorites. *A coincidence?*

Cristopher picked fresh herbs from the window box, adding them to olive oil and lemon juice from Gran's tree. He put Adrienne to work dicing green onions and tomatoes. At first the companionable hush was broken only by the chopping of their knives. Then he hummed, as her grandfather often had. Adrienne found that she was smiling.

They sat at a small iron café table and ate the bright, cold meal among the live tanks that kept the day's catch. The breeze brought the rotted salt smell of low tide through the mangroves. Oddly, it was a scent Adrienne loved.

She glanced at her watch, startled. What she had intended as a terse visit had slipped into a pleasant lunch, the minutes whisked away by laughter. Adrienne hoped to bring the conversation back around to her grandmother's situation and the fact that Christopher was the proud owner of everything that ever mattered to her. But he was good at keeping her off topic. Instead, they chatted about all the gossip she had missed, the changes to the town he had witnessed. They even did some light reminiscing, keeping their distance from the darker bits. Adrienne's stony guard crumbled enough to allow her to laugh. She had almost forgotten what that felt like. A strange, airy feeling filled her.

Finally, Adrienne shook her head, staring at her empty plate. She and Kali had survived on quick meals and leftovers from the restaurant for far too long. She couldn't recall the last time they'd had a real meal together.

"I've failed her."

She confessed her regrets to Christopher then, about her lackluster dinners with Kali, and the rest of it. This wasn't a side of herself she usually shared. But Christopher had a way of drawing out her truths.

"Maybe. Possibly." Each word seemed precisely chosen, as if he were handling a fragile piece of glass. "This new chapter will be good for both of you."

He slid her a shot of tequila to smooth his comment. His gaze held a knowingness that seemed misplaced given their near-stranger status.

"Tequila won't help me figure things out," Adrienne joked as she brought the glass to her lips.

He countered, "Maybe, but it has a way of sanding down life's roughest edges. And it cuts the seafood's sweetness."

"He can cook and make drink pairings? Will wonders never cease?" Adrienne raised her brow.

"A piece of fish, a perfect scallop. It's a beautiful thing. You should make it the best experience."

"The poetic fishmonger." She closed her eyes and let the warmth of the alcohol seep through her body. "No wonder Tessa and the townies are infatuated with you."

"Maybe. A little."

She imagined he was smirking. With a shake of her head, she sighed in bewilderment and opened her eyes. "I've never understood your fascination with this town."

"The market, it just . . ." He paused, looking around fondly. ". . . reeled me in. Seeing people come and go, hearing their stories, the liberty of it all makes me happy."

"I guess I will never know how a writer's mind works." Adrienne reached for the tequila bottle and quickly refilled their glasses. "I'm guessing you never married Rachel? It was hard to imagine her making this place her home."

"And you would be right. Rachel left me long ago. Never married."

"That explains your fan club."

Christopher blushed as he adjusted his spectacles on his nose. "Kali—I'm curious why you named her that. I'm guessing it's symbolic, but I wouldn't want to make an assumption."

He was good at changing the subject.

"A child born from death and destruction," Adrienne said softly.

In the years that followed Kali's birth, she cringed whenever she called out her daughter's name. The name was conjured during the drug-induced aftermath of labor when Adrienne was torn and exhausted. All she could think of was Lucas. His lifeless stare haunted her dreams—that filmy echo of the life that once sparkled within them. When they asked for the child's name, somewhere in the deep stores of her mind, Adrienne recalled the story of Kali Ma, which Lucas recounted one night out on the beach. The ancient name whispered from her cracked lips. A fitting name for a million reasons she couldn't remember the next day. She woke to find the pink, wiggling child in a bassinet next to her hospital bed with the name on the placard.

"But also, rebirth," Christopher added like it was some silver lining.

She offered him a strained smile.

He got up and took their plates to the sink. "Come and work here while we figure out everything with your Gran?"

Adrienne came beside him, her hands picking up the washed plates and methodically drying them.

"And do what? Sling fish and make light conversation with the old biddies?" Her lips puckered. "You seem to have cornered that market without my help."

"I have a kitchen, and you are a chef, right?" Christopher waved toward the fancy range and fridge. "We could open for dinners. Cook what you want. The gala is coming up. It would be great to launch something new, a new partnership."

"I'm not a chef. I never went to culinary school. I'm just a cook." Adrienne placed the last dishes on the high shelf above the sink.

"Semantics." Christopher brushed off her protests. Each rebuttal met with immediate counterpoints. He had come prepared. "You were already a fine chef at sixteen if I recall correctly. Culinary school be damned."

"So, you want to start serving dinners at the fish market?" Adrienne folded her arms across her chest.

Christopher turned to face her. "That was the dream, was it not?"

Their bodies existed in a thin space that crossed the boundary of personal comfort. Tenderness washed over her, her defenses thawing slightly as she realized he had remembered her dream.

"The town has changed. The locals are much more sophisticated than you remember. They will come. I have been doing some light fare on weekends and take-out stuff, but we could ramp it up to full dinner service."

"The town is different." Adrienne considered how the ladies in the market had pressed her and added, "But it doesn't feel any different."

"You're wrong." He leaned into her, his mouth close to her ear. An electrifying pulse shot through her thighs.

It was as if the universe had rewritten its laws in an instant.

Adrienne quickly took a step back, hoping he wouldn't take it as coldness. "I guess I always had the idea to make a go and turn it into a restaurant."

How long has it been since I touched a man?

Adrienne didn't have time to dwell on such things. She had to leave before she did something she would regret. She wasn't going to screw up on her second day in town.

"It's like riding a bike." He gave her one last glance, one more chance to do something foolish, before turning to the kitchen island. "As Mrs. Miller mentioned, the summer gala is coming up. I've got a whole bunch of things I'm heading up. You could join me, and we could test the waters."

The gala, a multiday event culminating around Independence Day, was the highlight of the summer in Harbor Point and Gran's claim to fame. Artists came from all over to win ribbons and hock their wares. But the real prizes were the blue ribbons handed out for the best pies, cakes, and whatever category Gran could dream up. The contests became more elaborate over the decades, and the stakes grew. And though Gran was in charge of the baking and cooking competitions, she always broke protocol. She entered her own dishes and somehow won every category. It wasn't until Adrienne was fifteen that the gala council forbade Gran from entering. That's when Gran began forcing Adrienne to enter the competitions to "keep the ribbons in the family."

Adrienne might have enjoyed the events otherwise.

The final dinner, traditionally orchestrated by Gran, had a reputation for being the gala's star attraction, its brilliance illuminating the previous decades. The whole town would gather at the lagoon gazebo, a vast covered space in the middle of the Back Bay's small alcove. A swanky band would play while the mayor gave out the ribbons. After the awards, Harbor Point's people feasted on an endless array of dishes donated by all the best cooks in town. Gran stood at the helm for years, cooking for the event with Adrienne, a hapless victim forced to work alongside her.

"I don't know." Adrienne studied the pattern in the terrazzo floor.

Christopher came over and took her hands into his. "Give it some thought. No need to make a decision today."

Their eyes locked. A noticeable sag in his shoulders painted a picture of surrender. His hand came to her face and tamed a wayward clutch of curls.

"For what it's worth, I'm glad you're home."

She was aware of her rapid breathing and the warmth of his hand on her face. Conflicting emotions flickered across his face. Instinct took over, and she smacked his hand away, as surprised by her reaction as Christopher was. They both stood gawking, unsure of the next step, until Adrienne breathed, "I'm sorry. I don't know why I did that."

"No, don't apologize. I'm embarrassed by my forwardness."

Christopher fidgeted with his glasses. "Too much tequila, too many memories."

"I should go." She grabbed her purse off the counter and headed for the door.

His plea, "Don't leave like this," came as a whisper, stripped of its earlier confidence.

The bell above the front door suddenly jingled

"I must have forgotten to turn the lock," Christopher said, his body relaxing.

They emerged from the back together, Adrienne following Christopher. Caught in her confused thoughts, she almost collided with his back when he abruptly halted by the cash register. She stood on her tiptoes to peer over his shoulder.

There, standing in the middle of the market, was Quinn Merritt. It was an older version of the boy she once knew, the boy she would have followed anywhere, but Adrienne would know him blind.

What little scaffolding held her up crumbled. All bets were off. Armageddon had arrived on a blazing chariot, and Adrienne found herself laughing hysterically without effort. As she moved toward him, a desperate flutter in her chest grew more potent by the moment. He was the sun, and she was helpless in his gravity.

Quinn stood with his hands in the pockets of his tan shorts, resembling an escaped convict.

In her memory, he was a static figure, stuck forever as the boy in the picture tucked into her dresser mirror. Smiling and free, with wild dark hair blowing in the wind and stormy blue eyes. He laughed with his mouth wide open and cartwheeled on the beach at night.

He was forever her Peter, the boy who never grew up.

But the Quinn who stood before her was a stranger. He had cut his hair short and spiky. Dark circles blushed the thin skin below his eyes. Time and stress had etched tiny lines at the corners of his eyes and mouth, signposts of an unkind journey. A hardness dwelled in his expression.

Yet he was still beautiful in that heartbreaking way that some men carried into adulthood. Just enough of the boy lingered behind his eyes to reduce her body to ash, and at that point, she welcomed the wind to carry what remained of her away. Far away. Anywhere but there.

"Quinn?" His name emerged as a raspy croak. Her mouth opened and closed in vain attempts to form further words. *What do you say when you have waited fourteen years to speak?*

She wanted to hit him. She wanted to fall into his arms like she used to. Deep down, Adrienne knew that even now, if Quinn told her everything would be okay—that all that mattered was right there, and that would be all that did matter as long as they were together—Adrienne would have lapped up his words like warm milk.

"When you left the house this morning, I followed you." His voice reflected his turmoil. "I shouldn't have done this."

He's folding.

She realized she didn't want him to go. "It was you in the house last night? The light was on in your old room," Adrienne said, trying to pull him back to her.

He looked like a cornered animal. "I didn't want to go to the house. Your grandmother was never fond of me."

"I don't understand. Why are you here? Why were you in the house? This can't be a coincidence that I return and you're here. Not after all this time." Words flooded from her now. Her head spun with desperate questions she had obsessed over. But it was like he hadn't heard her.

"The girl with you. She looks like Lucas," he said.

Quinn's words shattered her illusion. He wasn't there for her. He was there to get answers.

"She is mine," he said more to himself. His words came with a funny twinge.

"Yes." Adrienne closed her eyes. "She is yours." After all the years of being mute, it was like a rebirth to finally say it out loud.

Quinn's rigid posture softened discernibly, and he took a cautious step toward Adrienne, eyeing Christopher as if he were an interloper. But something made him pause, and he backed away once again.

For a while, no one spoke. Adrienne's senses heightened. Every tick of the metal clock on the wall punctuated the silence while Christopher loomed behind her at the counter. Quinn stood beside a small table by the front window, nervously tapping his slender fingers on the metal top, syncopating with the clock.

"Why are you here, Quinn?" Adrienne finally asked.

He expelled a sigh, his shoulders wilting. "I never really left" was all he gave her. "I come and go."

Adrienne couldn't cry, but her entire body juddered. He had been right there, in this goddamn town, the whole time. "I tried to find you."

"I know." A shadow of shame fell across Quinn's face, his gaze darting away.

Look at me! she wanted to scream, but time and space made her hesitate to lash out at the fragile creature Quinn had become.

She turned to Christopher. "You knew?"

He was frozen behind the counter, wide-eyed. "No. I swear. If he's been in town, he's done a good job staying hidden."

She turned back to Quinn. He had left the table and was edging toward the door.

"Why are you here?" she asked again.

"I . . ." Quinn began, but someone came inside, the doorbell jingling like a warning.

It took Adrienne a few moments to realize Kali was standing next to Quinn, not knowing he was her father. She had on paint-splattered coveralls, her arms dotted with reds and blues. With her hair pulled away from her eyes, there was no denying she was a Merritt.

With an eye roll and the effortless nonchalance of teenagers, Kali declared, "There's no food at the house. Gran told me to come find you."

"Kali, go back. I'll be there in a few minutes with groceries."

Quinn pressed against the wall, trying to shrink away from the girl. Of course Gran had told Kali to come. Elizabeth Harris was a fire starter.

When Kali noticed Quinn, recognition flashed across her face. She backed away and sized up the terrified man in the corner.

"You're my father," she said. She waited for Adrienne's confirmation. All Adrienne could do was nod. The lies had come to an end.

"I guess I am." Lines creased Quinn's brow as he silently studied Kali.

Christopher came around from behind the counter, and the four stood in an awkward circle, with no one knowing what to say. Adrienne gazed longingly at the ceiling, half expecting a meteor to crash through and kill them all.

"I shouldn't have come. This was wrong. I'm sorry," Quinn finally sputtered, then slipped out of the market with all the talent of a bumbling cat burglar.

Who is that man? His familiar features were all there, yet his eyes, once suffused with life, were now voids of fear. Quinn as she knew him was lost somewhere within.

"Mom, what the hell is going on?" Kali demanded. "And who is this dude?" She nodded toward Christopher.

"Hi, I work here," Christopher chirped. "I can make you a sandwich."

"That was my father." Kali ignored the greeting and offer of food. "Why didn't you tell me he was here?"

Adrienne dropped into a chair, overwhelmed. "I didn't know until now."

"You're not telling me things." Kali shook her head. "It can't be some crazy coincidence he's here."

"No, it's not." Adrienne buried her face in her hands, a silent surrender to the weight of their past crashing into the present. "He lives next door in the big white house. He was supposed to be gone. He left a long time ago."

"So he wasn't just some boy or just some fling? All this time, you knew where he was, who he was. I had a father and the whole other half of my family sitting here, and I never knew about them. I asked so many times." Kali began to cry. "Why did you leave? Why did you take me away from him? Why did he run away from me?"

Adrienne wanted to wipe Kali's tears away and take her daughter into her arms, but she didn't have the strength. Kali's eyes shimmered with a pitiful mix of betrayal and confusion. Adrienne was left grappling with her own paralysis, her instincts at war.

There was no simple way to respond to Kali's questions. For nearly fourteen years, Adrienne had meticulously packed away every memory, every piece of the past, into a corner of her mind. But now the dust was unsettled, and every ghost was awake, refusing to be ignored.

With a shake of her head, as if trying to dispel the lies, Kali turned and vanished onto the bustling sidewalk outside.

Adrienne had no words for Christopher either. Taking her cue from Kali, she spun on her heels, surrendering to the urge to escape.

CHAPTER FOUR

By the time Adrienne trudged in from a summer storm with bags of soggy groceries that evening, Kali was locked in her room. It would take time, and maybe some big gesture, but Kali would come around, Adrienne assured herself.

On the second day of the silent treatment, amid the rhythmic rumbling of the washer, Adrienne found a soothing mantra: *This isn't the end of the world.* She could have waited a few more days for a full load, but the garage offered a refuge from the silent house and Gran's calculating gaze. The old woman's every action was a chess move, from the innocent errands she'd send Kali on to the minute changes in her routine. Adrienne was all too familiar with the game.

The knowledge that Quinn was mere yards away flitted about her brain like a pesky fly. At times, she batted at nothing to shoo away the incessant thoughts. As if her problems could be so easily resolved.

The orderly folding of clothes was her answer to all the strife, not the hollow clamor of "taking action." *It's worked so far. Why not now?*

A knock at the front door sent Adrienne springing up from her stooped position, a startled gazelle in her domestic wilderness. Rather than go through the house, she pushed the garage door clicker. The mechanism whined as the door tucked itself into the ceiling. Christopher's face poked around the corner.

The man did not know the meaning of giving someone time to cool off. Her hands found their way to her hips, her glare fixed on him with steely intensity. *Would the garage door kill him if I pushed the button? Maybe just bang him up a bit?*

"I know you don't want to talk to me right now." Christopher held his hands up in surrender as he entered the garage.

"Correct, but here you are." Adrienne returned to the washing machine.

"I am. Take a walk with me?"

He stood with his hands jammed into his shorts pockets and a sheepish look. Before she knew it, her head bobbed in reluctant agreement, opening a gate into uncharted territory.

"I'm only agreeing to go because I don't want Kali to hear us talking. She's mad enough." Adrienne grabbed her straw hat off a hook.

They strolled down the shore toward the public beach to avoid the Merritt house. She couldn't bear to think that Quinn could be peeking out from the large two-story windows that faced the Atlantic.

At first, neither Adrienne nor Christopher spoke. There had been a finality to their exchange the previous day. Walking beside him on the shore was strange. It was as if nothing had happened. She could not decide whether he had lied about not knowing Quinn was in town. If she had known that singular piece of information, she would have stayed away.

"You knew more than anyone how important this news was." Pivoting toward him, she wrapped her arms around herself. "Did you keep it from me?"

His gaze skated over the vast beach, a palpable evasion. "It's been years since I've seen him around here. And even then, it was for a fleeting moment, here and there. It's been so long, I figured he'd finally moved on."

His words landed with an unsettling simplicity. Instinct murmured to Adrienne that there was more beneath the surface.

"If you really cared about me, you would have told me this long ago. My kid hates me, Christopher. Hates me because I lied to her all these years about her father. She thinks I knew Quinn was here and I kept her from him." A great sob formed within. "Maybe it would have been bad. Maybe he would have crushed what little I had left, denied his child, rejected me, but at least I'd have closure."

Tears welled up, breaking the emotional dam that had stood unyielding since Kali's birth. When the nurses left her with her cherub baby, she had clutched Kali to her and mourned the end of everything. Once the ache dulled, though it would never leave entirely, Adrienne vowed to hold in the pain and the tears, for they would do no good and change nothing.

Christopher pulled her to the shade of the lifeguard tower and held her. A demand for honesty perched on the tip of her tongue, but fatigue stole the strength she needed. She leaned into him, pushing her face deep into his shirt. Pushing him away would be wrong. In the tumult of her world, he stood as the only constant.

"I'm sorry, Adrienne. I couldn't bear to tell you. I made a mistake thinking it was better if you thought he had vanished for good. I hoped you could make a fresh start with him out of the picture."

"It was stupid of me to believe he wouldn't return. Deep down, I knew he would, but I was scared he would reject me . . . and Kali." Her fingers tightened on Christopher's shirt, bracing herself against the bitter truth. "That was worse than thinking he was simply gone."

Adrienne sniffed back the snot and wiped her tears away.

"You know, Kali is nearly the age you were when you met Quinn and Lucas," he mused. She pulled back to look at him. "I remember what you were like at that age. It sounds like she is a lot like you were. You certainly never let me off the hook, not for one second." He regarded her fondly. "If you remind yourself of what it was like when you were her age, I bet you'll find the key to mending this rift. You wanted the same things she wants now: for the adults to see her, hear her, and not brush her off."

His words resonated within her, leaving her to marvel at the wisdom time had given him.

"I've tried to forget those years as a survival tactic."

"You shouldn't have to get by only surviving, Adrienne." His smile emerged, shaded by melancholy. "Come on, let's go back to the house. I've brought the Harris ladies dinner."

"Aren't you staying?" Adrienne let go of him and wiped her face again. The last thing she needed was Kali or Gran to see she had been crying.

"Let's revisit that another day. I assumed Kali wouldn't appreciate company tonight. I moved the contractor's visit to next week."

They walked to the house. With nimble strides, Christopher ascended the steps first and picked up a basket.

"Dinner is served," he chirped, handing it to her. The basket was heavy. "All you have to do is heat it up. I left a small electric burner in the kitchen."

"What on earth is in here? There's enough for a week." Adrienne pried the lid open to find many containers of food, all labeled with instructions. She smelled lemon and dill.

"Well, you are without a stove for the time being." Christopher nodded toward the basket.

"Very true."

ADRIENNE GOT TO work reheating the various goodies from Christopher's basket as evening settled. She had opened all the windows on the first floor, and though the air was hot and sea-sodden, the crosswind blew out the dusty stagnation of the house. She stood barefoot at the small hot plate, her face bathed in the fragrant steam of seafood stew.

As she spooned the cioppino into her bowl, Adrienne cradled Christopher's advice like a precious stone, hearkening back to her youth. She grimaced as she recalled the summer she first met the Merritt brothers. Lucas Merritt was sensitive, creative, and talented. Quinn Merritt was strong and beautiful. So full of excitement and desire. That summer, the brothers unlocked a hidden door, and the world opened its wide maw, revealing the secret realms of privilege and adventure—and swallowing Adrienne whole.

CHAPTER FIVE
Summer 1996

The new, gleaming estate next door to Adrienne had grown in width and breadth throughout the year and was completed on the 1st of June. Finally, the mysterious Merritt family was due to move in at any moment.

The town was abuzz with gossip. At Hairspray Heaven, ladies prattled on about Mr. Merritt's widower status, his wife having been claimed in an unfortunate car accident and leaving him to raise his two young sons. Harbor Point was their "fresh start." Others in town believed Mr. Merritt was moving his family to town in search of a shipwreck off the coast.

The wreck of the *Nuestra Señora del Carmén* was a local legend often retold by old men playing card games on the bait shack stoop. Rumored to have been lost at sea carrying millions in gold bars and jewels on its way to the New World from Spain, the ship seemed to bring a new prospector to town every decade. But none of the previous treasure hunters had put down roots in Harbor Point, building the grandest home in town.

As June waned, the town's intrigue simmered. No glimpse of Mr. Merritt yet. From her bedroom window, Adrienne Harris was the estate's most frequent audience. She loved to sit, elbows on the windowsill, face in her palms, and stare for hours. Her eyes traced the clean square lines and large, dark windows, her mind shaping and reshaping the face of the enigmatic Mr. Merritt. Who was the man who built the brilliant white house? The ladies pestered Adrienne at the weekly Junior League luncheons, demanding news, but she had nothing to offer.

Dear old Gran was blatantly unimpressed. A steady stream of complaints had flowed from her lips during construction. The noise was too loud, the machines were dirty and dusty, and the burly workmen trampled her prized flowers. Adrienne recognized the envy in Gran's eyes, a longing stirred by the phantom Mr. Merritt's wealth and notoriety. The big house seemed to harbor everything Gran prized yet did not possess. Adrienne kept this observation to herself and grew uneasy as she imagined her new neighbors clashing with the formidable Elizabeth Harris.

Still, Adrienne found herself riding the same wave of mystery and anticipation that had captivated the others. Even General Boynton, the town founder, had never lived in such a dazzling estate. Her mind sketched out a treasure hunter's life filled with international adventures. She compensated for her lack of experience by stitching together scenes from those glamorous old movies Gran loved to watch late at night. Mr. Merritt resembled Clark Gable. His sons were the spitting image of a young Frank Sinatra and Errol Flynn.

Adrienne found herself drawn to the beach on that side, yearning to witness the faintest stirrings of life. *What would it be like to live in such a place?* The scorching wind buzzed with energy. Dizzy, Adrienne would fall into the sand and, staring into the washed-out blue sky, imagine the depths of the sea and its hidden treasures.

Without fanfare, the Merritts finally moved in. The only warning was the subtle invasion of moving trucks threading through the empty streets. Expecting a spectacle, most locals missed it entirely. Even Gran, always the first to sense change, did not hear the trucks turn up the gravel drive and park in front of the house. Adrienne was in fact up and about, but she was oblivious to the convoy, too busy trying to keep her tackle from falling as she pedaled up A1A to the marina to meet her grandfather. Her fishing gear balanced precariously across the handlebars of her bike. She had a lot of poles, each one for a different fish.

The days she worked on the boat with her gramps glistened like jewels amid Adrienne's routine. She would wake, drawn out of sleep as the sun peeked over the horizon, throw on the dirtiest, grimiest pair of jean shorts she could find, pairing it with some holey, threadbare T-shirt that perpetually stank of fish guts and turpentine, and head to the marina. Her sun-bleached deck shoes glittered with dried fish scales. Dried fish blood spotted her lures. Her worn-out beach cruiser's continued survival stood testament to her grandfather's handiwork.

She locked her bike up on the chain-link fence, took the gear off, put it in the old wagon next to the gate leading to the live wells, and headed toward the mangroves beyond the market parking lot. A little path through the green tangle led to the Back Bay and her secret spot, where the canopy preserved a refreshing coolness against the sun's assault.

The smell of rotting things floated up from the muck as she slipped out of her shoes. She headed for the water, dragging the little wagon behind her.

Mangrove roots jabbed through the sand, blackened fingers reaching for the water's edge. The little baitfish darted in the shallows, playing hide-and-seek in the roots. The water was clear, but a few feet out, where the sand dipped sharply, it turned coppery black, full of tannins from the dead mangrove leaves. Undeterred by the specter of gators, Adrienne stepped into the water without hesitation. Nothing could pass her keen senses without detection. Mudfish gulped for breath on the mucky banks, and ballyhoo skimmed the water's surface. An egret tiptoed through the brambles.

She nestled a few folds of her net between her teeth, freeing her hands to tame the rest of its wild expanse with practiced ease. Standing sideways to the water, her left eye on the black pool, she sought the telltale shimmer of a school, a shudder on the surface. When she found her mark, she hurled the net over the dark water. It fanned out into a disk before settling on the surface with a *thwap!* She hurried to pull it in, bringing the metal weights together like puckered lips to keep the fish inside. When the net reached the shore, hundreds of silvery bodies frantically danced in its clutches. She tossed them into her bait bucket, her hands moving swiftly. She didn't lose one fish.

When her bucket brimmed with bait, she traded its weight for the lightness of her bamboo pole and threaded the hook with a small ball of bread. Wading through the clear shallows, she found her spot, a small bowl of deeper water where the blue crabs congregated, searching for food. She let the dough ball sink into the pit, and the crabs scuttled over to inspect it. Adrienne held her breath and listened to the pulse of her heart. When one of the crabs latched on, she yanked the line, and the crab popped out of the water, still clutching the ball. Adrienne grabbed the crab by its backside with her free hand so it couldn't pinch her and stuffed it into a burlap sack hanging from her shoulder. She refreshed the hook with a new dough ball and persisted in her casting, not ceasing until each crab from the bowl had been consigned to her bag.

With her quota of bait secured and blue crabs destined for lunch, she surrendered to the embrace of the wet sand, where the mudfish perched on her feet. She fed them bits of the bread they took from her hands. Piercing the leaves, the sun created a kaleidoscope of light and shadow. Adrienne let her eyelids fall, immersed in the quiet warmth of the late morning. It was here she was connected to everything. Here, she could lie back and be absorbed into the sand and the water. What bliss to evaporate into all things alive and green, she daydreamed.

An unexpected ripple to her left shattered her serenity. She sat up, her clothes wet, her arms sugared with the refined grains, and spied a red-ribbed fin cut out of the water for a moment. The hunt was on.

A snapper, too large for the shallows, had followed the baitfish and stranded itself in the mucky bay, the mangrove roots acting as a makeshift prison cell. Adrienne crept through the water, making little wake or sound. The fish was too disoriented to notice her approach. She stretched her arms into the tannin-soaked pool as if to hug it. Cool, smooth scales slipped across the tips of her fingers, and she gently encircled the fish with her hands, bringing the tired thing out of the water. There was calm acceptance in its eyes.

She brought the gasping face close, smelling the sweet, fishy scent. Its eyes bulged as it spied her, its beauty not lost. For a suspended heartbeat, she was entranced by the mosaic of red and white scales, their luster unmarred by the struggle. Then she laid the snapper on the sand and swiftly slit its belly, the entrails spilling out. She threw these to the baitfish in the bucket, who churned furiously to claim a morsel. The snapper went into the big ice chest by the live wells up by the market before Adrienne turned toward the marina.

The cars on A1A drifted by like giant, lazy fish, matching Adrienne's sluggish pace. Occasional hands fluttered in greeting from car windows. She held on tightly to her shifting load, trying to keep from spilling all the fish onto the sidewalk. Twyla's flower shop, Maddy's Café, the Hurricane Bar, and the new pizza shop that didn't have a name slipped by in her periphery on her shortcut through the former Frank's Auto-Rama, now an abandoned lot where beach daisies were slowly breaking up the concrete, returning the patch of land to something wild. Fat yellow-and-green grasshoppers sprayed up as she barreled through with her wagon and sloshing buckets of bait. *The Dolly*, bobbing cheerfully in the bay by the gas pumps, came into sight.

Christopher Crane stood with hands on hips at the back of the boat where Adrienne expected her grandfather to be. A groan slipped from her lips, carried by the salty air directly to Christopher's keen ears. He laughed as if they were playing a game where she didn't find him the most annoying person in the world. He even threw in a little wave to make it worse.

Adrienne hiked up her soggy jean shorts and trundled closer.

"Are you coming out with us?" She surveyed the boat, searching for clues. Happily, he had not brought his gear. He was too clean for boat work, wearing a crisp white polo shirt paired with tan khaki shorts, his dark hair just washed and brushed.

Casting a shadow with his hand against the sun's glare, he measured up her silhouette on the dock. "I'm only here to lend a hand," he replied. His British accent fought to disarm her, but she stood fast against it. He grasped the outrigger and leaned into it.

"I put a snapper in the ice chest. There's a bucket of blue crabs up there too." Adrienne launched onto the boat, landing with a satisfying thud.

"A good morning haul, I see." Christopher eyed the wagon, pulled himself up to the dock, and handed her the live bait buckets. She decided not to grumble about how she could handle it, instead waiting for the right moment to pin him with the day's complaint.

"I'll pop them in the steamer when I return to the market. Want me to fix the fish, too? Maybe some lemon? Garlic?" He nodded to her as he handed the last bucket down.

It was hard to stay mad at him, especially when he was always helping her grandfather run the market, steaming her crabs, and offering to prep her fresh-caught fish. With her grandfather's health waning, their reliance on Christopher was an unwelcome necessity. But all she had to do was remember the latest news article he had written for the *Harbor Point Star*, where his "real job" was as a beat reporter.

Adrienne chose to ignore his kind offer and get to the point. "I really enjoyed yesterday's article about Gran." Swinging around, she dumped the last squirming fish into the boat's live well.

"Oh, Adrienne," Christopher said in a singsong tone he reserved for her, no doubt knowing it made her feel like a kid, which no fifteen-year-old wanted. His feet hit the boat's bow, causing her loose fishing poles to fall over. "It's my job to report on the happenings around town, and we both know it's a small town with not much going on."

She glared, waiting for a better explanation.

"I can't help if one Elizabeth Harris tends to be the main source of 'happenings' in this town." He opened his arms as if asking for some consideration. She wouldn't give it to him. "I must report on the disputes. My hands were tied."

Yet again, a scandal had rocked the annual Harbor Point Historical Society chili cook-off fundraiser. The previous year, Gran had lost first place for the first time when Paola Suarez, Harbor Point's butcher, had snatched the title away; the very next year, Paola's prize-winning chili verde gave the panel of judges explosive diarrhea.

Smelling something beyond mere culinary intrigue, Paola dispatched a sample to a food lab. Lo and behold, the test showed traces of ex-lax in her pot of chili. Pete Spicer, a bashful figure known to hover over Ocean Boulevard Bridge, only found the courage to step forward when the lab results were illuminated. He claimed he saw Gran lurking around Paola's hot plate the day of the event. The Harris family had been banned from the chili cook-off for life.

The relentless gossip was already a torment, but to witness her grandmother's mortifying antics etched in ink was a burden Adrienne struggled to shoulder. Anyone could go into the Harbor Point Library and search archived issues of the *Star* and read about the terrible crimes Gran had committed. Adding insult to injury, Gran herself kept a scrapbook, a disconcerting tribute to her notoriety, bursting with clippings of every article where her name featured. The book would appear late in the evenings whenever Gran hosted some to-do at the house.

Slumped in defeat at Adrienne's unrelenting stoniness, Christopher turned to the hatch leading to the boat's cabin. "You think he's okay to be on the water today?"

"He's going to die. He might as well enjoy what he has left. I'm taking him out if he's feeling up to it." She cringed at her own frankness, but it was the truth. Gramps was going to die sooner than later. "He had chemo yesterday, but he slept through the night. So far, he's holding up."

"You're too young to care for all these old people. You know you can call me if you need help."

Her tense posture melted in resignation as she nodded. Christopher's simple kindness threatened to undo her carefully constructed defenses. The dedication he showed by working at the fish market for paltry wages revealed his deep affection for Gramps. She had to be brave for her grandfather, but who would be brave for her?

Gramps always had a kind word to say and a song to hum. His storytelling would fill the market with old men in the late afternoon. Before cancer, he proudly served as the unofficial grill captain at all community picnics. And his shy version of Santa at the Women's Club holiday fundraisers was a town favorite. It made Adrienne beam with light to be near him, to call him her grandfather.

"I'll be up at the shop. Stay close to the shore, okay?"

"Sure. You know I can handle this." Adrienne creased her brow as Christopher hopped onto the deck. She couldn't give him too much leeway.

"That's right. Your birthday is next week." He tapped his chin thoughtfully.

"How'd you know that?"

"Come on. I'm a reporter. It's a big one, sixteen, right? It'll be strange seeing you driving around town rather than pedaling that rusty old bike."

Adrienne rolled her eyes.

"I have another tidbit for you, something you'll want to know from this ol' reporter."

"Sure."

"I happen to know that the Merritt clan is moving into that grand house next door to you today."

Adrienne straightened abruptly. She had been counting down the months. Now that the day was here, thoughts flurried within, leaving her in a state of ambiguous exhilaration.

"Ah, thought that might be of interest." Christopher winked before heading up the dock. He turned to her one last time, shielding his eyes from the sun. "I'm off to meet with Mr. Merritt for an interview, but fill me in on anything interesting you might spy?"

"Sure," she replied again, but she wasn't present. Her mind had wandered over the Back Bay to South Road. *What's happening at the big white house?* It was impossible to focus.

Gramps came out on the deck. He smiled at Adrienne. His face, a map of years lived out in the elements, brightened whenever he found himself on the water. His sparkling blue eyes rivaled a child's on a joyous summer day. Adrienne cherished the sight of him: his shock of thick white hair slicked back with a dab of VO5, his chest still trim and browned through the gaps of his unbuttoned, faded Hawaiian shirt.

"A short trip today, Dolly." Gramps put a hand on her shoulder and gave Christopher a salute. "Not a good idea to leave Gran alone with the new neighbors."

They all chuckled at the idea.

—

LATER THAT AFTERNOON, they pulled up to their small wooden dock. The surrounding jungle cloaked the Back Bay in dappled shadows as Gramps started the familiar ritual of cleaning and readying the boat for the next day. His arms trembled slightly, the broom in his grip brushing feebly over the deck. Adrienne bit back words of concern. Instead, she quietly took over when he relented and slunk to his captain's chair.

The bottom of the bay, a concoction of mud, sand, and who knew how many years' worth of mangrove roots and leaves, squished between her toes as she scrubbed the hull. The tide drew toward its peak ebb, and the air seemed to ferment, viscous with the stench of rot and heat.

As they headed up the narrow dock and through the tunnel of mangroves, Gramps draped an arm over her shoulders and slid something into her palm. Her fingers closed around a crinkled bit of paper. When they emerged into the sunlit expanse of the grassy field adjoining the road, Adrienne looked at the fifty-dollar bill in her hand and kissed his cheek.

"For your birthday. Don't tell your Gran. You know how she is. Put it toward that car you're saving for." He placed a kiss on the top of her head.

She smiled. "It will be our secret."

Her eyes darted to the moving van outside the gate of the mansion. Her feet suddenly rooted in place, tethered by a bout of apprehension. Then she followed Gramps home. It wasn't as if she could simply march up to the front door and ring the doorbell. The thought made her skin crawl. Unsaid words fluttered in her mind, but not one of them felt right.

CHAPTER SIX

Days ticked by after the moving trucks left. Gran wore a mask of anxiety. Her words often dissolved into grumblings about lack of neighborly courtesy. A stream of antsy Junior League and botanical society ladies came in and out of the house daily. They sat in the living room in their finery, sipping iced tea from tall iridescent glasses and speculating about when Mr. Merritt would show himself.

After a week of conspiring ladies and nonexistent Merritts, a disillusioned Adrienne carried her surfboard through the seagrass and reasoned that nothing genuinely exceptional ever happened in Harbor Point. They would probably never see much of the Merritts. The family was likely not the kind to immerse itself in the rustic charm of townie life, to laugh over shared dishes at potlucks, or to contribute their voices to the local clubs. They would zip in and out, elusive interlopers, always on the fringes, like the rich in Palm Beach.

Adrienne plopped her board on the hot sand and spread her towel, carving out a little refuge among the afternoon beachgoers. Facing the glass-smooth sea, she tried to conjure the moist heat to rise and congregate with the uncertain winds where land met the ocean, turning and twisting into a rare summer set. But her powerful gift of premonition did little to stir the waves, so Adrienne closed her eyes and contemplated a paddle to the reef for a free dive down to the coral. There, she could seek the good shells that never reached the shore or gather sea urchins to sell at the market.

Gran had taken Gramps to the clinic for his chemo treatment.

He went three times a week, and the sessions wore him out. Adrienne tried not to ruminate on the neon poison they pumped into his veins. The first treatment shattered her—watching the vibrant spirit fade to a flicker. His life force seemed to retreat, making way for the ruthless fluid, itself waging war against the cancer that dared to claim him. That first night, he had been sick, and now he was something delicate and quickly snuffed out. After that, she couldn't bring herself to go. Surprisingly, Gran was sympathetic and allowed her to stay home. Death was Elizabeth Harris's Achilles heel. It terrified her so much that she banned the topic from the house.

A cold tremor seized Adrienne's body, a harbinger of the void Gramps's absence would leave. She pushed the chill away and surrendered to the sun, its rays painting her skin for hours on end. By August, she would be a brown crisp, and Gramps would jokingly call her "the native," referencing the drops of Cherokee that surfaced in the summer.

Focused on each searing skin cell, Adrienne soon sank beyond the towel into the dark place of sleep. Yet, like a cat alert to its environment, her ears tuned to the waves, listening for a sea change.

She stirred when the temperature dipped, signaling the sun's march west. Gran and Gramps would be home soon, exhausted after the hours of treatment. With her eyes still held captive by sleep, she propped herself up on her elbows, already planning the simple dinner she would prepare. Something bland and straightforward that Gramps could handle. Soup and some bread. She would gather the last vegetables from the garden as she went in and plop them all into a pot.

A subtle shift in the atmosphere pricked at Adrienne's senses, and her eyes shot open. No more than a yard from her, a boy about her age sat on a towel, bent over a large sketchbook. His face was cloaked by a sizable sweetgrass hat and sunglasses. Though a long-sleeved white sun shirt hid his torso, she could tell he was tall and thin by his long snow-white legs.

A tourist, for sure.

The boy's quick, agile strokes with the black charcoal mesmerized Adrienne. She stretched, trying to peer over the edge of the paper and see the mysterious work.

"It's impolite to spy," the boy said without stopping his work, the accusation wrapped in a warm voice that hinted at camaraderie.

"It's impolite to sit this close to a stranger. Especially a girl on the beach," she returned, matching his playful tone.

"You snore, by the way, but not in an awful way." He dragged his thumb across the page, smoothing some hidden edge.

"I mean, look." She spread her hands out wide, gesturing to the shoreline. "The whole beach is empty; you have your pick of places to sit."

"This spot was the perfect angle. I can't help you were in the way. I didn't want to disturb your snoring." His strokes, once assertive, softened into a tender dance across the page, echoing the thoughtfulness in his voice.

"I don't snore," Adrienne muttered.

He stopped sketching and turned to her, peeling his sunglasses off and revealing a face as pale and round as the moon. A child's face, save for his eyes, which struck Adrienne with the force of a thunderbolt. They were a shade of undiscovered blue and carried profound wisdom contradicting his youthful features. A blush crept over Adrienne's cheeks as she realized she was ogling him.

He tore the sheet from the book and handed it to her. A seagull faced out to sea, the wind ruffling a tuft of feathers on its back. The fine detail of the drawing seemed too advanced for someone their age.

"You must be some kind of art genius," Adrienne marveled.

"Keep it," he said as he stood and brushed the sand clinging to his shorts.

He offered his hand to Adrienne. It seemed like such a formal thing to do. She hesitated at first but then accepted.

"I'm Lucas." He didn't let go of her hand, instead peering down at her as if she were an intriguing specimen, his face shadowed by the hat.

"Merritt?" she asked as the clues locked into place.

"Hmm." He nodded and removed his hat, revealing a head of black hair that stood out in every direction. He was every bit the all-American boy, with a dusting of freckles across his nose and cheeks that seemed to be lifted straight out of a Norman Rockwell painting. "The younger."

Confused, she simply nodded. "I'm Adrienne."

"Adrienne," he repeated, making her name sound elegant. The sun dipped behind the cottage, bringing a notable difference to the light.

She turned to inspect her home for movement, knowing time was running short. "I have to go." She turned back to him, apologetic.

"Maybe we could build a fire out on the beach tonight? Be neighborly?" He raised his brow. His invitation hung between them, as unexpected as a snowflake in July. Yet something about his earnest expression nudged her to nod.

"It will be late, like eleven?" Adrienne picked up her board and towel, shaking the sand off. "I think I have some wood up by the shed."

"Don't worry about it. My dad has a whole pile up by the pool."

"Well, welcome to South Road." Adrienne gave him a quick, self-conscious smile and headed for the cottage.

When she reached her yard, she glanced back and found him in the same spot, his hands now in his pockets. *Is he making sure I make it home?* She gave him a wave, and he returned it. His idiosyncrasies seemed harmless. *And aren't all artists a bit peculiar?* She remembered the art kids at school, all gangly arms and legs and paint-splattered jeans, their heads crowded together in a frenzy of whispers and creativity. They lived in a world of their own, oblivious to mundane reality.

And aren't I odd too, in my own way? A smile tugged at her lips as she imagined Lucas's reaction to her morning triumph: wrestling a wriggling fish from the water with her bare hands. He'd probably mark her as the strange one then. A switch flipped inside her, and she relaxed in a pleasant yet painful way, as if someone had pinched her skin and then let go.

DESPITE THE SMALL kitchen's oppressive temperature, Adrienne scooped the vegetables, onions, and tomatoes with zucchini in a pot absentmindedly, her thoughts elsewhere.

Loneliness, once a welcome ally, gave no comfort now. The only girls she socialized with were the Junior League children thrust upon her. Boys loved to ask about secret fishing spots or the best bait for grouper but never asked her to the movies. But Lucas was blissfully new and ignorant of Adrienne's family history or strange hobbies. She was not yet labeled as Elizabeth's granddaughter, nor reduced to the "fish girl." Summer, with its promise of reinvention, opened up a million possibilities. *Who will I be?* Whoever it was would have to measure up to the Merritts.

The car pulled into the driveway, crunching over the gravel. A few moments later, Gran and Gramps came through the front door. Hunched over, Gramps made his way to his favorite chair in the living room. Gran entered the kitchen with a flourish, complaining about the clinic and the nurses.

"My God, I do not know how that place stays in business." She tossed her purse on the kitchen table.

Adrienne found her grandfather cocooned in a blanket. Setting the soup on the side table, she watched Gramps recoil from it as if it contained something sinister.

Together, they peered out the bay window at the shore, contemplating the sea as the last colors in the sky faded to gray blue. She knew one day she would sit alone. She turned to plead with him to eat but found him asleep. His face wore the look of a man at war who knew only a tentative type of peace. She tucked the blanket under his chin and took the bowl back to the kitchen.

Gran ate soup at the table as Adrienne busied herself washing out the soup pot. The wind, once crisp and salty, had shifted. It blew in from the west, bringing a stagnant odor through the window slats.

The cicadas sang their final cries in the dense, interlaced branches of the trees.

"I have a headache," Gran said. She scooted her chair from the table and stood, smoothing the creases in her bright-pink slacks. "The clinic has drained me. I will never know how anyone gets well in such a horrible place."

Adrienne leaned against the counter, taking in the swirl of colors that made up Gran's ensemble. Her grandmother would be a pulsating beacon of unconventional charm in any setting less vibrant than South Florida. She thought nothing of pairing purple with orange or hot pink with electric blue. Her makeup palette was a storm of hues, with powdery blue often smearing her eyelids and cheeks in a defiant ruby on either side of bright-orange lips. It was Elizabeth Harris in her full spectrum.

"Tomorrow, we have the Junior League meeting at three." Gran left her bowl at the table and headed toward the living room. "Make sure you are clean and presentable."

Adrienne's eyes trailed after Gran, executing an exaggerated roll before she scooped up the bowl and dumped it with the others in the sink.

The rows of pill bottles taking up residence in her grandparents' medicine cabinet, each name a tongue twister, would ensure Gran an uninterrupted night's sleep and leave Adrienne an opportunity to escape later. Each little pill was part of Gran's army against whatever health battle she faced.

When Adrienne peered out the window at ten to eleven, she caught the distant glint of a fire. A sure sign that Lucas was waiting for her. She went to it like a moth, and he welcomed her with a friendly smile. They settled side by side on the quilt he had brought, letting Adrienne's marshmallows, laced onto sticks of dried seagrass, turn toasty brown over the fire. Words tumbled out of her, detailing the travails of Diana—her mother—and the affliction that seemed more like something from a poorly written script than an actual illness.

Beneath the layers of narratives and excuses, the stark truth stood exposed. Diana had been just a girl, too young and overwhelmed to navigate the mazes of motherhood.

"I have heard of it," Lucas said, perhaps trying to diminish the sting of her mom's abandonment. "I think it's called disembarkment syndrome. When your dad's business is the ocean, you get to know the strange things that happen to people on the water. People get so used to the sea that they find it hard to stay on solid land. It's like they live in a constant rocking boat."

So, her mother's affliction had a name. *It's real!*

"I wish my dad would get it. Then he would stay out on the boat all the time," Lucas said with a snort.

Adrienne gazed into the blue heart of the fire. "Yeah, my gran too. That would be great."

They exchanged glances and giggled together at their wicked thoughts of casting the adults out to sea.

As the night deepened, Lucas shared his own mother's story. The rumors about the town were correct. She had died two years before in a terrible car accident. His words wove a tragic tale, spoken with choked-back desperation.

"He was driving." Lucas poked the fire with a bit of driftwood. "He never told us what happened. He won't say anything about that night."

"After the accident, we all kind of lived in our own worlds." Lucas turned toward the dark sea. There was no moon, and everything flickered in shadows cast by the fire. The only sound was the shush of the waves. "He sent us to boarding school because of his travel demands, but I think it's easier for him not to be around us."

Lucas turned to her and touched his cheek to her hand. "It's strange, but I feel like we have been friends forever," he said, his childlike manner endearing.

"It does."

The notion of a friend—someone she could bare everything to—

had always seemed a mirage. But with Lucas, that mirage might be an oasis. Her arms tingled, and warmth filled her belly.

"I never really knew my biological parents," Adrienne mused as they stretched out on their backs and took in the night sky. "It's pretty much just been me and Gran and Gramps. I feel more like an adopted kid. I mean, I know my mom is still out there. I get postcards once in a while or a phone call when she's in port. But it feels like Gramps is my real dad. He's taken care of me my whole life. I don't know anything different."

Every few minutes, the darkness was split by a streak of light, fleeting but dazzling. They picked out the faint summer constellations they knew and created new names for the leftover stars.

"I guess we both have abnormal histories. So much for the 'nuclear family' and stuff." Lucas sighed deeply. "Maybe that's why we feel so connected to each other."

"Sometimes I pretend my grandmother is dead and it's just me and Gramps. She controls my whole life. I feel like I'll never escape her." Adrienne realized she was picking at her cuticle, and blood was seeping into the space between her nail and pointer finger.

"I feel it too. My father wants me to go into the family business." His bitterness flavored the air around them. "It's not enough for the golden boy to run things. I have to be there too."

The town gossips had put the number of sons at two; it seemed they were right.

"The golden boy, meaning your brother?"

"Yes, Quinn. The firstborn and heir to the Merritt adventure-travel empire." Lucas rolled onto his stomach facing the water and flicked at the sand, tossing bits of wood and shell. "We are only fifteen months apart, but you would think we lived in different worlds. Don't get me wrong, Quinn's great, and I love him. My sarcasm is reserved for my father."

"The town thinks your father is a treasure hunter," Adrienne said.

"He likes to think he is. The business funds his 'hobbies.' I was five when he caught the fever. Found his first piece of gold on a dive off the coast of Bimini. That's all it took to hook him."

"Is that why you moved here? Because he's after the wreck off the coast?"

Lucas laughed. "This town is a real gossip garden. I think he wanted to leave Ohio and our old life behind for a fresh start, now that we are older and hardly home. But yeah, he picked this place because of his theory about the wreck. His crew is doing preliminary dives this summer to see if they find anything."

"That sounds like a big gamble. Moving here and building this huge place without knowing if the gold is here." Adrienne gestured toward the water. "I've spent my whole life in these waters and never found anything more than starfish and shells."

Lucas crossed his arms on the sand and rested his chin on them, his eyes distant. "My dad believes in the whole risk-and-reward system. He likes to go big and bold." A sigh escaped. "Treasure hunting is like the lottery. You have got to be in the right place at the right time. You can walk by a gold coin a thousand times and never see it. Most treasure gets corroded from the salt. You hardly ever find shiny stuff. That means you need to know what you're looking for."

"You sound like you know a lot about it. Do you go with him?" Adrienne reoriented herself to the ocean and rolled onto her side, propping her head on her hand. "To find the treasures?"

"Nah, I'm more of an indoor person, unlike you, sun-kissed mermaid." His finger lightly jabbed her arm. "I can see you don't share my aversion to being outside."

"Salt water runs in my veins."

"I guess we will have to find a happy middle ground." He nodded.

"I don't get much free time. Tonight is a special case." She unfurled the intricacies of her life to him—tales of her grandfather, their bustling fish market, and the relentless web of social obligations that tethered her to her grandmother's side.

"I get it. You and my brother are a lot alike. Dad always has something for him to do. He's also the lead diver on the hunting crew. That's why you haven't met him. My dad has him out on a survey today."

Behind Adrienne's eyes, plans and schemes whirled, all crafted to dodge Gran's summer workload. As she nestled beside Lucas, the fire's glow painting them gold beneath a tapestry of stars, a realization dawned. This teensy taste of life tonight was woefully inadequate. Adrienne was hungry.

The day had stretched its hours to their limit, yet within her, a vibrancy pulsed, her senses heightened, her spirit defiant in the face of sleep. By midnight, the pair was slaphappy, telling jokes that made no sense. In companionable silence, their heads met, a soft point of contact as their eyes traced the dark curve of the shoreline. Only when Lucas stopped mid-sentence of a terrible limerick did Adrienne notice someone approaching them.

"Quinn, you're home," Lucas said. Adrienne detected a trace of disappointment.

"I saw the fire. Thought you might be down here," a voice sang from the shadows. The fire played light games with the brother's features, a face gradually forming. "I never imagined I'd find you out on the beach with a girl," the boy teased, his voice much more resonant and dynamic than Lucas's.

"Quinn, this is our new neighbor, Adrienne." Lucas touched Adrienne's shoulder and smiled at her.

Quinn folded his frame onto the sand; the circle around the fire was now complete.

He didn't possess the round, all-American looks of his brother, though they shared similar features. Quinn's face was more angular, his chin a hard line in the light. His eyebrows were darker and slanted, which made him seem contemplative, and the blue of his eyes was not as striking as his brother's. They were darker. Stormy. They locked with hers, stirring an unfamiliar queasiness within. He was broad and muscular, and the salt, wind, and sun had started to age him prematurely, as the elements did anyone who spent their life on the sea. He could pass for twenty, at least.

Adrienne was acutely aware she was gawking, but no matter how hard she tried, she couldn't stop. She could look at his face forever and find new things to admire. A part of her was terrified that the boys would sense how Quinn's arrival had rattled her. She glanced at Lucas, his demeanor betraying no hints of suspicion.

"The girl in the tree," Quinn said with a devilish smile. "Nice to meet you."

Lucas dropped his gaze.

Adrienne wanted to die right there, burn to ash, and be carried away by the wind. What a babyish thing to do, climbing trees and peeking at the people next door. She had only done it a handful of times and thought the banayacado hid her completely. Plus, she had only ever spotted the movers.

"I told him to keep his mouth shut," Lucas muttered.

"Nothing wrong with climbing a tree. God, Lucas, chill out." Quinn laughed and patted his brother on the arm with force.

While Lucas nursed his shoulder, Quinn's attention veered toward Adrienne. "I can be a real ass sometimes. I didn't mean to make fun of you."

"It's fine," she stuttered, her instincts poised at the edge of flight to the safety of her home.

"Well, catch me up. What did I miss?" He glanced at Lucas and then at Adrienne.

"We've been telling each other the stories of our lives," Lucas said, relaxing. He skewered a fresh marshmallow, extending it to Quinn, who gleefully accepted it.

"I'm sure Lucas got some things wrong. He has a terrible memory. And . . ." Quinn put his hand on her knee, making sure her attention was entirely on him. "I'm sure he told you awful lies about me."

"Actually, he never mentioned he had a brother," she said, trying to sound nonchalant.

Quinn's laughter was a roar reverberating through the still night. Loud enough that Adrienne feared Gran might wake from her drug-induced sleep. But she didn't care. For the first time, she had drawn laughter from a boy—not just any boy, but this mesmerizing, radiant creature.

The rest of the night, the spotlight was on Quinn, his presence a powerful undercurrent not allowing her to break free. It wasn't as if she put up a fight, either. He had effortlessly charmed her with a touch and a single chuckle.

Unlike Lucas, Quinn could not stay still. He was prone to bouts of animated talking and walking. His hands conducted an invisible orchestra, articulating tales of far-off lands, intriguing individuals, and close calls with danger. He would then flop onto the sand, seemingly exhausted, but the quiet spells lasted only a few moments. As the night wore on, it became evident Quinn was a master weaver of tales. His soul was tethered to the ocean, and Adrienne was enchanted by him.

She glanced at her watch, the neon digits blinking *4:00 AM*. A long yawn escaped, and fatigue washed over her in a slow wave.

"I need to catch some sleep before work," she said, her words laced with reluctance as she glanced at the brightening horizon. "It's already tomorrow."

"What are we doing today?" Lucas asked. He kicked sand onto the fire's embers.

Quinn rubbed his hands together. "I'm free. We should find some trouble to stir up in this sleepy town."

"It's my birthday," Adrienne said, more as a realization than to make it known.

"You must have plans then?" Lucas folded the quilt up. He sounded disappointed.

"None. It's never been a big deal in our house." Adrienne hoped he didn't press. The mention of her birth always cast a cloud over Gran's already cranky countenance.

"Okay. Then it's set. We'll pick you up at seven tonight. I just got my license, and we can cruise the South Florida scene," Quinn announced. Adrienne had the feeling most people went along with Quinn's plans. His natural dominance was clear.

"Sure," she heard herself say, knowing there was no way her

grandmother would allow her to drive around with strange boys. But it was plain as day at that moment, and she had no silly notions about it: She would always say yes to Quinn.

They parted ways, Lucas touching her shoulder and uttering a goodbye. She watched them head to the big white house, the whole scene wrapped up in a halo of light. Quinn bounded ahead of Lucas, leaping over the seagrass and laughing. They were two sides of the same coin, different but undoubtedly brothers.

Once in the safety of her bedroom, with the door closed, Adrienne went to the window. The Merritt estate loomed in the dark. The wild drumbeat of her heart filled the night. Her breaths came in short, quick gasps, struggling to keep up, and lightheadedness threatened to topple her. The familiar contours of her world seemed to have rearranged themselves, as if she had walked through the mirror into a place filled with possibility.

A light appeared upstairs in the big house, and a shadow moved across the drawn blinds. Adrienne held her breath. The shade went up, and Quinn appeared. He opened the window and placed his hands on the sill, staring out.

Curled into a small, unnoticeable figure, Adrienne watched him, imagining the furrowed lines on his forehead, the distant gaze. All a cryptic language she yearned to decipher. She stood there until the blinds came down and the light went out.

"Goodnight, Quinn," she said to the night.

She got into bed, but there would be no sleep. Her eyes remained wide open as the sky grew pink with morning's blush. The spot on her knee where Quinn had touched her stung like a burn. And another kind of burning crawled through her. In Quinn's wake, he left blazing turmoil. Yet the raw intensity of her newfound urges sent a shiver up her spine.

CHAPTER SEVEN

At nine the following day, someone knocked on the front door. Adrienne bolted from her bed and hurried to open it before the noise woke her grandmother. Gran was a storm cloud before noon, especially if last night's pills lingered in her system. Gramps was awake, his eyes faintly shimmering, but he seemed to have grown roots in his chair.

A robust, aging man greeted her with a bouquet of stargazer lilies. He was short with a square frame and wore a crisp white Ralph Lauren polo, his salt-and-pepper hair slicked back with gel. He reminded her of a sailor from those pirate movies on PBS, with deep-brown skin cured like leather.

Startled, she accepted the flowers, and enigmatic blue eyes twinkled at her through the stems. That was when she knew the man must be the fabled Mr. Merritt, treasure hunter. Though the brothers shared nothing in form with their father, their eyes connected them. Her previous grand visions of him crumbled like dust. All credit for Lucas and Quinn's tall, lanky bodies and pleasing faces clearly went to the late Mrs. Merritt.

"You must be Adrienne. The boys told me about you this morning."

He stuck out his hand, and she feebly took it. His palms were rough and calloused. She could tell that Mr. Merritt had toiled to make his money, rising as the American fairytale foretold. He seemed too blue-collar and plain to be a wealthy businessman and treasure hunter.

"Call me Bob," he said, letting go of her hand. "I was hoping to speak to your grandmother. Introduce myself and all."

"She's sleeping. Then there's the Junior League this afternoon . . ." She trailed off, wondering how long she could keep Gran from Mr. Merritt. Adrienne could almost hear the clashing cymbals of confrontation from the not-too-distant future.

"Well, please tell her I came by. These flowers are for her. I heard she's into plants." Mr. Merritt—she would never be able to call him anything other than that—winked at her and then nodded at the lilies. "I have some things I'd like to talk to her about. We want to put a wall between your property and ours. The problem is, the tree seems to be growing on both sides of the property line."

Adrienne's jaw practically unhinged, her expression no doubt approaching a horror that only cartoon characters could convey. "You want to cut down the tree? That tree is Gran's most prized thing in the whole world."

This statement carried not an ounce of hyperbole; the tree held an unrivaled position at the pinnacle of Gran's affection. It was a tree of local legend and lore, an oddity of the botanical world that brought her a sort of fame. She held lectures and picnics beneath its canopy. A plaque at its base retold the tale of its beginning. Of how Gran's father had planted an avocado tree in that spot, and somehow, a banyan sapling grew simultaneously, twisting and melding with the avocado until the two trees were one. Just as she did with articles about herself, Gran kept a scrapbook containing any article mentioning the tree. She reserved the earliest pages of the album for the articles crystallizing her moments in the limelight. It sat in a place of honor on the coffee table in the living room, in reach whenever company came to the house.

"We would build around it, but it is a big tree. Plus, the root system extends almost to my house. It's giving my contractor a pain in his side." Mr. Merritt laughed, a sound ringing with mirth that found no echo in Adrienne's stone-faced expression.

"Mr. Merritt, you should know that Gran doesn't listen to reason. Ask anyone." Adrienne spun around, scanning the corners for Gran. "Trying to get her to cut down that tree means big trouble . . . for all of us."

"You leave her to me, honey." Mr. Merritt gave another great chuckle, and Adrienne jumped. "I'm throwing a housewarming party on Saturday and want to invite you and your grandparents. I'm sure I can charm Mrs. Elizabeth Harris into compromise."

Mr. Merritt gave a little wave as he turned toward the path.

Adrienne remained on the porch for some minutes longer, the cool tingle of her peculiar gift spreading through her.

A storm is coming.

AFTER DINNER, ADRIENNE stood at the kitchen sink, washing the dishes and plotting her escape from the house. Her frustrated sighs, escaping her lips like trapped birds, caught her grandfather's attention over the crinkle of his newspaper. When he tottered into the kitchen, Adrienne let the floodgates unleash a torrent about Quinn and Lucas and her wish to join them that evening.

"Go, have fun. I can handle Gran," he said with a wink and a pat on her arm.

"I can't. She'll end us both." Adrienne sighed. She threw the dish towel on the table. "It's her worst nightmare, me out with boys."

"You shouldn't worry so much. You're young. Go and do teenager stuff. Get in a bit of trouble. You mind the market and take care of us old bats. You deserve time to be a kid. I'm sure the boys are nice." Gramps leaned in, his eyes holding the glint of a secret ready to be unveiled. "Don't tell Gran I told you, but I took her for a drive when she was a young gal."

"In a million years, I'd never picture Gran driving with boys." Adrienne's head swiveled, her lips curling into a brief smile before she rose and returned to the sudsy dishes.

"Your gran was quite a wild one when I met her." His hearty chuckle warmed the room. "Don't you tell her I said that either."

"I don't believe you."

"Sometimes, I feel bad you got stuck with us old farts," he said softly.

She paused as she dried the last plate. "You got it the wrong way around. I'm the one who screwed up your retirement. If you hadn't had to take care of me . . ."

"Ah." He brushed away the sentiment. "Go, get ready, and I'll deal with the fearsome Elizabeth Harris."

Planting a kiss on the sparse hair adorning Gramps's head, Adrienne darted away to her room, keen on beating Gran to the proverbial punch. Heeding her grandfather's words did not come guilt-free, but the urge to see Lucas and Quinn again won out over any hesitations.

The problem was that she had nothing to wear. Her wardrobe consisted of worn T-shirts and jean shorts. The three outfits Gran forced her to wear to the Junior League and other social functions were all skirt suits and ridged shifts, not something a girl wore out with teenage boys. She was going to be sixteen in a few hours. Adrienne reasoned that boys probably didn't care for girls who walked around in clothes with fish blood on them.

Who will you be, Adrienne?

A chaotic ten minutes saw her closet upturned and her spirit teetering on the edge of surrender. Then a plan formed. A quick trip to the little general store next to the grocery market with Gramps's birthday money would get her a new dress. The alien thought trilled through her.

The good thing about living in a small town was that Adrienne could walk anywhere in Harbor Point. Muting her footsteps, she eased out of the house, tossing a casual wave to Gramps, and headed for Bill's General Store. Bill's carried a bit of everything.

As she scurried to the sanctuary of the changing room with a yellow dress, Linda, the cashier, eyed her inquisitively.

At first, Adrienne didn't even realize that the image in the mirror was her. The dress made her tanned arms appear even darker. Her dark-brown eyes shone from within a cascade of curls let loose from their usual ponytail. She was getting boobs. The thin material outlined the faintest curve.

Unfortunately, covering up everything wild about her would be impossible; her arms bore a series of healing scrapes and bruises from working at the market and skulking among the mangroves, and Band-Aids adorned her legs. But the sundress was a good start.

Adrienne took a deep breath and exited the changing room, heading for the cash register. Linda's lips spread in a broad smile.

"Got a hot date, huh?" she said. She clipped the tag from the dress and rang it on the machine.

A laugh dribbled from Adrienne's lips as Linda gave her a bag for her "old" clothes. She fled the store before the woman could press her.

As she skipped over the bridge back to South Road, Quinn came into view, leaning against the driver's door of a pristine white Bentley convertible. Adrienne admired the gleaming white-and-chrome machine, taking in her sleek lines. *The car costs more than our house.* Quinn appeared nonchalant. *This must be a typical day for him.*

Quinn smirked and nodded approvingly. "Ah, she likes cars." He was as beautiful as the car, wearing a blinding white polo paired with dockers.

"Dad likes pretty things," Lucas said from the back seat, his tone more sarcastic than joking.

"Who wouldn't like this pretty thing?" Adrienne replied, touching the polished hood ornament. Last night on the beach, her previous, dull life had ended, and she was stepping into a new life where fancy cars were the norm.

Quinn moved to the passenger side of the car, pulling the door open with a bow, his movements fluid and gallant. "Your chariot, m'lady."

A giggle bubbled up as she awkwardly slid into the front seat. *Is Quinn looking at me differently?* Turning to Lucas to say hello was all she could think to keep from saying something dumb to Quinn.

Lucas had an arm stretched across the back of the seat, his posture exuding detached comfort. His sunglasses hid his blue eyes and any hint of his mood. His lovely red-and-blue checked button-down shirt made his pale skin luminescent. The brothers seemed to dress similarly yet in different colors.

"Let's get out of here." He nodded to Quinn, who scampered back to the driver's side and jumped over the door, sticking a perfect landing on the seat.

"Yes, let's go find some trouble." Quinn rubbed his hands together in what was becoming a familiar gesture. A thrill tangoed up her spine, partnered with terror at his enthusiasm.

"You're going to find that hard to do. Nothing happens around here. Everything closes by nine o'clock, even the police station." Adrienne shook her head at the foreseeable monotony of the evening. They would drive around, probably end up at the marina pizza place, and then get bored and return to the beach like the night before.

"We're from Ohio. We know what boring is," Lucas said, leaning between them.

With a turn of the keys, Quinn awakened the car, its engine purring like a sunbathing feline. "Correct, brother. And that means we are experts on finding fun where no fun is to be found."

Adrienne had never before gone looking for "fun" or "trouble"—two destinations always forbidden by her grandmother. Yet here she was, being chauffeured by teenage boys on an evening ripe with summer's charm. A vision of Gran swaddled in her night coat, curlers in her hair and arms crossed defensively, squatted in her head. The eerie waltz of red-and-blue lights from a police cruiser painted the scene.

She pushed the image aside and resumed focus on Quinn's cheerful face as he zipped over the bridge.

Ultimately, they drove to Palm Beach, the legendary town of privilege and money that stood against the Atlantic, with its polished mansions and whitewashed shops. Everything on the island was tidy and clean, the verdant grass and hedges all trimmed just so. Quinn eased the sleek convertible into a parking spot on Worth Ave, where the glittering windows of designer boutiques hinted at the area's reputation for high-end shopping.

The magic of the strip did not fade after closing time when the shops went dark, the expertly trimmed ficus trees catching the light like fireflies. Beyond the street were hidden gems, gardens and grottoes tucked behind the arcade of shops and linked by pedestrian vias. Many of the art galleries placed pieces in secret courtyards. The trio walked the empty paths, admiring the bronzed figures of children climbing trees and flying kites. They found an enormous blue porcelain fish in an alcove. Quinn mounted and rode it like a horse, making Adrienne laugh. He swirled his arm as if it held a large cowboy hat.

They came upon a ghost tour about to begin. Lucas pulled out a wad of cash as thick as a folded dish towel and peeled off some bills, handing them to the perky tour guide. The guide's voice rose and fell as she wove the tale of Addison Mizner, the famed architect whose spirit was said to wander his Palm Beach creations on Worth Ave long after night had fallen.

Following her account, both boys started whispering in Adrienne's ear, saying they thought they "saw" a ghost. Whenever Quinn leaned in, goose bumps traced her arms.

"I'm starving," Quinn said as the tour disbanded.

Adrienne's eyes flicked to her watch, the hands pushing toward eleven. She considered the dwindling chances of finding an open restaurant on a sleepy weeknight. But they followed the faint moan of a violin and ended their quest at a place with a French name nestled in one of the grottos. Tiny tables dotted the patio, encircling a bubbling fountain. In the corner, a couple was lost in each other, sequestered within the overhanging fronds of a palm tree. The violinist stood nearby, readying for the next song.

Quinn approached the hostess standing guard at a polished podium by the entrance, engaging her in hushed conversation. Two men in crisp white aprons and black shirts escorted Adrienne to a table by the fountain. The server handed her a sizable menu. Of course, it was all in French.

Lucas leaned in, his voice dropping to a whisper. "I can read it to you if you don't understand. We were forced to learn French."

A knowing smile crossed Adrienne's lips. "Thank you, but I know French cuisine. I've pored over every line of Escoffier's cookbooks."

"Really?" Quinn leaned back in his chair, his eyebrows arched in surprise and admiration. "You want to be a chef?"

"I think so." Adrienne dipped her head behind the menu, not wanting him to see her blush.

His eyes twinkled. "You'll have to be brave, Lucas, and eat whatever Adrienne makes you, or you'll hurt her feelings."

Lucas scanned his menu. "I can be a bit of a picky eater."

"That's okay." Adrienne reached out and squeezed his arm. There was a thoughtfulness about Lucas that reminded her of Gramps. "I can make you anything you like. I like to experiment when I'm working at the market."

He gave Adrienne a sheepish smile.

They got to the business of dinner. Everything on the menu was tempting, and anything Adrienne mentioned, Quinn ordered. When the dishes arrived, there was no room on the table. They ate and laughed for what seemed like hours, only slowing when they became stuffed. Then they quieted and listened to the music.

Adrienne peeked at the couple in the corner as they leaned into each other and whispered things that made the other smile. The idea of being in love, of romantic whispers and knowing smiles, was so novel that she had difficulty imagining trading places with them.

She turned to Quinn and caught his eye. Heat bloomed in her cheeks under his gaze. He responded with a wink before turning his attention toward the hostess, signaling her with a subtle nod.

The serene ambiance was punctured by lively strains of music, and a giant chocolate cake materialized before Adrienne. The servers and the hostess circled their little table and began to sing. The candlelight from the cake cast a carousel of shifting shadows across Quinn's enthralled features.

"Make a wish, Adrienne." Lucas's voice echoed like a distant melody in the haze of her thoughts.

She turned to him, nodded, and focused on the candles. A wish crystallized within her. *An endless summer with Quinn and Lucas.*

———

AFTER LEAVING THE restaurant, they went to the beach, running along the shore as the moon rose over the ocean. The world around them simmered in a coppery glow. The water was inviting. They kicked their feet up, splashing each other until a patrol cop told them to go home: It was too late for kids to be on the beach. Such were the unspoken rules of Palm Beach—transient moments of joy abruptly curtailed, leaving a sense of not truly belonging.

No one was in a rush to get home. Quinn navigated the Bentley with a leisurely grace along the empty A1A. Adrienne claimed the world as her own, tracing the squiggly line of the shore with her finger as they sped along. The ocean's balmy scent made her want to close her eyes, but she forced them to stay open. Every blink was a potential lost moment in this ephemeral experience.

She held her breath as they neared the end of their journey. She had done an excellent job of forgetting about Gran as they gallivanted around Worth Ave. The countdown on her magical Cinderella night was nearing the inevitable stroke of midnight.

There were no police cruisers with their lights on when the Bentley stopped on her street. Gran wasn't out in the driveway in her night coat and curlers. A silent prayer of gratitude for this reprieve slipped from Adrienne's heart. As she exited the car and closed the passenger door as gently as possible, Lucas crawled into the front seat. He leaned through the window, a smile playing on his lips.

"Want to come swim at our pool tomorrow?" Lucas asked, his moon face cherublike.

Adrienne glanced toward the quiet and dark cottage. "I have to open the market tomorrow. Come by if you want, and I'll cook for you."

She looked past him at Quinn in the driver's seat. He was turned toward the Back Bay, gazing at the dark line of mangroves hiding the water. His voice when he spoke bore the weight of obligation subtly straining against an undercurrent of rebellion.

"I'll be gone until the housewarming party. Dad has a new mission for me."

The disappointment left a sour aftertaste. It would feel like forever until Quinn returned.

"Sure, I'll come by," Lucas said with enthusiasm. "I'd rather be inside than at the pool anyway. You can show me how to sell fish."

The image of Lucas the socialite slinging fish ignited a shared ripple of laughter among them. It was a high note on which to end the night.

Adrienne turned to the boys once she reached the path's edge and waved. A flush rose in her cheeks when the boys patiently waited until she disappeared before driving away.

She found Gran sitting at the kitchen table with a cup of coffee, waiting for her. Of course. Her "night on the town" wouldn't be without penalty—but it would be worth it.

"You think you got away with something tonight, using your poor sick grandfather as a means to go out with boys," Grand said flatly. "Don't think you can go out with strangers all night. That's how your mother got into this mess in the first place. I won't let you ruin your life as she did. I won't raise another illegitimate child dumped on me. No. If you get pregnant, you are out of this house."

Gran's words burrowed under Adrienne's skin, stirring up the old sting.

Adrienne clamped her tongue between her teeth. The metallic taste of blood filled her mouth. Arguing with Gran was a quicksand trap. The more she struggled, the deeper she'd sink. Eighteen was just two years off, and then freedom. She would go to culinary school. It would be okay to break ties. Gramps would be gone, and Adrienne would have no reason to stay in Harbor Point.

"They are nice. They are our new neighbors, and they are my friends. They come from a good home and go to good schools. They are everything you would want my friends to be." Adrienne chose her words carefully, trying to think like Gran would think, painting the brothers in a good light.

Gran shook her head. "The rich don't understand rules. They take what they want, bending the world around their whims. Even 'good' boys think they rule the world, Adrienne. They pluck desires like low-hanging fruits, never considering the consequences. No boy will ever think you are worth more than ten minutes. You should focus on your studies and make something of yourself without any boy in the picture. They will bring you down. They will be the end of you."

"We're invited to their housewarming party." Adrienne laced her voice with cheerfulness, attempting to steer their conversation away from dangerous shoals.

"Yes, a formal note came today. I guess we will finally get to see what all the fuss is about when it comes to Merritts. I've asked the ladies from the Junior League to accompany me." Gran set the mug on the table, took the note from her coat pocket, and slid it over to Adrienne to inspect for herself. The cardstock's weighty feel and texture spoke volumes of Mr. Merritt's penchant for luxury. This would be no casual affair.

I'll have to buy another new outfit.

She would ask Lucas about the dress code when he came by the market.

CHAPTER EIGHT

As preparations unfolded, not even the most seasoned Harbor Point residents could predict what kind of spectacle the Merritts' housewarming party would shape into. The day before the event, trucks of various sizes began delivering items to the big white house. Folding tables set with crisp white linen, crystal goblets, and silver were erected around an impressive poolside dance floor. Thousands of white twinkle lights crisscrossed over the festivities.

Adrienne glared at the banyacado tree from her grandmother's second-story bedroom window. It was a perfect vantage point, but the thought of Quinn catching her there again made her stomach flip. The din of the delivery people rushing about and the workers preparing for the party made every nerve in her body tingle with excitement.

When she spotted Lucas in the driveway, she boldly called out to him.

"Come over!" he shouted and waved.

Adrienne found his invitation impossible to resist.

"The caterers are working in the kitchen," Lucas said as she neared. "Want to watch them?"

With a nod, she fell into step behind him as they were swallowed by the sprawling grandeur of the Merritt mansion. She was Alice, stepping through the looking glass into a strange world filled with unfathomable lives. The grand living room boasted a wall of windows that looked out toward the sea. A sweeping staircase curled up to the second floor. Yet the lively symphony of the kitchen—the clatter of pots and pans, the tempting aroma—was what drew her in, an irresistible siren call.

A gleam caught her eye, revealing a lineup of high-end stainless steel appliances for which most professional chefs would give their right arm. A mammoth Sub-Zero fridge stood guard beside a ten-burner Viking range. The counters were all made of brilliant marble. Images of golden and flaky pastries danced in Adrienne's mind as she gazed at them. A longing sigh escaped her lips at the bubbling pots, the sharp tang of garlic, and the ballet of the bustling cooks.

A great racket rose from the far end of the kitchen. A prep cook had sliced the better part of his thumb clean off. The executive chef berated him for not paying attention. "What am I supposed to do now?" The chef threw his bar rag on the floor. "We have no time for this."

Lucas spoke up, pulling Adrienne forward. "My friend is a great cook. Maybe she can help out?"

Under the chef's scrutiny, she shrank back, feeling like a lamb in the lion's den, and to him, she must have appeared just as comical. A laugh rumbled from his chest.

"Seriously, she runs the fish market in town." Lucas frowned and squeezed Adrienne's hand.

"Well, she can't be any worse than that idiot," the chef sighed, tossing her a clean apron.

Adrienne's heart hammered in counterpoint to the frenzied rhythm of the kitchen. She cast Lucas a murderous glance that promised revenge later. Lucas giggled, seeming to delight in her anxiety. Everyone's eyes were on her. She had no choice but to take the empty spot left by the injured cook at the counter.

It took little thought. Adrienne chopped the pile of vegetables awaiting prep, following the specific cuts the chef ordered her to make from his place at the stove. The kitchen fell away, and the rush of bodies around her melted.

The chef came over to check her progress. His approval emerged as a strange guttural noise.

"Take over on sauté. That woman is ruining my medley!" the chef barked. Adrienne jumped and skipped to the stove, where the mouselike girl shrank away from her and took over the prep station.

Drenched in sweat, Adrienne didn't leave her pan until the chef announced prep was over. When she turned to toss her spatula into the sink, she discovered Quinn behind her, leaning against the counter, wearing a goofy grin and nodding with approval. The spatula remained clenched in her hand, its weight suddenly alien.

Adrienne's insides popped and crackled like heat lightning.

"I like seeing you in action," Quinn said. "Impressive. Very Impressive."

"I'm sweating like a pig." A laugh tumbled from her lips.

"I guess we all need to get cleaned up. The party starts soon," Lucas piped up.

Adrienne's muscles relaxed as she mouthed a silent thank-you for Lucas's intervention.

THE PARTY STARTED at eight, when the sun dipped below the skyline. Adrienne twirled in front of the mirror. Her new dress—this one from the department store a few miles inland—rustled around her, its buttery yellow fabric contrasting with her dark skin. It had taken an hour to do her hair, something she never spent time on. She washed it twice and used a conditioner, then blew it out using Gran's ancient hair dryer with the frayed cord.

She had even footed the bill for some makeup, though she hardly knew how to use the products. Witnessing Gran apply makeup was like viewing a Jackson Pollock painting in progress. Adrienne elected to do everything she had seen Gran do, but the opposite. She applied the faintest hint of pink to her cheeks, a dab of something glistening to her lips, a swish of something pale to her eyes.

Her reflection became a stranger, the transformation unexpected and startling. A real girl had been hiding underneath all the dirt and fish guts. A smile spread across her lips. Yet, deep within, a tug-of-war ensued between the tomboy and the emerging young woman in the mirror. Was she ready to give up a life of trudging through the Back Bay, catching crabs?

A tentative but hopeful thought tiptoed into her mind: *Maybe I could be both.*

But this wasn't the time for meditation on what the next day would bring. With Gran and her posse of elderly socialites planning a grand entrance for later in the evening, Adrienne would slip into the Merritts' party without fuss or fight.

Her body was light as she skipped through the thicket that divided the two properties, yet she froze once she emerged at the party's edge. The band settled and tuned their instruments as the string lights came on. A knot of apprehension twisted in Adrienne's chest, tightening with each echo of raucous chatter. Though the world that would bloom into reality with her next step was not hers, her body ached to cross that line and never look back. Gramps was her only pull back, the silver string tugging her home again. Once he was gone, nothing in all the universe could keep her from the gravity of the big house.

"Adrienne," Christopher Crane called to her as he made his way over. "Is your gran joining you tonight?" He wore a beige suit with a white shirt, a significant change from his work shirts at the market. The transformation might have registered had her gaze not been anxiously darting through the crowd, hunting for Lucas and Quinn. Christopher seemed to blur into the background, his presence barely acknowledged.

"She's coming later with the 'granny mafia,'" Adrienne said casually. She had tried to abandon the fanciful notion that Quinn might see her as anything other than the girl next door, yet a flicker of anticipation ignited at the thought of seeing him again after so many days.

Will this feeling end? Will I ever feel human again?

"I heard about Bob Merritt's plans for the tree. Have you told her yet?" Christopher continued.

His words jolted her back to the conversation.

"No. I figure Mr. Merritt can handle her himself."

"Hmm." Christopher nodded as he sipped his drink. "You might be right, but I feel this won't end well."

Adrienne bottled up her agreement and gave him a dismissive eye roll before she spun on her heel, leaving Christopher behind. She refused to give him the satisfaction of knowing they were on a similar page.

Knowing that Gran's arrival could end her budding friendships, Adrienne resumed her hunt for the brothers. It was hard to predict how her grandmother would act in public. She sometimes kept up decorum when someone quasi-famous was in attendance or people from out of town were present, but she was known for losing it and making a scene. As she got on in years, the latter tended to be the case. The best Adrienne could hope for was a few more hours before it all came crashing down around her.

Quinn appeared amid the crowd, dressed in a creamy button-down shirt and long khaki pants. He was leaning against the bar on the lawn, surrounded by a cluster of young and expensive-looking strangers. Adrienne measured her pace, hoping to catch his eye before being snagged by the group's scrutiny. Quinn's boisterous laugh startled her. His tone was too deep and dry. This Quinn, she realized, was new. This Quinn was the one who worked for his father and had to mingle and network, the Quinn of fancy boarding schools and trips around the world. Even how he held his glass as he talked with his hands was different.

The group that encircled him all had glasses in hand with adult drinks. A maturity far beyond their years emanated from their poise and clothes. One girl with perfect blond hair and big green eyes stood too close to Quinn. She touched his arm each time she laughed at something he said. Adrienne tried to ignore how cheap and immature her own dress was compared to the other girls' glamorous and expensive outfits. She tried to forget her wild and unruly hair and her amateur attempt at makeup. Yet an overwhelming urge to retreat to the beach before the night unraveled tugged at her.

Before she could disappear, Quinn spotted her, a sudden light kindling in his eyes. Her name escaped his lips, a quiet summons, causing a ripple of intrigued faces to pivot toward her. In a flash, they pulled Adrienne into their fold. All eyes moved with her.

Where is Lucas?

"Adrienne, these are a few of my friends from school. They're here visiting. Came to surprise me." Hand on her shoulder, Quinn steered her around the circle, introducing her to his friends.

The group greeted her with a veneer of courtesy as they volleyed a string of cursory questions. Ann, the blond, held herself with an icy aloofness.

"Quinn, you should bring her to the polo tournament tomorrow. We have my aunt's tent on the east lawn. I think there will be a brunch," a redhead named Finn said after Adrienne had met everyone. "I bet she'd love to see the horses."

Quinn turned to her. "Do you think you could get away tomorrow?"

"I work tomorrow," Adrienne murmured, her voice barely rising above the ambient chatter.

"Have you been to a polo match?" Molly, a tiny brunette, asked.

"No, but it sounds like fun," Adrienne lied. There was no way she'd fit in with the crowd, and going to a polo match with them sounded far more daunting than fun.

"Polo matches are utterly boring, but they are a good place to meet rich guys and drink." A guffaw erupted from Ann, the infectious sound quickly spreading to the others. "I can let you borrow something to wear if you don't have anything suitable."

Quinn gave Ann a dirty look. "Ann, be nice."

"I am being nice, Quinton. I am offering her help. Do you want her to feel out of place?"

"Don't call me that," he muttered.

Adrienne's gaze finally fell upon Lucas, sitting at a secluded table beside the band. Latching onto the distraction, she waved. "There's Lucas!"

Lucas struggled to leave his seat, knocking over an empty glass.

"Great, here he comes." Molly rolled her eyes. "I hope he doesn't make a scene."

Her words perplexed Adrienne, disquiet settling in as Lucas approached.

"Run, Adrienne. Don't let these wolves corrupt you. You are too good for them." Lucas patted a guy named Alex on the back. His affability fooled none of those present.

"Let's not do this here." Quinn put an arm around his brother's shoulders. "Let's take a walk."

Lucas deflected Quinn's arm with a firm yet restrained push. "Buzz off. Adrienne, why don't you come with me? I hate to see you with all these fake people. It's not becoming."

"Sure," Adrienne said, cringing at the disapproving glares.

"You better put on your party face, Lucas," Ann said, smirking. "You don't want her to see what a mess you are. You can only run so far from your true fucked-up self."

"I won't hit a female, but I have no problem hitting a slut." Lucas took a step toward Ann.

Ann's boyfriend, Marcus, sprang into action, his fist connecting with Lucas's jaw. Adrienne sucked in a breath as Lucas stumbled back into Quinn.

Quinn scanned the party as he helped Lucas regain his footing, presumably to see if any partygoers had witnessed the altercation. Luckily, no one paid their little group any attention. The band had switched from Louis Armstrong to a Beatles number, and many of the guests were distracted by the dancing.

The goofy, affable Lucas seemed to have vanished, replaced by this tortured rebel. New mysteries about both brothers unfolded like some terrible flower. Adrienne felt a twinge of empathy; their double identities were as flawed and complex as hers.

"You better stop acting like an ass before Dad finds out and deals with you himself." Quinn spoke softly but decisively, pulling Lucas's arm to get him to leave the circle.

"You act all big and bad, but your mouth hides what a coward you really are," Ann hissed as she stepped away from the group. Adrienne considered the likelihood of Ann pursuing Lucas to continue her tirade.

Luckily, Marcus reeled Ann back, enveloping her again within the group's protective embrace. Lucas's whole body deflated, and he went willingly with Quinn up the gentle slope of the yard toward the pool. Adrienne was bewildered. *How could Quinn consider these people friends?*

"I don't know why they let him out. He should still be locked away," Molly said, crossing her arms.

Adrienne's heart pounded in sudden alarm. "What do you mean?" She wanted to go after the brothers, but curiosity made her hesitate.

"You don't know? He was in a mental facility last year for three months. It was voluntary, but I know he's on some serious antidepression meds."

"They should have kept him in there." Ann clucked. "He can be unpredictable. Watch yourself around him."

"Aw, she's just saying that because Lucas doesn't put up with her bullshit." Alex laughed and patted Adrienne on the shoulder. "Don't believe them. Lucas is a good guy. His mom died, and, shit, that's a lot to handle. He was depressed." He glared at Ann. "And he wasn't in a crazy bin for three months. It was an outpatient program. He went to school and everything."

"Quinn and I broke up because of him." Ann gave Alex a cold stare.

Marcus put his arm around her. "Yeah, but you upgraded with me." They shared a private smile.

"I should go check on Lucas." Adrienne smiled at Alex and gave the rest of the terrible, beautiful people a quick nod before she fled.

Lucas was finishing a large glass of ice water when she joined them. Quinn took care of him with a concern Adrienne found endearing, and she tried painting a picture of Quinn as a compassionate guy despite the abrasive company he kept. She wished Quinn had defended Lucas. But then a wave of uncertainty washed over her, reminding her of her limited knowledge. She ordered herself to trust her gut—as she prayed the brothers trusted in her character even as Gran's imminent arrival threatened to unhinge everything.

"Hey, will you sit with him while I distract my father?" Rising from his seat, Quinn cast a lingering glance over his shoulder at his high school friends, their laughter fading into the night.

"I'm good, bro. I'm feeling better." Lucas patted the seat next to him, motioning for Adrienne to take it.

"You're not," Quinn muttered as he left.

"I can't believe the whole gang showed up." A slow, despairing shake of Lucas's head sent loose strands of hair fluttering around his face. "I thought we'd gotten rid of them after school let out. I guess everyone was curious about the new house. The rich travel in packs, like wolves."

"I understand." Adrienne's fingers toyed with the delicate hem of her dress.

"Yes, I imagine you do." With a sigh, Lucas lowered his head onto her shoulder, his hand seeking hers in a plea for comfort. "Quinn has the terrible habit of seeing the good in everyone. It's that, or he doesn't have to worry about them like I do. He's popular. He doesn't know the world I know. I love him, but we live on different planets." Lucas pulled away from her and let his head fall back against the chair, eyes scanning the night sky.

"You can't let them get to you. Like you said, Quinn's friends don't matter." Adrienne rested her hand atop his, their fingers intertwining again in solidarity. "You can't decide to stop taking your medications."

"So easy to say, isn't it? Don't let them get to you," Lucas said, trailing off as he glanced toward the band. Then, he turned to her.

"Anyway, I made you something for your birthday. Sorry it took so long to get it to you."

Lucas pulled a folded paper from his shirt pocket. She hadn't expected a gift; they had known each other only a handful of days. Adrienne shook her head.

"You gave me a wonderful night in Palm Beach."

"Don't say anything. Just open it," Lucas said. A spark in his eyes melted away the frost of melancholy, revealing the boy she first met.

She unfolded the paper and beheld a beautiful drawing of her grandfather in black and white. The likeness was startling. A tremor swept through her.

"It's so realistic," Adrienne marveled. She touched the lines of her grandfather's face with her fingertips, expecting to feel the rough scratch of his chin whiskers.

"I started it the other day when he came to the market. He is a good man, your grandfather." Lucas's voice dipped to a whisper, each word heavy.

"This is the perfect gift. I could never do anything like this. You are a true artist." Her eyes burned with unshed tears. Something in her core shifted.

"I'm sure you do great things, Adrienne." With a tenderness that stole her breath, Lucas brushed a loose curl from her temple, tucking it behind her ear. "I can see it in you. Beautiful, wonderful things."

"You don't even know me." She shook her head again.

"I think I'm beginning to."

"Lucas," she said. Affection swelled within her.

"I'm glad we met," he whispered.

"Me too." She laughed and wiped away the tears on her cheek.

Lucas laughed with her. "Who knew that something good would happen moving here?"

"Yay. Everyone is happy," Quinn said rather dryly. He slid into the seat next to Adrienne. The turmoil with his group of friends had temporarily doused the wildfire of her hormones, but now that the evening had calmed, the unforgiving chemistry returned. She steeped in the awareness of Quinn's presence beside her, in the distinct, subtle aroma of sunscreen mingled with Ivory soap. A moment ago, she was crying and bonding with Lucas. Now she only wanted to bury her face in Quinn's chest and have his arms around her.

The glow in Lucas's eyes had dimmed. He monitored the party scene. "Did your crew leave?"

"Yep, on to bigger and better things. They wanted to go to South Beach." Quinn handed Lucas another glass of water and held out one of the two beers he had set on the table to Adrienne. She peeked to see if anyone was watching. The party was in full swing, and the adults, under the spell of the lavish soiree, had no care to patrol the children. With a tentative smile, she took a sip, hoping the bracing liquid would anchor her emotions.

"Don't worry about tomorrow," Quinn said hesitantly. "I've let the gang know we're skipping the polo match. Knowing them, by morning, they won't remember tonight."

"And that's supposed to make me feel better?" But the strain on his face was quickly smoothed over by indifference.

The band switched to swoon-worthy top-forty numbers, and the trio relaxed. A warm breeze blew off the Atlantic, bringing the biting smell of salt and sea. Everything glittered around them.

"I love summer," Quinn said. He clinked the tip of his beer bottle to Adrienne's, smiling. A smile she was convinced had been created only for her. It set the world spinning. The lights flashed by like swarms of fireflies in the background.

"Me too," Adrienne said, feeling something inside her pelvis groan with need. She met his gaze with the same intensity he gave. Her secret hope was that he might see the truth within her. She was irrevocably his, lost in the labyrinth. Undone. She had signed up for the duration, whatever that was.

As Adrienne prayed for the magic never to end, the time came for Elizabeth Harris to make her entrance. Her grandmother appeared under the strings of white lights, wearing a garish crop-sleeved dress that boasted large fuchsia and emerald-encrusted poppies. Her black hair, swept into a fierce french twist, was held in place by a turquoise hair pick. Her shoes were a bright-yellow low heel. She was the perfect aging starlet. Her baubles, bracelets and earrings, peacock necklace, and hairpin all twinkled like the lights above her.

Behind Gran trailed the gaggle of society ladies, all dressed in slight variations of the same Lilly Pulitzer summer dress. They fanned out on either side of Gran with such pageantry one might think their whole entrance had been choreographed. They called themselves the Junior League of Harbor Point; however, every member had long surpassed the traditional age limit, clinging to any scrap of youth they could. The town's lack of willing young people didn't help the matter.

With her hands on her hips and a masterfully arranged look of surprise, Gran entered the crowd as if the meeting had been predestined and not by invitation.

"Well, ladies. What a show," she said, dripping saccharine. Adrienne cringed.

By now, Mr. Merritt had ventured over to greet Gran and her entourage. The women, tightly clustered, broke form and floated toward the newcomer like Fred Astaire's backup dancers. Questions flew at a fierce pace, marked by shrill stabs of giggles at every charming remark.

Boy, Adrienne could see where Quinn had inherited his charm. It oozed so thickly out of Mr. Merritt that she could almost taste it. Dozens of dinner invitations assaulted him. Propositions for private tours of the ladies' home gardens came in symphony.

Adrienne let out a resigned sigh, her shoulders drooping. "I suppose it's time for you to meet my grandmother," she said.

"That is Elizabeth Harris?" Quinn was wide-eyed.

"Wow," Lucas added.

"Yeah," Adrienne said, exhausted before the introductions even began.

Quinn and Lucas took it all in stride, having far better manners than she would in the same situation. They smiled politely and shook each of the old ladies' hands, responding to questions in that instinctually formal tone the rich used.

"So, you are the boys who kidnapped my granddaughter the other night?" Gran said with a sternness that no one could be sure was in jest.

"Mrs. Harris, I assure you, she came willingly." Quinn gave Gran his most dazzling smile. "I have heard all about your magic in the garden. Adrienne told me about how devoted you are to the Florida landscape."

At that moment, something akin to alchemy took place. The stern lines of Gran's face softened, her eyes glinting. Adrienne bit her lip to hold back a laugh. She found it almost absurd how Gran lapped up Quinn's blatant show. Yet he was something to be in awe of. A true master of conversation.

"Speaking of gardens," Mr. Merritt interjected, "I was hoping Mrs. Harris and I could speak about the tree that grows between our two properties." He gestured dramatically toward the tree. "Of course, not tonight. Maybe over lunch tomorrow?"

Here it comes.

All the Junior League ladies and Adrienne turned to Gran with hesitation and concern. The pleasant mask slipped from her face at the mention of her beloved tree. Her brows knitted together, forming a deep "V" that shadowed her eyes.

"That tree is one of a kind." Gran stepped out from the cluster of ladies, holding her hands above her head like a tour guide might when highlighting a point of interest. "When my father built this house, he planted the first avocado tree in this town right in that very spot. Unknown to him then, a small banyan tree sapling was also taking root. The two trees grew up together, twisting into one. In fact, the DNA from each tree merged to create a new hybrid. People have come from all over the world to study this marvel."

"It's been in the newspaper," Lottie Bismarck added.

"And on television too," Bell Townsend slipped in.

"Ah, I see, well." Mr. Merritt cast a measured glance over the group, his hands seeking refuge inside his shorts pockets as a thoughtful furrow divided his eyebrows. "You see, I plan on building a wall around my house. Unfortunately, the survey results prove the tree grows equally on each of our properties. I was hoping we could discuss its removal."

Gran let out a howl of laughter, causing the partygoers to turn her way. "It's over a hundred years old. Its trunk alone spans fifty feet in circumference. We could never possibly move it."

"I wasn't suggesting moving it but *removing* it. A big tree like that could threaten our houses if a bad storm arose. My landscaper said the branches are brittle and could snap off and fly through our roof," Mr. Merritt said, concern threading his voice. His act was well rehearsed but transparent as glass. "Again, this might be a conversation for tomorrow."

"That landscaper of yours better not lay one finger on my tree," Gran continued, wagging her finger. "It's a historic and important landmark in this town. You will have to build your wall around it."

Adrienne and the other ladies retreated a safe distance. Even the Merritt brothers took a few steps back, feeling the heat of Gran's barely restrained fury.

"Is there a document stating this tree is a historical landmark?" Mr. Merritt folded his arms across his chest like he had bested Gran. "Because if there is none, then I have the legal right to clear my side of the property line."

"Well, Mr. Merritt. There will be one in place before you can lay a hand on my tree."

Gran folded her arms, mimicking Mr. Merritt's stance. Her resolve was stern enough to shut him up for the moment.

"Well, this is really not the time or place to continue this conversation." Mr. Merritt said once more, putting on a showy, fake smile.

"I assure you, Mr. Merritt, the conversation is over." Gran nodded firmly. "Adrienne, time to go."

The old ladies fell back into rank and file, marching through the grass after Gran as she barked orders to her white-haired minions.

"Call the police, the mayor, and a lawyer!"

Adrienne turned to the brothers and shrugged. She was out of options.

BY MORNING, GRAN had hatched a plan. Adrienne woke groggily with salt-crusted eyelids and emerged from her room to find Gran flitting about the house before nine, dressed in her finery. Catching sight of Adrienne, she stilled, and a slow, triumphant grin split her features.

"The mayor has pledged to help designate the tree as a historical landmark!" Gran clapped as she spoke, her eyes ablaze. A new crusade. She paced with frenetic energy.

It was only the beginning.

Judge Harry Lassiter would hear the case on the 30th of June, which gave Gran only a few days to prepare her arguments. It was either the 30th or they would have to wait until September when the judge returned from his annual two-month recess. Anything civil got put on the back burner while he was gone.

In the days leading up to the hearing, the phone seemed to ring incessantly, each call accompanied by hushed urgency. Gran and her posse spent hours poring over historical documents in the stuffy archives at the public library. Adrienne's fingers clacked furiously at typewriter keys night after night, transcribing Gran's endless stream of researched "support." The brothers' absence grew ever more tangible. She hadn't spoken to them since the night of the party. For all she knew, they both hated her guts, thanks to Gran.

Their living room transformed into a hive of white-haired women carrying folders full of so-called evidence in one hand and fruit-filled danishes in the other, determined not to let the rigors of their mission wear them down. Most of their "evidence" came from newspaper articles written about the tree over the years, many penned by Christopher. Several of the ladies vowed to testify to the historical significance. There were documents showing other trees given the same status due to their unique nature. Two were within the town limits.

The hearing was open to the public, and the townspeople packed into the courtroom. Adrienne saw in their eager faces the morbid anticipation of disaster unfurling.

"It's damn hot today and one day before my summer recess. I'm sweating like a newlywed on his wedding night, and my bunion is barking, so let's make this quick." Judge Lassiter eyed Gran while he said the last part. "Well, we will hear from Mrs. Harris first, and then Mr. Merritt will have a chance to counter."

Gran stood and smoothed out the wrinkles from her dress. She wore a bright-orange quilted shift accessorized with an orange rhinestone necklace and bangle bracelet. She had let her dark-dyed curls hang loose, making her appear more ferocious than usual. Despite her petite frame, the sheer force of her personality made her appear as a titan among the courtroom's inhabitants. Her war paint for the day consisted of bright-blue eye shadow and two severe swaths of burgundy rouge.

"The tree that we have lovingly come to know as the banyacado is threatened by my new neighbor, Bob Merritt. Unfortunately, the tree grows between our two properties, but there it grows and should be protected from harm for as long as it lives. I'm not doing this for personal gain." Gran turned to the rows of townspeople listening to her every word. "I am doing this for our town. This tree symbolizes the town's history, a history rooted in my family. The tree has grown with the town, becoming a powerful symbol of Harbor Point and its people."

Gran's speech rang with a cadence that Adrienne found uncharacteristic. She turned to Christopher, who was mouthing Gran's words. It clicked. The eloquence bore Christopher's unmistakable tone.

The passionate speech stretched out, turning minutes into eternity until, finally, it ended.

"Judge, to be considerate of time and the heat, I will be brief," Mr. Merritt said to open. Judge Lassiter's features eased into a near smile at the promise of brevity. "I understand that the tree is an integral part of this town. Though I'm new here, I can see that you all value the history of this gem of a community. Now that this is my home too, I want to assure all you good people that I appreciate the same things you do. It was never my intention to destroy something of importance. I merely seek to create a safe home for my two young boys. I am prepared to have the tree relocated to Mrs. Harris's property, at any expense, so that we might both leave this courtroom getting what we want."

Gran stood, interrupting Mr. Merritt. "Impossible. You cannot move the tree. It is over a hundred years old. The root system is too extensive to uproot. The tree will die if you try to relocate it."

"Some people do this for a living. I have found a company confident they can relocate the tree without injury," Mr. Merritt shot back, his cool facade beginning to crumble. "They have surveyed the tree and taken proper measurements. They have moved bigger and older trees than this one."

"Your Honor, this is a one-of-a-kind tree. We don't know how it will react to being moved. We cannot predict how the tree will fare. We need to declare it a landmark and protect it from destruction." As she spoke, Gran waved her arms wildly, Christopher's carefully scripted argument falling out of play.

"Waterfront property comes at a premium. You can't expect me to throw money away on land I bought and am the rightful owner of?" Mr. Merritt stared down the judge as he rolled up his sleeve. Sweat dotted his reddening complexion, painting a picture of exhaustion.

"Your wall will ruin the water view for us who live on South Road. Your wall shouldn't be allowed even if the tree wasn't growing on the property line," Gran snapped.

"That's enough!" The words exploded from Judge Lassiter,

punctuated by the resounding smack of his gavel against the bench. "I will allow Mr. Merritt's team to submit a proposal for relocating the tree. We will have experts review the proposal, and then I will decide when the court resumes in September. That should give everyone enough time to approach this matter sensibly. Until then, the tree is temporarily protected. Mr. Merritt, your wall will have to wait."

With this decree, Judge Lassiter tapped the gavel once more. The room erupted in chatter.

Mr. Merritt pushed through the crowd toward the exit. Catching sight of Quinn and Lucas waiting at the back of the room, Adrienne flushed with mortification. Gran hugged Christopher, saying she was sure that, in the end, the tree would be saved. Adrienne followed behind them.

Victory painted Gran's face with an unquenchable glow. She raised her arm and gave the remaining onlookers a royal wave as she passed.

Adrienne hoped the Merritts were long gone when they left.

—

THAT NIGHT, ADRIENNE couldn't sleep. The house throbbed with trapped residual heat as the hearing's agonizing scenes pranced across the stage of her mind. To make things worse, Gran had forbidden Adrienne from seeing Quinn and Lucas. "They're no good, those boys. The apple doesn't fall far from the tree."

A shadowed face appeared right outside the window above her head so unexpectedly that Adrienne didn't even startle.

"Hey there," the face said. The fuzzy image came into focus, pressed against the screen.

Adrienne sat up, pulling the sheet to her chest. "What are you doing here, Quinn?" she whispered.

"Come outside." He was sitting on the window ledge, trying to pry the screen out of the frame. Adrienne got out of bed, keeping the sheet close. Quinn finally wiggled the panel free and let it slide to the ground. He stuck his body halfway into her room. "It's too hot to be stuck in there. Let's go swim."

"It's late." But her body was already moving to get her swimsuit.

"We'll meet you at the beach," he said, knowing she'd come.

Slipping into her swimsuit, she made sure the bedroom door was locked before leaving. Adrienne couldn't recall the last time Gran had checked in on her, but with the threat of teen boys living next door, it was a new possibility. Then she seized the window frame and hoisted herself through the open gap with an anxious energy.

When she made it to the beach, Lucas was planted in the sand close to the seagrass. The remnants of their last fire still blackened the earth next to him. Quinn was out in the water, his head bobbing above the small waves.

Lucas watched his brother splash around. "No matter what they do, your grandmother, my father, it won't change things between us. Quinn isn't the sort to say emotional stuff, but it's the same for him." His smile was soft.

Adrienne nodded and sat next to him.

"Fuck them all," Lucas added, surprising a laugh out of her.

"Yeah, fuck them all." She leaned over and gave Lucas a quick kiss on the cheek. He touched the spot where her lips had been. An invisible thread spun between them, knotting in a pact that needed no words.

"Don't get eaten by a shark out there." He started to pull his sketchbook from a burlap bag.

"How can you see to draw?"

"I don't have to see. I just know." He sounded amused.

"And I'm not scared of sharks." She sprang up, charging toward the embrace of the sea.

"Hey," Quinn said. He welcomed her into the sea with a spray of water to her face.

She giggled and returned the splash, hitting him right in his open mouth. "Hey yourself."

"Climb on and I'll take you for a ride." Quinn turned to hoist her onto his strong back.

Though it was night, he wore a rash guard, which Adrienne found odd. Her arms curled around him. With the weight of her secure, he plunged into the welcoming darkness of the water. Adrienne put her face against his neck and breathed in his scent, that mix of soap and salt she loved. There was no fear or nervousness; she melted into him as they floated. He emulated the deep, echoing calls of whales, each bizarre sound sending ripples of merriment through her.

"I wish summer never ended," he told her.

"Me too," she replied, feeling a sharp pang at how quickly the summer would pass. Once July came, the season rushed to the finish. In September, the brothers would return to boarding school.

"You're a great kid. I'm glad you live next door."

Adrienne's shoulders slumped slightly, but she vowed to prove him wrong. *You will wake up, and that kid who catches fish with her hands will be gone, and there will be a girl standing there, a girl you could love.*

A contented sigh escaped her as she burrowed into him, the strands of his hair curling around her fingers. The waves gently carried them back to the shore.

SUMMER PASSED LIKE a flash fire. Adrienne and the brothers never mentioned the people who came to survey the land and dispute property lines. They uttered no words about Mr. Merritt and Gran's daily yelling matches. They hid from the warring adults.

As if by surprise, the brothers' last day arrived. Promises as delicate as spiderwebs were spun—to write every day, to try to come home for winter break—but Adrienne's intuition told her not to hold out hope.

"Goodbye, Adrienne, the girl of summer." Quinn's bittersweet farewell haunted her. She was sure he felt her tremors as he held her close.

Lucas's pain mirrored her own, a silent empathy reflected in his glossed-over eyes, in the words clinging to his throat. As they parted from their last fire on the beach, he slipped a piece of sketch paper into her hands before turning to follow Quinn home. She tracked them until their silhouettes disappeared like a mirage in the mist. Adrienne unfurled the precious piece of paper. A sketch of her, alone, gazing out at the ceaseless sea, leaped off the paper in sharp relief. Though it was beautiful, it was a mournful foreshadowing.

CHAPTER NINE
Summer 2012

Words had become scarce commodities in the Harris household, rationed and hoarded. Kali kept to her room or left early with her sketch pad, disappearing down the beach before Adrienne could catch her, and Adrienne avoided Gran as best she could. It was a trifecta of silence. The trio roamed the house like lonely spirits. Gran anchored herself to the kitchen table for hours, cradling mugs of coffee in her weathered hands. Her presence devoured the space, leaving Adrienne confined to the stifling guest room.

At first, Adrienne welcomed the absence of confrontation. With each passing day, though, the feeling of constriction grew, as if a transparent glass bowl were closing around her. Finally, she could take no more of the quiet and the hiding. She began hatching a plan to escape Harbor Point with Kali before the town sucked them in for good. They would fix up Gran's house, doing all the work themselves—with some help from Christopher. The second step would be dealing with Gran, which would be the hardest.

There was only one option. Adrienne called the family lawyer, Mr. Goodrich, a man who possessed the same unique ability to tolerate Elizabeth Harris as Christopher. He had seen Gran through all of her courtroom battles and civil cases. If anyone knew how to solve the Gran problem, it would be Mr. Goodrich.

"Well, Adrienne." Mr. Goodrich cleared his throat. "It's not easy to take over someone's life while still living. If your grandmother refuses to move out of the house, you must get her deemed incompetent. It's not an easy process . . . or cheap."

The thought of the kitchen fire and the possibility of getting stuck in Harbor Point made her skin crawl. "Start the paperwork. I'm sure you understand I'm not the right person to care for her." Adrienne worked to steady her voice. "She cannot live on her own. She has spent all her money on frivolous things."

"I ask you to take some time to consider this move. Why don't we chat next week after you think things over? Also, consider the retainer fee. It's an expensive endeavor. You should also speak to another lawyer about going forward with this. I have ethical issues going against your grandmother's wishes. I have someone in mind."

A harsh "Fine" escaped through clenched teeth. "Give me their contacts."

—

ADRIENNE'S FRUSTRATIONS METAMORPHOSED into determination, propelling her to breathe life into the timeworn cottage. She wanted to be ready if they ended up selling the house. It was the only way she could afford to get Gran into a home, but she kept finding more things needing repair. Adopting a systematic approach, she decided to tend to one room at a time, starting with the den.

A disgusted sigh prefaced Gran's words. "You will kill me with all this dust in the air." She stood in the center of the room as Adrienne pulled the remaining white sheets off the furniture. "Maybe that's what you want, eh?"

"She speaks," Adrienne mused flatly as she batted a cobweb out of her face. "Maybe you should go sit outside while I clean." She worked to sieve her words through the filter of calm. "It has to be done. We've been here weeks, and I need to get this house in shape."

"No, no. I want to ensure you don't get rid of anything I want to keep. I know you. You'll throw out perfectly good things when I turn my back."

"This house is falling apart. You want it to collapse like Mr. Merritt's?"

Adrienne could see Gran working on a comeback. *That took some wind out of her sails.*

She softened. "There is no money to care for your needs. We might have to sell, even if that is a hard thing to do."

"You're here. You can stay and tend to . . . *things.*"

"I can't stay in this town. That wasn't the plan."

"Why not? Christopher offered you work at the market. That's a job. Your child is almost in high school. You need to stay put and let her get a decent education."

"It didn't work out the first time." Adrienne's head swung from side to side, a silent dismissal of the notion.

"What other option do you have, Adrienne? You talk like the world has its hand out for you, and you have the pick of the crop." Gran threw her arms up.

"There are options," she lied to herself more than Gran.

"Such a silly girl," Gran huffed. She followed Adrienne around the room with the keen eyes of a suspicious headmistress but said little in protest. It was progress. The question crept around the peripheries of her mind. *Does Gran want me to stay?* She would never admit it, but she wasn't hurrying them out the door.

Adrienne washed the windows of their greasy salt-cured film as a strong wind off the ocean brought the smell of seagrass into the house. She scrubbed years of foot traffic buildup from the travertine floors on her hands and knees with a little brush, as Gran had said good housekeepers did, revealing the small fossils of sea life. Adrienne loved the spirals and flutes of the ancient shells preserved in the limestone. The old ocean forever trapped. Perhaps she would get trapped here, fossilized for some future excavator to find.

Moving on, Adrienne ran her fingers over Gran's lifetime collection: the musty chiffons, matted fur wraps, and muddied rhinestones; the eerie Styrofoam heads crowned with wigs in forgotten styles, silk shawls—their fringe yellowed from neglect—hanging like tails. These relics spoke of a family that had faded before Adrienne's birth, of places she'd never stepped foot in. Gran's history was a cryptic puzzle. It was one topic she refused to talk about.

Adrienne took a break, grabbing cold lemonade from the fridge. The picnic table in the backyard offered refuge from the swirling dust motes.

She was distracted by movement out on the beach: her daughter. As she spied on Kali sharing a light moment with a tall, tanned boy, a spectral thread of déjà vu wove through her. On this very beach, Adrienne, barely sixteen, had fallen for Quinn. Kali's world was simple, defined by the orbits of school and art. The sight of her as the star of such a familiar scene sparked a protective instinct Adrienne scarcely realized she possessed.

She hollered a happy hello, waving as she approached the pair. God, she must look like a total dork, like one of those dopey parents in sitcoms. Helicopter parents. As Adrienne neared, Kali rolled her eyes and took a noticeable step back from the boy.

Good.

"I thought I saw you out here, Kali," Adrienne said with a plastered smile. "Who's your friend?"

The boy, who introduced himself as Tam, seemed to be years beyond Kali. His brown curly hair, soft eyes, and air of maturity hinted at Pacific Islander lineage.

"Oh my God, Mom. Did you need something?" Kali said curtly.

"I was hoping you could come in and help me clean." Adrienne picked her words as though selecting delicate items from a glass case. "It's too big a job for me alone. You know Gran can't really help."

"I got to get back to my post anyway. I'll see you later?" Tam said, touching Kali's shoulder.

With a barely perceptible nod, she threw a guarded glance at Adrienne, her eyes brimming with unspoken thoughts.

IN THE LIVING room, mother and daughter tackled the towering stacks of magazines and scattered papers. Kali was a fortress, her aura shimmering with resentment. Adrienne tiptoed on a thin ice sheet, contemplating when to bring up Tam.

"How did you meet Tam?" she finally blurted.

"He saw me sketching at the public beach a few days ago," Kali said, leafing through the yellowed pages of a *Life* magazine. "He'll be a sophomore at the high school in the fall."

"What did he mean, he'd see you later?" Adrienne leaned back, her weight settling onto her heels as she observed her daughter, a mystery in the shape of a teenager.

"We were going to grab a pizza for dinner." The girl nonchalantly tossed the magazine into a trash bag.

"Were you going to ask me if you could go?"

"I didn't think I had to. I've never asked before."

A cold knot tightened in Adrienne's chest. "That was different. You were with your girlfriends. This is a boy you obviously like."

"Mom, I've been out with boys before. You just never paid attention," Kali countered, defiance in her voice.

"You are only thirteen," Adrienne protested. "I'd feel better if you were in a group of kids than alone with him."

"I don't know anyone else here." Kali's voice dropped, her shoulders sinking as she took a deep breath. "I was alone with him last night anyway. I am still here, alive and kicking."

Adrienne's eyes went wide at the realization. "I didn't know you were out last night."

"You know nothing about my life." It was a simple, gutting statement devoid of hostility. "Moving here hasn't changed that. You are still a million miles away, even when I'm right in front of you."

Adrienne swallowed hard. The ghosts rose all around her.

"Are you having sex with him?"

Kali paused, looking thoughtfully into the dusty air. "I'm thirteen, Mom. I'm not stupid."

"Kali." Adrienne licked her lips. "I don't want you alone with this boy. This age is hard, with all your hormones raging. You might end up doing something you regret."

"Like having a baby at eighteen. Like you did?" Kali's voice hitched in her throat.

"Yes." Adrienne sighed. "I made many mistakes. I would have had you when I was older when I could have . . . been a better mom." She scooted across the floor on her knees toward Kali. "You are not the mistake, though. You are everything good in my life."

She reached out, her hand seeking the comfort of Kali's, but Kali pulled away.

"I am not you. You can't treat me like I'm a screwup. I've always done the right thing. You can't keep me from seeing Tam. He's my only friend."

"I won't have you ruin your life like I did—like my mother did before me." Gran's words reverberated through time, emerging through Adrienne's lips. "You can ask him here for dinner and have pizza out in the backyard."

"It's not me. It's you who ruined my life. It was ruined from the day I was born when you lied to me. I went to the house," Kali sputtered. "I had to since you don't want to tell me anything about him."

Her sharp accusations hit like projectiles, but Adrienne was drowning in the implication of Kali's visit to Quinn.

"You've talked to him?"

Kali nodded, near tears. "I had no choice."

Adrienne's knees gave way, and she found herself sitting on the floor, her mind a whirlpool of shock. So, her gut had been right. Quinn was hiding out in the house, even though it had stayed in darkness since their confrontation at the market. *Is he roaming around with the light off to make me think he's gone?*

"What did you talk about?" Adrienne picked at a frayed edge of the rug.

Kali turned away. "I don't have to tell you anything."

"I don't want you alone with him." Adrienne's voice shook, a lump forming in her throat. It was an equation she had never considered. *Is it safe for Kali to be around him?* Quinn, once a vibrant man full of charm, now seemed spooked, timid. A stranger.

Kali didn't acknowledge her last statement, and Adrienne was too terrified to push it. The tension gradually faded into the silent rhythm of their cleaning. Adrienne moved to the den to put some space between them. Doubt gnawed as she scrubbed at a stubborn stain, her mind churning with questions about the new boy and the reappearance of Kali's father. She couldn't project her own mistakes onto her kid. Kali had never given her reason to worry.

At the bottom of the den closet, Adrienne pulled out a box of quilt supplies and revealed Gran's large red lacquer recipe box. She had forgotten it existed. She lifted the box with reverence, dust swirling in the slanting light as she wiped the grime off its lid. Two ornately carved doves nuzzled on the cover, nestled among the filigree branches of a pear tree. Gran's mother had brought the box from Hungary when the family made the long sea voyage to America in 1905, seeking a better life.

It had always been just a recipe box to Adrienne as a child, but now she could appreciate its meaning through older and wiser eyes. The Harris women came from a long line of accomplished cooks. The recipe box held the best dishes from each generation.

"I'm done in the living room," Kali announced, appearing in the den with an apple in one hand, her face pinched in a scowl. She pointed to the recipe box tucked in Adrienne's lap. "What's that?"

"It's Gran's recipe box. There are recipes that your great-great-grandmother created." Adrienne took the lid off and found a hopeless tangle of index cards and pieces of torn paper with faint lists of ingredients penciled in. "I loved to read each one. I learned to cook with these recipes, and when I got older, many of the dishes I created were inspired by these."

Her fingers traced the faded handwriting on the tea-stained recipes as she gazed fondly at the familiar names. Her taste buds seemed to stir from a deep sleep, each dish's memory unfolding on her tongue. An ache filled her at this reminder of how she had stopped cooking, really cooking, after running away all those years ago.

"That is a treasure." Gran shuffled into the den and leaned over Adrienne to inspect the box. "All of my best dishes are in there."

"Why did you have it buried in the closet?"

"I was worried one of those biddies in the Junior League would snatch it. You know how they all love to snoop around. Now that I don't get around much, they all have been asking for copies. Like I would share anything with those sharks!" Gran pursed her lips and tapped the lid of the box. "It was a good place to hide it."

Kali plucked a recipe from the box. "Mom's never made anything like this before."

She was right. Adrienne's meals had long mimicked the uninspired menus of touristy beachside joints. Relying on restaurant leftovers or frozen dinners from Publix, Kali had never tasted the history of the Harris family.

Adrienne leaned back against the worn couch cushions, watching Kali and Gran, their heads bent together over the recipe box. One recipe fluttered to the shag carpet next to Adrienne's feet. She unrolled the curled paper to find it held the ingredients for a dish that used to soothe her like a warm blanket.

An irresistible force summoned her to the kitchen, and she rummaged through cabinets, emerging victorious with ingredients to make palacsinta. The sweet, tangy aroma of simmering apricot jam wafted into the den, coaxing Kali and Gran toward the kitchen. They slipped into their chairs at the table as Adrienne cooked.

Gran watched her ladle out the batter, eyes glittering with approval as each paper-thin pancake took shape.

"My mother was a cook for a family when she came to this country. I was a girl when she gave up her job at my father's insistence. He was independently wealthy and used his wealth to build this town. But we always had parties, and my mother oversaw everything. She would make everything by hand. I remember how warm the kitchen would be. And the smells! I would help, too. Everyone would be talking and laughing."

The light in Gran's face eroded to shadow.

"But that all ended when my father died. It had all been an illusion. There was no money, no bank account or trust. It was up to me to work and care for my brothers until they were old and smart enough to leave this town and never look back.

"Cooking is in our blood, Adrienne." Gran examined the food set before her. She pushed the folded pancake around the plate with her fork. "It has been a blessing and a curse."

"Don't you enjoy cooking?" Adrienne asked.

"It was all I could do to survive and keep my brothers in clothes and food," Gran said quietly. "I had dreams too. I never wanted to get stuck in this town, but there was family duty. With my brothers off to work on the oil rigs in Alaska, I was the only one who could keep our family's legacy alive. The Harrises were something once. We were the heart of this town." The sudden clatter of Gran's fork striking the plate sounded like a discordant note in a tranquil symphony. "I couldn't let us be forgotten, wiped off the face of the map."

She exhaled a sigh that seemed to come from a well deep within before delicately lifting a small bite to her lips. Her eyes closed in reverence as she chewed. A low murmur rumbled out of her chest.

Adrienne felt similar satisfaction as she savored the sharp eruption of fruit, a delicious assault, and then the papery, featherlight bitterness of the pancake. The food had cast a spell, causing Gran to spill some of her carefully guarded secrets. Instead of feeling burdened, Adrienne felt lighter at this revelation of what they had in common—an unspoken yearning for more, their silent desires echoing off one another in a chorus of longing.

—

WITH THE TRANQUILIZING effects of a hearty meal spreading through them, Adrienne felt a shift in the atmosphere. It was as though they'd emerged from the storm. After the last forkful of palacsinta, Gran floated off to bed, leaving Adrienne and Kali in the kitchen.

"I want you to pause spending time with . . . Quinn." She wasn't even sure what to call him in front of Kali. "I need to talk to him before you do. I know you think I've neglected you, but this is big. I need to make sure you are safe."

"He isn't some crazy person. He just seems sad," Kali protested, but there was little fight in her now.

"Promise me you will wait." Adrienne extended her hand toward Kali's, only for her fingers to again graze empty air as her daughter jerked away.

Kali let out a sigh, her eyes performing a dramatic role. "Why can't you just tell me what happened? I can see it was bad. You both are like ghosts."

Adrienne slouched in defeat. Maybe it was the meal. Perhaps it was that Gran had revealed some truths about her painful past. But now, in raw honesty, Adrienne discovered the words that had eluded her since that fateful day when Kali stumbled upon her father.

"I loved your father from the moment we met. He made summers like a dream I never wanted to wake from. That is, until his brother died. After that, we both died too, in our own ways. Everything became a nightmare." The grief rolled over Adrienne. She looked down at the pile of napkin filaments she'd been shredding unconsciously.

"I read the newspapers," Kali said, bending her head as if in prayer. "He killed himself, right? But why?"

An invisible force threatened to choke Adrienne. "Death never makes sense, even when it's expected."

She shied away from the phantom of past mistakes, the ones that had pushed Lucas into the water. He had wanted his death to hurt as much as she had hurt him and chose the path he most feared. *How do you say these things to a child?*

"I'm not proud of lying to you. I am sorry." A molten tear traced a path down Adrienne's cheek. "Just promise me you will let me speak to Quinn before spending more time with him."

"Fine." Kali's agreement came out as an expelled breath, a reluctant surrender she'd been holding in.

If she was agreeable to holding off her meetings with Quinn, maybe she would be willing to compromise on the new boy in her life too.

"Now, about Tam . . ."

Kali shot her a murderous glance. Adrienne wasn't about to give up, but she'd humor her daughter a bit longer.

As she packed away the leftovers and scrubbed clean the kitchen, she realized that the quaint charm of the town, subtle and sly, had been weaving its tendrils around her, drawing her in without her notice.

CHAPTER TEN

Adrienne lay wide awake as the night deepened into the wee hours. She found herself again at her window, lost in the daunting silhouette of the house next door against the backdrop of the moonless night. Quinn roamed the dark rooms just feet from her bed. The thought of him so close and yet so removed made her stomach do flips.

With the first light of dawn barely touching the sky, Adrienne meandered through the dew-spattered grass toward Quinn's house, which was still swallowed by the pre-morning gloom. She shimmied through the cracked stucco wall Mr. Merritt had eventually built only to be crumbled by Gran's mighty banyacado.

She stood amid the waist-high grass, her gaze drawn to the large windows gazing out pensively over the ocean. *Does Quinn see me?* In the shade, a giant monarch fluttered by, and birds sang above.

The decay was much worse the closer she got. The white lacquer-like finish on the stucco of the outer walls hung in giant flaps like peeling flesh. Bougainvillea dug clawlike roots into the walls, creeping toward the roof. It has been less than twenty years since it was built. Without rescue, the salt would swiftly reduce it to ruins.

Adrienne crept up to the front door and knocked so hard that her hand throbbed. Her heart threatened to break free from its ribbed cage. Five minutes passed, and no answer. She wasn't giving up.

She went to the kitchen door at the side of the house. On the stoop, a beach daisy languished, wilted and desolate. A memory flash assaulted her mind: Lucas's outstretched hands bristling with daisies. His otherworldly blue eyes cresting the sunny yellow field.

A strong urge to retreat scraped at her. But her hand went to the doorknob.

It didn't budge. Her body led her to the loose brick at eye level, where she found the spare key. The latch groaned. As she nudged the door open, a gust of cool air rushed from within the house.

The drone of an air conditioner reverberated down the darkened hallway.

"Quinn?" she called out. "I'm here."

The maid's quarters stood like a tomb of memories. She touched the brass knob, feeling the raised carving under her thumb, and withdrew quickly as though burned.

An empty glass stood on the counter in the vacant kitchen. Adrienne made out a thumbprint by holding it to the light. The fridge bore a collection of cold cuts, a half-eaten loaf of bread, and two eggs nestled in a dish. Elements of daily life, their implications cryptic. Adrienne thought she heard something: that soundless din of a quiet room and yet the presence of something. Something trying to be silent.

"Quinn, I'm not leaving till we talk," she called out again. "I know you're here."

A newspaper from that morning lay on the kitchen table. It was open to the Arts & Entertainment section, with the summer gala taking up the whole page. It was obvious that Quinn had been there, but now all that remained was a mausoleum.

A final plea: "Quinn? Please."

Adrienne headed up the winding staircase. Arriving at Quinn's door, she pressed her fingers against the solid barrier and nudged it open.

The bed was neatly made with navy-blue sheets. A whitewashed wood lamp stood on the nightstand. But there was no trace of Quinn here. All of his photos from around the world were gone. The surfboard she had helped him buy was absent. The shelves of peculiar shells and artifacts he had found diving had vanished.

A small pair of binoculars sat on the windowsill. One plain light-blue polo shirt hung on a hanger in the closet. Adrienne clutched the shirt and brought it to her face, breathing in Quinn's scent—the ocean, Ivory soap, sunscreen, the sun itself—trapped deep in the fibers.

Shaking, she sat on the bed with the shirt on her lap and surveyed the room. These were the things one left behind, not worth being taken or remembered. A pair of binoculars. A shirt. A lamp.

A girl.

She hung the polo back on its hanger, closed the closet door, lowered the shade, and smoothed out the crease on the bed, then retraced her steps through the house. This time, she did not touch the knob of the maid's quarters. She locked the side door and returned the key behind the loose brick.

—

KALI AND GRAN were still asleep when Adrienne returned. Heat clung to her like a persistent housefly, with no brush of wind to offer relief. She decided to pack up the leftovers from the night before and pay Christopher Crane a visit.

Christopher greeted her at the market door as if he had been expecting her. His sunny mood was a welcome distraction from the morning's unsanctioned house visit, mending the jagged edges of her anxiety. Of course, he wasn't hurt by her elusiveness. Christopher had a way of shaking off the world's worries.

The market offered a rare serenity this time, not a single soul rustling about. The sun slanting through the big front windows made everything warm and golden.

"I brought you something to eat, to thank you . . . for the picnic dinner. It was delicious. I'm sorry it's taken me so long." Adrienne returned the picnic basket in addition to her palacsinta.

Christopher went to the door, turned the sign to Closed, and pulled the white vinyl shade over the door window.

"You just opened." Adrienne hovered by the counter, her eyes darting between the stools, the vacant tables, and the door like a bird, uncertain where to land.

"Mondays are slow. I'm sure no one will notice." Christopher brought his hands together as if anticipating something delightful. "Remember how I'd beg you to close early in the summers?"

She smiled. "How could I forget? It was a daily request."

"Hmm, Hungarian pancakes?" Christopher scratched his bristly chin. "My favorite."

"Gran told me. I mean, Gran mentioned that you liked them after I had already made them," Adrienne said, tripping on her words, as she went into the kitchen. "I hope you're hungry."

"I'm always hungry," he said from close behind her. Anticipation tickled her nerves.

"I guess I'll take you up on the offer to cook here," she said as Christopher attacked the pancakes with childlike enthusiasm, smearing bits around his mouth in a way she found endearingly messy. "We can see how it goes."

"So, you're going to stay?"

"For the summer. After that, the road blurs a bit."

"Good, I've missed having you around barking orders at me." He smiled.

A giggle escaped her, a youthful and carefree sound that had ever been a stranger to her, even in her school days.

"It's your place now. We can bark at each other."

"That, my friend, is a deal."

He held out his hand, and she took it.

"I guess we should plan how to execute this. And what this is."

They got down to business planning, intending to open for dinner service on the first night of the gala. Christopher oversaw a food tent they would use to promote the service. The new menu would highlight the market's seafood. Their culinary visions were in sync, and the first night's menu came together quickly. As she propped her feet up on a stool, satisfaction washed over her, and she sank into as she would a hot bath.

"So, do you cook extravagant and labor-intensive meals and leave them at the doorstep of all your fans?" Adrienne threw the tease his way, her words buoyant.

"My fans?" Christopher said before stuffing the last bite of palacsinta into his mouth.

"Those women who were here the day I came in. They seem to enjoy your fishmonger skills." The memory conjured a fresh wave of giggles from Adrienne, her laughter ringing out like unexpected music.

"Oh, them," he said with a smile.

"I don't know if I can work here if the place will always be overrun with your groupies."

Adrienne went to the fridge and grabbed the bottle of tequila from their previous lunch, the early hour be damned.

"I forgot how funny you are." Christopher leaned back into his chair, arms folding behind his head in a relaxed pose. "You always made me laugh."

"Yeah, I'm a regular stand-up comedian." She handed him a glass and poured them each a shot. With a swift tilt of her head, she let the liquid slide down her throat.

"Don't tell your Gran, but you are the better cook," he whispered as if Gran would somehow sense his betrayal.

The apricot filling decorating Christopher's nose, an unexpected artistry on his otherwise serious face, inspired her to reach over and wipe it away.

"You said Kali is a painter," he mentioned. "The gala has a high school division for the art show."

"I'll tell her when I get home." Adrienne let out a heavy breath, wanting nothing more than to be able to share the information with Kali without everything else rising to the surface. "I want to see her happy. She's been so moody and angry since we arrived. Painting has always been her refuge. She's met a boy. I overreacted, and now she hates me even more. He's a lifeguard at the public beach."

"Ah, I bet it's Tam."

"Yep."

"He's a good kid. Works two jobs. I wouldn't worry about him." Christopher chuckled. "He also has a fan club."

"Not what a mom wants to hear. But he is quite a sight." Adrienne shook her head. "I'm worried about her, about us."

Her troubles crept back into the room, persistent as shadows at sundown. She threw back another shot. "She visited Quinn. I don't know what they talked about. This morning, I went to his house and broke in. He wasn't there. Maybe he skipped town for real."

She sighed, not looking at Christopher, acutely aware of how she must appear. Vulnerable and unsteady. "Have you seen Quinn?"

"I haven't. Maybe he did take off. I wouldn't blame him. I'm surprised you stayed." Christopher put his hand on top of hers. His easy smile faded, replaced with a seriousness that Adrienne hadn't seen before.

"Where would I go?" She stood and went to the window. The mangrove forest was a black line against the azure sky. "What a can of worms. No money to my name. Driftless."

Christopher approached and nudged Adrienne to turn around. He touched her cheek.

"I want to help. Tell me what I can do to help."

He was always there, a comforting presence at every family gathering, a helping hand in every crisis. It was more than could be expected of a friend, and sometimes Adrienne wondered if his feelings ran deeper. Despite the secrets he held close and the half-truths he told, his actions painted him in a noble light.

"It makes no sense why you stayed. But here you are, in this annoying little town." Adrienne shrugged. "You could have done anything."

Christopher reached for a kitchen towel, using it to methodically clean the smudges from his glasses.

"Why did you give up on writing? Why did you stay here?" Adrienne prodded when he failed to respond.

"I like Harbor Point. And I didn't give up on writing." He moved to the sink, turning his attention to the mound of dishes. Avoiding her gaze, he scrubbed each plate with more focus than necessary. "Shitty stuff happens to everyone, Adrienne. You are not the only one. I've had my share. I roll with the punches. I carved out a comfortable space here."

"I'm sorry I upset you." Adrienne leaned against his shoulder. "It's me. I'm all wrapped up in my own self-loathing."

The room fell silent except for the clink of dishes and the soft swish of water as Christopher scrubbed the plates and glasses, his brow furrowed in concentration. His glasses slid down his nose, and he pushed them up with a quick, habitual gesture. Adrienne couldn't help but smile.

"What happened to Rachel?" she finally mustered the courage to ask. God, she couldn't give the poor man a break.

"She went back to England." He pulled the drain out of the sink and tossed the dish towel onto the counter. Then he turned to her. "After you left, she told me she was pregnant. She lost the baby a few weeks later. It was the last straw. She wanted to be home, near family, and I couldn't leave with her."

"I'm sorry to hear that."

"Surprisingly, I wasn't sorry at all. I think we clung to each other longer than we should have. We were a little bit of home to one another, but this town became my home, and Rachel never could make peace with that."

The corners of his mouth turned down in a subtle grimace, and her eyes lingered on his face. He was starting to acquire those fine lines in the corners of his green eyes that came with age. Something in her chest tightened, and she realized she wasn't looking away this time.

"This place never was home to me. I was always someone on the outside looking in, even when the whole town's eyes were on me."

"This place is in your DNA," Christopher said, shedding his solemnity. He leaned close to her. "You forget all the other things about this place that are deeply ingrained in you. You may have been cut down like your Gran's beloved tree, but the tree didn't die, and neither did you."

"Now I'm a tree?"

He laughed, a rich and joyous sound, and Adrienne lit up inside.

"Yes, chef," he said shyly as he bowed his head.

His words were a soft surprise, flushing out a hidden truth she'd always known but never acknowledged.

They came together simultaneously. Adrienne's arms circled his neck as he wrapped his arms around her waist. The kiss was the most natural thing in the world. The room seemed to tilt slightly, a woozy effect of the alcohol, but a new sort of pleasure suffused her, clear and sobering, sweeping her into a different reality. His lips were full and gave under pressure. The faint taste of apricots swarmed her senses. She sank into his body as Christopher's strong arms drew her deeper into him, knitting her hands through his thick black hair. Their breaths came faster, hearts pounding in unison, and every touch seemed to ignite a spark, driving them closer with a desperate need that neither could deny. Adrienne knew if she didn't pull away soon, there would be no way to stop going down a dangerous road.

She found the strength to push away from him, unlocking their bodies. The world spun around them, moving too fast, and the bubble of their shared moment burst. A torrent of worries and fears drowned the sweetness of their connection. Though kissing him had been the most enjoyable thing to happen to her in . . . decades, the annoying British man had always been her one bastion of normalcy. Now he was swept up in the storm with her, a new complexity in an already chaotic existence. Doubts mingled with the taste of his lips.

"I'm sorry. I keep fucking up." Adrienne's hand swirled, her fingers grasping at words that seemed to evade her. "It has zero to do with you. I hope you know that."

"Adrienne, you don't have to explain anything to me." Christopher straightened his shirt collar, his fingers trembling slightly. "I hate to admit it, but I have difficulty controlling myself around you. I hope you know this *thing* surprises me too."

"Oh my God, Christopher, stop being such a gentleman. I kissed you too, and I didn't expect this kind of . . . reaction, but I wanted to kiss you. My life is in utter shambles right now."

Her body started to quiver, a violent tremor that seemed to originate from her core, and she grasped the counter's edge for support. Vomit raced up her esophagus, but she forced it back down. She felt the crying coming.

"Lucas killed himself because of me."

She hadn't planned to say that, but it was the root of all things.

After she found Lucas in the water, numbness became her shield from the past. She'd packed away that final summer with grim determination, sealing it in a corner of her mind where it lay ignored but never forgotten. The path of least resistance was a gift. She pitied those who held on to ghosts. In an absurd display of hubris, Adrienne convinced herself she was immune, but since returning, the facade had crumbled. In the cozy market kitchen, she tumbled into the abyss.

"I betrayed him. I didn't see the warning signs. Quinn hates me for it. I know he blames me."

"No, Adrienne." Christopher's eyes widened, his head shaking with conviction. "Lucas struggled with depression long before you ever met him. Quinn blames himself. It's why he's 'Havishamed' himself in that house. All the clocks stopped the day Lucas died. Don't you see, Adrienne? Both of you live in these little worlds of false truths."

"He threw me away." She clutched Christopher's shirt, pulling him closer. Her voice cracked. "You can't want me, Christopher. You can't want someone else's trash."

Her legs gave way this time, and she slumped to the cold tile floor, her energy spent. Christopher followed her down. Time lost meaning as she sobbed tears of loss, regret, and exhaustion into his shirt sleeve.

His silence spoke louder than words, his understanding a balm to her bleeding edges. When her eyes finally dried and drooped from exhaustion, Christopher carried her up the narrow stairs to the tiny studio apartment above the market. His shadowy outline against the small window was the last thing she saw before falling asleep.

———

ADRIENNE WOKE NOT knowing where she was. The web of hair clinging to her face divided her vision into segments. Memories of her meltdown crept into her consciousness, each confession and tear pulling into sharp focus. The apartment's small bedroom above the market—the blue walls, the flood of late-evening light through the east-facing window—became familiar again. Thankfully, the chair Christopher had occupied during her breakdown was now empty.

She smoothed her hair as best she could and sat up. Her head throbbed. The chill of the shower offered refuge, temporarily washing away the pain.

Coming out of the bathroom, Adrienne noticed the plate on the nightstand. Christopher had left her a croissant, two aspirins, and a glass of water. Propped against the glass was a card with his elegant script.

I had to meet the evening boats. Eat this and take these. They will help. Everything is going to be okay.

Adrienne glanced in the mirror, her eyes no longer bearing the inflamed vulnerability of the previous day. That part of her was tucked away, hidden behind a mask of determination. With its routine and demands, work beckoned as a path forward, a way to mend what was broken. She flipped the card over and scribbled a reply on the back:

Going to schedule the vendors for Saturday. Call if you think of any final items to add to the order. One week till the gala means one week till we open for dinner.

Adrienne's eyes traced the words of her note, searching for a hint of sentimentality. Her pen hovered, poised to make changes, but finally, she sighed and left it as it was, placing the message on the cash register downstairs.

CHAPTER ELEVEN

One week later, Adrienne and Christopher were in the thick of prep for the market's opening night. The clock struck noon, and the doors would open at four.

The decision to have their soft opening on the night before the gala's street festival began suddenly seemed like a gamble. The gala ran for a full week, offering classes, talks, workshops, and demonstrations on nearly every type of art that existed. Who would even show up to eat with so much happening all over town? The street festival was a big food and art show with rows and rows of white tents lining the green space by the marina. And Adrienne and Christopher had a string of commitments starting early the next morning, including competing against the other food vendors for customers. Plus, Christopher had encouraged her to do a demonstration in the arts tent.

"It would be good for business," he said, hopeful.

"Have you lost your mind?" Adrienne's lips flattened in disbelief. "As if I don't already have a mountain of tasks to conquer? How do we even manage all this?"

Another reason to lie low for the gala was Tessa. The thin blond had taken the helm for this year's festival and seemed to be everywhere at once. It was odd speaking to Tessa about gala matters when all Adrienne could think about was the kiss. The question of Christopher's relationship status gnawed at her. She wanted to ask, to know, but the words stuck in her throat, held back by fear.

As the dinner hour neared, Adrienne was drenched in sweat with her hair matted against her cheeks, despite spending a good deal of time fixing the mess into a bun. Splatters of sauce painted her shirt with bright Picasso stains, and a fire burned within her. At first, she had hesitated, but muscle memory never dies. Amid the chopping and sautéing, everything melted away, leaving only the sizzle of the pan and the melding of flavors.

She moved around the kitchen, in her groove. The ocean breeze whispered through the window, carrying a faint fishiness. Adrienne closed her eyes, and for a moment, she was sixteen, tinkering in the old kitchen when the market was slow.

"Everything is fish," Adrienne said as she scanned the kitchen. She held the menu Christopher handed her. "Maybe we should have added alternatives?"

"No worries. I trust your capable hands. Look at this guy." Christopher held up a glistening red snapper. "He is perfect. There's little you have to do to him. Everyone will want to eat him."

He waxed poetic on each fish, each crab.

"Look at this scallop. It was plucked out of the Gulf this morning. My friend drove them across the state so we could have them."

He dipped his finger into the brine, where the medallion of flesh rested in the half shell. He held it up, a tantalizing invitation. Adrienne hesitated before taking his finger into her mouth, tasting the intense saltiness underscored by a lingering sweetness. Their eyes met for a flash before she pulled away.

"That is the essence of the sea. Everything I love about this town—the sea—is there."

"You should write about that, about fish and crabs," Adrienne said admiringly as she sliced mushrooms with practiced ease. "Share your passion with the world."

"A cookbook?" Christopher came beside her and began mincing garlic.

"Maybe something with more memory and meaning?" she said, poking him in the side with her elbow.

Christopher nudged her back. "I've missed this. Cooking with you. The kitchen has been too quiet since you left."

Adrienne set down her knife and simply watched him, cataloging his different expressions as he worked. Her gaze drifted to his lips. Then she smirked as she recalled Gran's demanding presence in the kitchen. "It's like we've just come out of a war under a five-star general. So nice and calm now," she said.

"You know, she never ran another gala after you left. I think you took the wind out of her sails."

"She was the one who kicked me out."

"She did . . . in the heat of the moment. I think she would have taken it back if you had stayed. She has never been the same since."

Adrienne held the chef's knife up, using it to punctuate her words. "Elizabeth Harris's motives are a mystery better left unanalyzed."

They settled into final prep.

"When you asked me to stay all those years ago," she blurted out. It was not the best time to ask, but the words kept coming regardless of tact or timing. "You didn't want me to leave. Why?"

Christopher's eyes darted around the room, his hands fumbling with a kitchen towel. A nervous laugh escaped him. Their gazes locked.

Adrienne yanked off her apron and headed for the door. "We're out of olive oil. I'll run to the market and get some."

Her feet led her aimlessly down the aisles of the Winn-Dixie, her hands trailing along the shelves. For the first time since returning home, she wasn't ruminating on Quinn, Gran, or even Kali. Her every thought circled back to Christopher. His smile, his touch, his words, all-consuming.

Doesn't Christopher just hang around out of some weird fascination with Gran? He was a writer, after all. Writers were drawn to the strange and unusual. She paused in the frozen food section, a puzzle piece locking into place.

The cart, filled with groceries, seemed trivial now. She abandoned it in the middle of the aisle, her mind racing with newfound clarity, and fled the store, forgetting why she had come.

—

OPENING NIGHT SWEPT away Adrienne's concerns in a whirlwind of activity. Time lost meaning as orders flew in and plates were filled. The line of eager patrons never seemed to dwindle. Each moment blended into the next, leaving her with a dizzying sense of accomplishment and exhaustion.

Around seven, Adrienne made a frantic call to Kali for help serving and busing tables. Begrudgingly, Kali appeared in all black. Behind her was Tam, smiling and happy to help. Adrienne didn't have time to deal with anything other than cooking.

By eight, her hands were slick with sweat as she juggled plates and entrées, fighting to keep pace. When she turned to find Tessa and her mother standing in her kitchen, a surge of disbelief and fury nearly overtook her.

"I'm looking for Christopher," Tessa said matter-of-factly.

"Well, he is not in here, so get out!" Adrienne barked, stunned that the woman would invade her sacred space without permission.

Tessa's eyes widened, her body jolting. Thankfully, the mother-daughter combo fled the kitchen.

Adrienne knew exactly where Christopher was—out back scooping up blue crabs to go into the pot—but she wouldn't tell Tessa that. Once the crustaceans were bubbling away and the next round of dishes had left the kitchen, Adrienne finally alerted Christopher to Tessa's arrival.

"Your girlfriend is here," she said curtly over her shoulder as she sautéed shallots at the stove. She immediately cringed. She sounded like a high schooler, so smarmy and vindictive. The cold hand of jealousy had seized her.

"Excuse me," he said quickly as he rushed to the door and slammed through it.

Adrienne tasted the bitterness of her actions on her tongue.

That second summer, when Quinn and Lucas returned, flooded back, each scene—the beautiful new girl in town, all of Adrienne's threatened hopes—playing out again with Tessa and Christopher.

She ripped off her apron and headed out to the front room. Tessa and her mother were seated at a table, poring over the menu. A laugh threatened to escape Adrienne's lips as she watched Christopher loom over the duo. His arms were folded across his chest, his stance rigid and unyielding, like a prison guard watching over his charges. Tessa's eyes seemed to find Christopher at every opportunity.

"I wanted to apologize for snapping at you back there. I get caught up in the rush when I'm cooking," Adrienne said as she arrived at Christopher's side.

"Let me apologize too," Tessa said sweetly. "Christopher invited me, and I wanted to ensure he knew I had arrived." The blond reached up and put a hand on Christopher's arm for emphasis.

"Well, I hope you enjoy your meal. We have been working endlessly to ensure it is perfect." Adrienne leaned closer to Christopher. His face remained unreadable, but his eyes betrayed a hint of alarm, the sense of being trapped between two strong-willed women.

Tessa smoothed the napkin on her lap. "Yes, he told me about your plans for the gala tomorrow. The town is eager for a taste."

"It looks like the town couldn't wait till tomorrow," Adrienne said, surrounded by crowded tables.

"Yes, you will be busy all summer at this rate." Tessa smiled at Christopher. "How will we ever find time to see each other?"

Smiles faltered, glances were averted, and an awkward silence settled in. Christopher pushed his glasses up on his nose, a subtle gesture betraying his discomfort. "Ah, the pitfalls of success" was his only response.

"Well, it looks like a new ticket is coming in." Adrienne gave a little wave, seizing on the excuse to escape the conversation.

Christopher appeared a few minutes later and got to work on

his side of the island. The last rush of dishes went out without any mention of Tessa.

Adrienne cracked the crabs, each forceful snap releasing a bit of the frustration building inside her, and shucked the oysters vigorously, channeling her emotions into her work for the late crowd. The final rush was soon over, followed by the predictable lull. The town still fell asleep by nine. That it was gala week made no difference.

Adrienne was ready to follow suit. Kali and Tam whipped off their aprons and headed out without a goodbye. She let them go, making a mental note to pay them for their time the next day. Tam had turned out to be a competent server, and by the night's end, Adrienne was warming up to him. Her brow furrowed, though, at the thought of her thirteen-year-old daughter having a boyfriend. She had long ago resolved to guide Kali away from anything that might jeopardize her bright future.

Tessa's face appeared in the kitchen entryway, her eyes wide, lips pressed into a tight line. The confident charm from earlier was gone. Christopher ushered her out to the dining room to say their goodbyes.

Adrienne leaned against the lip of the sink, wanting nothing more than to follow and see just how much of a "goodbye" Christopher gave her. But she didn't warrant an explanation from him. They had shared one terrible kiss. *Why would he want to get mixed up with me?* Tessa could give him everything Adrienne could not. An easy life without doom and gloom. Before the kiss, Christopher had stood at a safe distance, watching the Harris family madness unfold like a spectator. But now, with that simple intimacy, he seemed on the brink of being forced to step into a role.

Welcome to the madhouse.

"I think we are safe to close at ten." Christopher breezed into the kitchen and plopped a fry pan into the sink bowl. "Most of the town has been and gone already."

"How did Tessa like the meal?" Adrienne asked, feigning indifference as she flicked away a stray crumb.

"No complaints," he said in his careful way. "I told her we needed to talk. I'm going to go meet her after we clean up."

"I hope you're not breaking things off with her on my account."

God, that was awful. She needed professional help. She finally looked at him and found his eyes fixed on her, his face clouded with disappointment. *Is this how I always act around him? Cold and dismissive?*

She couldn't find the humility to utter an apology.

"I'm going to tidy the front." Christopher's voice wavered, and he hastened out of the room. Watching him, a hollow ache condensed within. She wouldn't blame him if he walked out of the market and never returned.

Only it's his market now, not mine.

After that exchange, neither said a word the rest of the evening. As they reached the parking lot, Adrienne turned left and Christopher right, their paths diverging silently, like two ships sailing away into the obscurity of the night.

That night, so ensnared within the thought of Christopher's kiss days before, her mind couldn't help but meander down memory lane. In half sleep, her lucid thoughts settled on the summer when everything changed. The summer the new girl breezed into town like an impending storm, her presence threatening to unleash chaos.

CHAPTER TWELVE
Summer 1997

Christopher's satisfied sigh that night lightened the heavy air as they clinked glasses of ginger ale, toasting to the end of the grueling application process. Adrienne had officially applied to join the new culinary magnet school.

"I can't say I'm sad it's over," he admitted.

She had finished her last cooking intensive that morning. A local chef had been the guest who demonstrated how to make the five "mother" sauces of French cuisine. To be a great chef, one had to master all five: béchamel, velouté, espagnole, hollandaise, and tomato. Adrienne and the small group of hopeful students did their best to replicate them. Their results were tasted, and scores were given, but no one knew their standing yet. She would know by July 30.

Adrienne's heart was still racing. She had spent the previous summer mastering all the mothers. By the time she reached the market after the intensive, she was practically walking on air. Her sauces had turned out perfect, even the hollandaise, her nemesis. The guest chef pulled her aside and asked about her tomato sauce's secret ingredient. She was bashful to admit it was butter. A whole stick! The guest chef laughed heartily and confessed to using it in his own recipe. Adrienne caught Gran's eye, and for the first time, a radiant smile spread across the stern woman's face, aimed directly at her.

"If I don't get it, I'll die." Adrienne's voice quavered as she set her empty glass on the counter. Restlessness took over, worries nipping at her heels.

Christopher's eyes narrowed as he studied her face. He rose from the stool and placed their glasses in the sink. "Why don't we take the boat out? It's early."

He didn't have to ask twice.

"I'll make sandwiches." Adrienne hopped off her seat and went to the fridge. Nothing could calm her better than being on the boat. She envisioned Gramps at home, his frail body cloaked in a woolen sweater, a futile shield against the inexorable chill of death. The doctor said time was growing short. Adrienne chose to pretend that was a lie.

"I'll meet you at the dock in twenty." Christopher gave her a salute as he went out the door. It was his new thing, along with calling her "captain," which she hated but rarely protested. In a way, Adrienne enjoyed her new role of ordering Christopher around. With Gramps's health waning, the weight of the market had shifted onto her shoulders, a burden she wore with pride and determination. Over the months, a silent truce had formed, driven mainly by Adrienne making an effort. Gradually, she even found herself laughing at his jokes. Their teamwork had become something she enjoyed.

The bell over the door jingled, and Adrienne groaned. A customer would delay her escape to the marina. She hoped it was someone decisive. A few seconds later, a face appeared in the doorway before Adrienne could flee the kitchen. It was Charity Talbot, the new girl in town. Adrienne's new friend by fate.

"Going on the boat?" The blond nodded to the chicken salad sandwiches on the counter. "Can I tag along? Can you believe there are no cute boys at the beach today?"

"Sure. Help me get all this stuff in the cooler," Adrienne replied with reservation, but her tone was lost on her perfectly sculpted and tanned new friend. Charity's eyes shone with self-assurance, her selective hearing always tuned to the frequency of her desires.

They had stumbled across one another during the final week of school. Adrienne did a double-take when she saw a new girl sitting at the bus stop. A new face this late in the school year? Charity's beauty acted like a shield she knew no one could penetrate. Before Adrienne could sort through her jumbled thoughts, Charity flashed a smile and extended her hand. They sat together on the way to school, and by the time Adrienne stepped off the bus, she knew she wouldn't be able to shake Charity Talbot.

The budding friendship was one of proximity. Charity and her family had moved into the old Scotia Plantation with her grandfather's intent to restore the crumbling mansion. The estate faced the water on the south side of the public beach, Adrienne's closest neighbor after the Merritts. Adrienne had played there as a child. Town lore said the place was haunted by the souls of the slaves who died working the pineapple fields. It was a grand and beautiful home, but Adrienne couldn't imagine anyone living there. Broken windows stared out like vacant eyes, and the overgrown lawn seemed to swallow the disintegrating facade.

"Papa likes an adventure." Charity had shrugged at Adrienne's concern, as if she saw something in the dilapidated mansion that Adrienne couldn't. "You learn to see the charm in the chaos," she mused, her face glowing. "We're like modern nomads, always chasing the horizon."

The family had finished a project in the Greek Isles before descending on Harbor Point. There, they had slept in a tent for months until the shell of their ancient villa was habitable. Charity coyly recounted her adventures with Greek boys, their silhouettes framed against the Mediterranean sky.

Charity had a magnetic quality, yet something in Adrienne's gut urged caution, like being entranced and warned by a fire's flickering flame. But when they first exchanged their stories, a weight lifted from Adrienne's shoulders.

"So, you're a 'leftover' too?" Charity had said. Her eyes were misty but understanding. "My mom couldn't stay away from the drugs. Yours?"

"Just couldn't stay," Adrienne replied, their shared histories uniting them.

The two girls headed to the marina with the cooler of food trailing behind them in the old wagon. Charity had shed her shirt and shorts, and she bounded through the empty lot shortcut in a skimpy bikini. What a pair they made. Adrienne in junky jeans and Charity looking like hot, fresh sex.

The moment they stepped onto the marina, Christopher folded across his chest. Wherever Charity walked, the boys' eyes followed like hungry seagulls tracking a hot dog at the beach. But not Christopher. And this was the man who liked everyone—even Gran.

Adrienne and Christopher struggled with the cooler. Charity was already at the bow, laying out her towel as if the labor before her was beneath notice.

"I don't know why you spend time with her. You two couldn't be more different," Christopher said under his breath as they undid the ropes from the dock.

"Believe me. I don't call her. She shows up on her own." Adrienne mopped her sweaty forehead and cast a sidelong glance at Charity. She was arching her back, her boobs bulging to capture the sun's attention. "I think she's lonely. What am I going to say? Go away?"

Christopher shook his head and turned the engine over. "Girls like that are never lonely."

Adrienne chewed on her bottom lip, wrestling with the uneasy blend of wisdom and inaccuracy. In the final days of the school year, she had witnessed the truth. When Charity walked the school hallways, the other girls parted like the sea, brimming with thinly veiled hostility. The tales she had regaled Adrienne with made it easy to understand. Every action Charity took, from her bold gaze to her unapologetic laughter, broadcast a life lived on her own audacious terms. She was a wolf among lambs.

As if to reinforce her lack of shame, Charity removed her top. She slowly turned onto her stomach without caring that she had exposed her sizable boobs to everyone on the water.

"They'll think we're running a floating brothel," Christopher muttered.

Adrienne nudged him. "Any ideas how to shake her?"

"Throw her overboard? Aren't the Merritts due home soon?" Christopher said over the boom of the motor.

She nodded. "Lucas said next Monday in his last letter."

A wordless understanding passed between them, a shared concern. Where did this new girl fit into their cozy circle?

Adrienne was still mulling over her dilemma after they docked. Her bottom lip throbbed from biting it. A selfish urge gripped her, making her wish she could keep her old life—Quinn, Lucas—sealed away from Charity's influence. *Is it even my choice?* In this small town, fate tangled lives together whether you wanted it or not.

"That boy, Scott, from school. He's having a party tonight, and we're going." Charity appeared from the cabin.

Adrienne's shoulders sagged. "I'm beat."

Ignoring her protests, Charity touched Adrienne's face and pushed the damp, matted hair from her cheeks. "You're going to let me make you pretty." Her blue eyes locked onto Adrienne's like tractor beams. Christopher's shoulders quivered, his lips pursing as he fought to hold back a chuckle. Adrienne shot him a glare, tallying a new score in an ongoing game.

CHAPTER THIRTEEN

On the day the Merritt brothers were due to arrive, Adrienne and Charity planted themselves on the beach, ready to put in a full day of doing nothing. Umbrellas were up, the radio was on, and a cooler was stocked with drinks and snacks. Adrienne had kept mum about Quinn and Lucas, yet there was Charity at her doorstep that morning, eyes twinkling like she'd sniffed out a secret. Adrienne fell into her default setting: coasting through the day on mental autopilot, thoughts stowed away.

Charity stretched out on a pink-flamingo beach towel outside the reach of the umbrella and applied coconut oil to every inch of her body. A few boys stalked her with their eyes from a patchwork of beach towels a few yards away. A black string number with four small triangles covering the places needing to be covered, Charity's bikini was more suggestion than garment, scarcely fulfilling its primary purpose.

Under the shade, Adrienne leafed nervously through a hefty cookbook, its bulk offering some cover for her daring new swimwear. Charity had pressured her to buy a bikini, and she relented. It was much more conservative, though, with thicker straps and a bottom that was more like a pair of underwear than a thong. It had a white background and giant green palm fronds as the print. Charity said it complemented Adrienne's brown eyes and dark hair.

Despite being the object of other girls' disdain, Charity had a knack for making Adrienne feel beautiful. This sensation might as well have come from another planet. Since childhood, Gran's eyes had scrutinized her, a disapproving sigh or a clucked tongue ever at the ready. It seemed to terrify Gran that Adrienne preferred to be encrusted with dirt.

Since meeting Charity, Adrienne spent less time fishing and wandering through the mangroves and more time at the mall. The moment Gran laid eyes on Charity, her face lit up with a rare smile of approval.

Toward the end of the day, as the sun sank behind the girls, a cool breeze slithered in. The brothers were not going to show. Adrienne glanced at the small stack of worn letters tucked into her beach bag, the only lifeline between them thanks to their boarding school's strict family-only phone policy. It was easy for plans to change faster than the postal service could report.

Charity yawned and headed out into the water for a swim. As Adrienne stood to join her, she turned toward the big white house and discovered two silhouettes against the low sun. Forgetting about Charity, Adrienne ran to them with childlike glee, and they clashed in a clumsy group hug, no one caring how silly they looked. She felt as though she'd been drowning in their absence and had just broken through the water's surface.

"Hey, missed ya," Lucas said, pulling her into a singular embrace. She had to tilt her head back slightly to look into his eyes, finding herself a perfect fit under his newly elongated chin.

"Likewise." She admired his cheerful face, now covered with scruffy bristles. They gave him a mature look, erasing traces of the boy she knew.

"My turn," Quinn said, opening his arms wide for her. "Come here."

Every muscle in her body stiffened as if electrified by his touch as they hugged. She was aware of his skin, his fingers pressing into the flesh of her shoulder blades, his suntan lotion, vaguely scented with coconuts, wafting off his skin.

He held her at arm's length, and she caught astonishment in his gaze. "I didn't expect to see you in a bikini. I wasn't sure it was you at first," Quinn teased. Seventeen was a good age for him. He was more muscular, his dark hair tinged with golden flecks.

The moment didn't last long. His eyes traveled beyond her toward the shore. Adrienne knew they would land on Charity, her new friend. Adrienne clenched her fists hard enough to cut half-moons into her palms. Her heartbeat pounded in her ears.

"Adrienne, friends of yours?" Charity said, embedding herself in the little circle. She looped her arm through Adrienne's and leaned in as if they were besties.

"Yeah, this is Lucas and Quinn Merritt. They live next door." Adrienne tried to sound casual, but it was hard. Quinn's eyes met Charity's, and it was as if the rest of the world had faded away. Fissures spindled through Adrienne's body, growing with every second that passed, a jigsaw puzzle inside her slowly falling apart.

"And you've kept them hidden this whole time? That wasn't very nice." Charity pushed Adrienne playfully.

"We just got home. We go to school up north." Quinn's hand shot up to rake through his hair, his movements unusually jerky, a sharp contrast to his usual grace. Around Adrienne, he always seemed relaxed and at ease. There was no version of reality where Adrienne could compete with Charity. The future flashed before her eyes. There would be endless days ahead of watching Quinn fall for someone else.

"Why don't you boys come over tomorrow, and we can get to know each other? We've got a pool. And I'm just down the beach." Charity's eyes remained on Quinn, a faint smile curving her lips.

"Sure, sounds great," he said, his eyes meeting Lucas's. Lucas gave a noncommittal lift of his eyebrows.

The boys headed back to the house, and Adrienne and Charity returned to the beach. Charity said nothing about Quinn as they packed their evening gear. Adrienne caught her lower lip in her teeth. *What should I say? Quiz Charity about her opinion on Quinn?* Charity would know in an instant that Adrienne was crazy about him.

"Come by around eleven, and we can make lunch for the boys," Charity said before going their separate ways. Adrienne's words stuck in her throat, and she nodded. The other girl's casual use of "the boys" struck a sour note. Adrienne had always used that term, wrapping it around Lucas and Quinn like a possessive embrace.

CHAPTER FOURTEEN

The next day, Gran waved Adrienne off with a smile, saying, "Enjoy your time at that wreck. I hope you don't get tetanus."

Adrienne entered the empty house and found Charity in the kitchen when she arrived. It was almost a given that Charity's grandparents would be absent. Adrienne had only met them once in passing as they headed off to some auction. Her eyes briefly scanned the unattended kitchen. She thought how liberating it must be to live without someone constantly looking over your shoulder.

"I got lots of things from the store. I wasn't sure what they would like to eat, and growing boys have big appetites," Charity said, winking. Adrienne blinked, unsure how to read the gesture.

"Lucas is pretty picky, but Quinn will eat almost anything." Adrienne recalled Quinn's crazy sandwich-making habits. He would burst into the market, starving from scuba diving all day, and spend a half hour in the kitchen piling strange combinations on his bread. Anything Adrienne offered went on the sandwich.

"Hmm, I had a feeling." Charity nodded, a smirk growing as she dumped pasta salad into a pretty glass bowl.

The boys arrived at noon. Quinn splashed into the enclosed pool with exuberance. Lucas, ever the observer, settled by the water's edge and lost himself in his sketch pad.

"This is a pretty cool place," Quinn said while gliding on his back.

"I guess if you like living in ruins. The whole property is falling down. My grandfather thinks he can fix and sell it for a good price in a year." Charity swam gracefully toward Quinn, her posture in the water casual yet clearly calculated to catch his attention. Her eyes roved over Quinn in an unabashed appraisal.

Adrienne slunk down into the pool.

Quinn rolled onto his stomach and disappeared beneath the surface. His hands clamped around her waist a moment later, lifting her out of the water. Then, she was airborne for a second before landing on the surface—right on her butt. She emerged to find Quinn cackling.

"I've been waiting all year to do that!" He splashed her. "Get you back for pushing me off my board last summer."

The spontaneous eruption of her laughter released a coiled spring. She lunged for him, scrambling up his back like a deranged monkey, trying to dunk him underwater.

"Not today," Quinn said, leaping as high as he could muster and making Adrienne fly backward into the water, the two of them attached. They sank to the bottom of the pool, her back rubbing the mosaic tiles. She pressed into him hard, enjoying the feeling of being wrapped around him in the silent underwater world. Far too soon, they bobbed to the surface and parted to catch their breaths.

"You two are too cute," Charity cooed from her raft.

Quinn's eyes darted toward Charity momentarily, his easy smile tightening at the corners. His gaze lingered a beat too long, enough that Adrienne felt the cool hand of death brush across her chest. She was navigating a minefield with a blindfold on.

"So, are you two some kind of item?" Charity asked as they wiped the water from their faces, laughing.

The question plopped over the laughter like a wet blanket. Adrienne's flinty eyes met Charity's. Charity met her stare unflinchingly as if daring her to say something.

"Nah, just best buds, right, Adrienne?" Quinn's words came out rapidly.

Adrienne swallowed hard and nodded before turning on her back, where they couldn't see her face.

Quinn got out of the pool and did a cannonball, rocking water onto the terra-cotta tiles and flipping Adrienne over on her belly from the wake. The three of them seemed to morph back into kids, swimming, splashing, and diving. Meanwhile, Lucas pulled his chair back inch by inch as if retreating from an invisible line of fire.

As the sun settled behind the old stucco building, filling the pool room with dappled light, the pool grew quiet, the splashes giving way to floating bodies and aimless strokes. Adrienne drifted on the back of a blowup alligator as Quinn swam lazy circles around her. Charity sat on the steps, never taking her eyes off the two of them. Lucas had put away his pencils and pad and closed his eyes. After a while, Charity left the steps and moved closer to Quinn.

"I'm bored. Let's play a game," she said. The room spun around Adrienne like a zoetrope as Charity's lips curled into a fiendish smile.

"What kind of game?" Lucas's eyes popped open.

"Truth or dare?" Charity offered as she backed up to the wall of the pool.

"Aren't we too old for that game?" Quinn chuckled. "I think I was eleven the last time I played it."

"You are never too old for truth or dare." Charity raised her brow. "Only a wuss would say that."

Adrienne had been waiting for it. Though she had not witnessed what Charity did with the boys she went out with, the blond girl had laid out the intricate games in detail for her. There was a glint in Charity's eye, a magician preparing their final trick.

I've already lost.

The words rang in her head like a bell.

Quinn was older, and Adrienne was sure he must have had sex before. She tried to block out the endless line of women Quinn had met while traveling. Adrienne was but a speck of dust in his wake. Her stomach churned as if a dark flower of injustice had taken root and was now unfurling its petals within her.

"Let's play," Adrienne found herself saying, tired of cowering.

"Okay, I'll go first," Charity said. She turned to Adrienne. "Adrienne, truth or dare?"

"Dare." It was as if someone else had spoken.

"Good girl." Charity nodded in approval. "I dare you to kiss Quinn."

Charity went right for the kill, her eyes gleaming with predatory cunning. Of course Charity knew Adrienne was crazy for Quinn. Girls like that knew everything.

"On the lips, no baby kiss," she added.

"That's not so bad, right?" Quinn teased, opening his arms wide and comically, waiting for Adrienne, his smile playful but devoid of more profound affection. His attitude confirmed her worst suspicions. She had been cast in the sister role rather than the leading lady.

Infuriated, Adrienne mustered up every ounce of courage she had and went into Quinn's open and waiting arms. She closed her eyes as she stood on tiptoes to reach his lips. The kiss made galaxies collide inside her, though it was hardly more than a peck. After it was over, she remembered that his lips had been soft, that his hot breath had brushed across her face. Adrienne would have morphed into a puddle if there hadn't been so many eyes on her. It was her first kiss, though she would never tell.

As the world snapped back into focus, a cold realization settled over her: Her heart had spoken its truth, but his silence was deafening.

She opened her eyes and found him grinning. Maybe even a little surprised. He messed up her wet hair. "A kiss to end the war?" He was referring to their ongoing battle to dunk the other underwater.

Adrienne nodded and smiled as best she could. Her chest burned as if a slow-burning ember had settled there, refusing to be extinguished. Her body had been altered. She wanted to leave, but leaving would make things worse. She glanced at Charity, once a friend, now reduced to a stranger she wished to forget. The girl could rot in hell for all Adrienne cared.

She cleared her throat. "Alright, Lucas, truth or dare?"

"It's getting late. We should head back. We have dinner plans with our father." Lucas's voice wavered, his eyes shifting away as he spoke. His fidgety movements betrayed his relief at the game's end.

As they all got out and dried off, Quinn's eyes met Charity's for a fleeting second, a silent exchange Adrienne couldn't ignore. Lucas approached Adrienne and put his arm around her shoulders, giving her a comforting squeeze.

"I haven't gotten a chance to talk to you," he said softly so the others wouldn't hear.

Adrienne leaned into him, as if love itself could be transferred through touch. "Come over tonight. We can go see the meteor shower from the beach."

As Lucas and Quinn left, Adrienne moved quickly toward the door, her face taut, desperate to put distance between herself and the day's memories, without even an offer to help Charity clean up.

GRAN WAS WAITING for her at home, sitting at the kitchen table and armed with her hefty party planner. Adrienne held the black book with a sinking feeling; it was the harbinger of busy, exhausting days ahead.

Gran had ultimately won the war over her beloved banyacado tree. Her army of botanical experts she strong-armed into making a case for the preservation of the tree had given Judge Lassiter enough to officially deem it a historical landmark by late November. Mr. Merritt's stucco wall was out of the question. But the great Elizabeth Harris's win did not mean that her personal war with Mr. Merritt was over. Something Adrienne couldn't quite name still seemed to buzz within Gran. A dark light appeared in the old woman's brown eyes whenever she glanced at the big white house next door. A bitter tang weaved through any words Gran spoke about the Merritts.

"We're having a party on the fourth. The whole town is invited. We need a proper celebration to dedicate the tree as a historical landmark. I expect you to help me prepare. We have a week to get ready. That won't leave us much time, but we've worked with less." Gran flipped the planner open to a new, clean page and began to make a list in her indecipherable scrawl.

As Adrienne sat across from her and listened to Gran give orders, it all became crystalline. A big old party to rub Mr. Merritt's nose in Gran's victory. Adrienne imagined a gaping mouth suddenly appearing and swallowing her summer plans. The idea of shopping, cooking, cleaning, and organizing alongside Gran made her bones ache. Charity would certainly get her hooks in Quinn, and any chance Adrienne had would burn away like mist on the morning sea.

CHAPTER FIFTEEN

By the end of July 3, Adrienne had cooked and prepared every conceivable food that held some nostalgia surrounding Independence Day. She rested at the backyard picnic table and drank a stolen Schlitz from the fridge.

The tension melted from her sore muscles, and her limbs went pleasantly limp. All she wanted to do was lie in the grass and fall asleep. An insufferable heat had descended on Harbor Point. No breeze, no rain.

It had been a week since the pool "party." Though Adrienne knew Quinn was away with Mr. Merritt, images haunted her thoughts—Quinn and Charity intertwined in an endless loop, each appearance more unsettling than the last.

"Hey!" As if summoned, Quinn's dark outline appeared where the edge of the grass met the sand. "Come swim. It's too hot!"

Adrienne shook her head in a pathetic attempt to sober herself. But Quinn was not some mirage on the scorching sand; he was still there, alone, when she peered through her tangle of damp hair, slick with sweat. She followed him instantly, not even caring that she was in jean shorts.

They swam in circles as Quinn told her about the latest treasure hunt excursion. Maybe, just maybe, he hadn't been having wild sex all this time, she tried to convince herself. She pieced together excuses for Quinn in the hopeful corners of her seventeen-year-old mind.

Love me, Quinn.

If she were brave, she'd kiss him again, and this time, he would know it had nothing to do with a dare. Her lips trembled, her courage faltering when she needed it most.

How does anyone do it? Take that step? Kiss someone without being dared?

"You know, my dad's having a party tomorrow too," Quinn said as he paddled.

"Lucas told me a few days ago. Nothing good is going to happen tomorrow night." Adrienne stretched out on her back.

"Wanna learn how to dive? I could teach you." Quinn rotated and floated next to her. "We have lots of gear. We can start tomorrow morning."

Adrienne laughed nervously. "It's the Fourth of July, and as we have established, your father and Gran have dueling parties."

"Fuck them, remember? This is summer. This is our time." She turned at the firmness in his voice. Though he smiled, she saw something dark and troubling in his eyes. Her internal intuition stirred. *Why is he asking me to swim?*

She agreed to meet Quinn at dawn on the dock in the Back Bay. She couldn't deny him.

—

ADRIENNE PACED FROM piling to piling on the dock, waiting for Quinn to show up. It was six thirty. He was a half hour late.

Maybe he's forgotten me. Maybe I'm not worth it.

Gran would surely rise early on party day. Each wasted minute twisted Adrienne's stomach with anxiety. Her mind whirred with endless to-dos, each task spawning another, like a never-ending fractal of obligations. Oh, but she would happily pay the price to spend an hour underwater with Quinn. Trapped in the blue silence, just the two of them.

In her mind, Gramps's voice echoed. *You're seventeen . . .*

Just as she turned to leave, a rustle from the mangroves caught her attention. There was Quinn, lugging a couple of tanks and a tangle of equipment. As their eyes met, it was as if someone had paused the world's hurried clock, leaving only endless possibilities stretching before her.

Behind him came Lucas with a beach chair strapped to his back and a large Panama hat on his head. A spasm of disappointment shot through her as her fantasy of frolicking alone with Quinn was dashed.

"Sorry," he said. "Someone was very slow this morning." He waved back at Lucas.

"I was ready on time," Lucas argued cheerfully, pushing past his brother on the thin strip of the dock.

He arrived in front of Adrienne, holding a yellow beach daisy. He tucked it behind her ear before hugging her.

"If you're short on help at the market next week, maybe I can pitch in. We can keep each other company. Dad has Quinn working all summer doing tours to the Bahamas. He won't be around much."

"Sure, that sounds great," she said as Quinn inspected the scuba gear.

"Let's get in the water." Quinn jumped off the dock into the Back Bay, then offered her his hand.

"I'm good," she said, scooting into the water next to him, afraid to touch him for fear that his touch would send fireworks through her thighs.

Quinn laughed and tossed her a mask. "Independent woman; I get it."

"Try not to drown her on the first day." Lucas pulled a large pad from the pocket on the back of his chair and bent his head, scribbling on it intently. He quickly encased himself in an invisible universe far removed from theirs. *Why did he come?*

Quinn pulled Adrienne out in the water until they were waist deep. He showed her how to put on the mask, clear it underwater, work the regulator, and control her breathing. He strapped her into all the gear and adjusted the belts and hoses, his hands brushing her bare skin. The scene blurred, and they were all alone in the dark water.

Quinn's voice took on a hushed, measured tone. Surrounded as they were by the vast, unpredictable expanse of water, he radiated a sense of security.

"Why doesn't Lucas come and swim?" Adrienne turned back toward the shore.

"Lucas is terrified of the water." Quinn's eyes didn't quite meet hers, and he kept tinkering with her gear. "He can't swim. Being in the water for him is a fate worse than death."

"That must be hard, with you always going to exotic places to dive." Adrienne let her breath out when Quinn released her, not realizing she had been holding it.

"Don't make a big deal about it. Lucas would hate that I told you."

She wished he weren't so close with his hands all over her. Quinn nodded toward Lucas, who was ignoring the two of them. "He'll probably brush it off. I'd leave it at that."

"Why is he so scared?"

Lucas's hand moved aggressively across the sketch pad, each pencil stroke betraying an urgency that his face tried to hide.

"Something happened when we were young." Quinn bowed his head to recheck some of her valves. "I think that is something you should ask him. If it ever comes up. He doesn't like to talk about it."

"You are very protective of him." Adrienne turned to Quinn. She studied the fleeting expressions on his face, a cipher begging to be decoded.

"He's my little brother." His tone left no room for questions. This was an irrefutable law of the universe. "We only have each other."

"I don't know what that's like"—it was Adrienne's turn to examine the valves—"to have someone by your side."

Quinn touched her arm. "Come on, let's get you under."

Adrienne dipped under the waterline, and the cloudy water disoriented her instantly. She couldn't see more than a few inches in front of her mask. Her body jerked toward the surface. Quinn followed her.

"We've stirred up the bottom, so the visibility isn't too good. Let's get the basics out of the way. Then we'll paddle over to the inlet where it's clear."

She gave a hesitant nod and trailed behind him. Quinn's hand clasped her vest a moment later, pulling her out further. The visibility was better now that they were away from where they had been standing. The tannin-stained water, full of decay, was not a place Adrienne liked to swim. She only got in when she had to clean the boat. Millions of filmy particles floated underwater, grazing the lens of her mask.

Quinn came into view as a hazy mirage directly in front of her. It was like she was in a movie about the Loch Ness monster. Quinn signaled to her to remove her mask under the water, then put it back on and clear it. They had spent a good fifteen minutes on the surface practicing.

Now it was time to go under.

She steeled herself to enter the murky depths and let her body sink beneath the surface. The shadowy lace of mangroves overhead faded, blotted out by particulates. Panic surged, every fiber of her being screaming, *Up!* as she kicked and clawed her way back toward the surface.

Quinn grabbed her by the shoulders and made her focus. They stayed buoyant for a while, her eyes locked with his. He let go of her arms and put his hands on her face, their warmth bleeding into her cheeks. He smiled and gently stroked her temples with his thumbs until she calmed. In Quinn's steadying presence, the water around her grew less menacing and the weight of her fears lifted. She couldn't understand why she had spooked.

Finally, she nodded to Quinn and gave him a thumbs-up. He released her. Alone now in the dark water, her chest tightened, but she breathed deeply through the regulator, consciously relaxing her muscles. With determination, she glanced over at Quinn. She wanted her movements, her composure, to shout confidence.

They spent the next half hour ensuring Adrienne knew how to work her gear underwater. Quinn made her clear her mask one more time, which she did as quickly as possible. Each maneuver came easier than the last, her movements growing smoother and more assured. Quinn's approving nods and thumbs-ups made it clear: She was getting the hang of it.

"Let's go out to the clear water. You can get familiar with buoyancy," Quinn said when they popped up to the surface.

They waved to Lucas and then paddled toward where the inlet let the ocean water into the Back Bay. Lucas followed, walking along the thin shore. Here, the water transformed from a cloudy soup into a crystalline expanse, the sunlight casting gilded rays down to the seafloor. A nice little reef had established itself along the deep cut. Adrienne had snorkeled around there her whole life. It was exciting to stay under and not have to come up to breathe. Lucas settled under a palm tree as Quinn and Adrienne stood in the shallows at the point.

She closed her eyes and took her mask off. The cool water hitting her face was a shock, though she expected it. She almost breathed—as Quinn had said she would feel the urge to do—but resisted. Carefully, she put the mask back on and blew air out her nose to force the water through the sides until the watery realm around her came into focus. Quinn nodded and motioned for them to return to the surface, and she eagerly followed him.

He showed her how to work her vest to add and release air to achieve the correct equilibrium when she was underwater. As he led her to the channel, the bottom dropped off quickly to about twenty feet. Adrienne eyed the swirling eddies and whirlpools forming as the tide retreated. Nature's warning signs belied the area's serene beauty. The currents could be wild when the tide went out. Boats were supposed to slow to a crawl as they went through, but few did. Adrienne had seen more than her share of vessels capsize and sink to the bottom of the channel. It came from driving too fast and getting caught in a crosscurrent.

They would be fine if they stayed close to the drop and didn't go out into the channel.

He echoed her fears. "Stay close to me. Don't go out past the drop."

This time, as she submerged, her heart maintained its steady beat, her lungs filling and emptying at a measured pace. The corals burst into view like a kaleidoscope.

They took some time to practice swimming and going to different depths. Clearing her mask with a swift puff of air, Adrienne met Quinn's eyes and offered a self-assured nod.

She took the helm and led Quinn around the various outcroppings when they got to the tiny reef, which was no more than a string of piled-up rocks that some corals and sea fans had attached to. She showed him where a remora eel resided between two rocks. They chased a fiery red parrotfish through a field of seagrass. Quinn took her down the side of the channel. A school of angelfish fluttered past them. As she floated, each exhale released another weight within until she was part of the water. It was a much more pleasant experience than the Back Bay. What freedom, not having to surface frequently, no nagging urge to draw in a breath.

Too soon, Quinn was tugging on her and pointing. When she checked her gauge, the air was low. She inflated her vest as Quinn took her hands.

There was nothing but the two of them, hanging in suspension, holding on to one another. Her lips tingled at the thought of tasting his. Her fingers clenched involuntarily around his hands. In a half-bold, half-instinctual move, she pulled her body against him. His eyes widened in surprise, but he didn't recoil. His gaze deepened, filled with an emotion she dared not name. His hand went to the small of her back, moving her closer to him. The pads of his fingers pressed against her bare skin.

They pushed their bodies together for a thousand years, as close as their equipment would allow. She wrapped her legs around his waist and put her hand on his chest. The rapid thumping against her palm mimicked that of her own heart. The shared pulse seemed to pose a question, filling the space between them with electric possibility. *What does it mean?*

Could Quinn feel the same about me?

Quinn checked his air monitor. There was no time left. They untangled from each other and headed to the surface.

There, the ambient noises of nature replaced the undersea quiet. Adrienne rolled onto her back, her chest rising and falling rapidly as she tried to harness her runaway heartbeat. A hush settled over them, their eyes meeting and darting away. Adrienne glanced at the shore. Lucas seemed engrossed, his pencil dancing across the paper, oblivious to the underwater drama that had just unfolded.

"Do you like treasure hunting?" she finally asked. It was a good neutral topic. The reef got her thinking of Mr. Merritt's shipwreck.

"I do it mostly because my father makes me, but I love the reefs with all the fish, the color of the coral. It's not a bad way to spend your summers as a kid, traveling worldwide and seeing the most beautiful places." He drifted beside her, their arms almost touching. "I could stay down there all day. Finding a gold coin or cup no one has seen in hundreds of years is exciting. It rarely happens, so it feels amazing when it does."

"A treasure hunter. I never thought I'd meet a real one." Subtly shifting in the water, she positioned herself close enough for their shoulders to brush. "I saw the Atocha exhibit too." The exhibit featured discoveries by a famous treasure hunter, Mel Fisher.

"It's a sickness. Dad can't stop. My father's holy trinity is treasure, God, and his family's image. In that order." Each word fell like a stone he wished he didn't have to throw. "He's been searching for gold, glory, and fame his whole life. He hasn't found anything. We know the Fishers. He hates Mel. We were one of the competing outfits. It was a dark time to be around my father. I was too young to hunt, but I remember everything."

Adrienne sensed a seismic change in their conversation—as if their ethereal connection had evaporated into the salty air. She sank back into the water, her legs swirling beneath her to keep her head above the surface.

"Wow. I didn't know your father was that serious."

"The tourism aspect is an excuse to sniff around new places for treasure. It pays the ridiculous bills that roll in from hunting. Dad has spent more than any fortune he hopes to find." Quinn remained on his back, his eyes fixed on the sky as if searching for answers among the rootless clouds. "I almost bled to death two summers ago, but father didn't care. He didn't want to take the boat back to shore to get me to the hospital." Quinn pointed to a line on his shoulder. "It's never been enough for him to have money and a nice family. When my mother died, he left for Brazil the day after her funeral."

Her fingers itched to reach out, to offer him comfort, but she pulled back. Their touch, she knew, was a live wire, unpredictable and intense.

"He's afraid he'll die before he finds a wreck. He's convinced it's offshore."

"Did something happen when you were gone this week?" Adrienne said with hesitation. "I don't know, I just got this . . . feeling last night when you asked me to come out here."

Quinn's brow furrowed. "It's nothing; I just had a stressful group. Being in the water always helps me let go."

"Hey, you guys, it's been two hours. Can we go?" Lucas called from under the palm trees, waving for them to come in. "I'm frying out here."

"It's nine? Shit." Adrienne's eyes widened. Her mental to-do list unfurled.

Quinn grabbed her tank and pulled her with him to the shallow water. "I'm sorry. I told you an hour."

She shrugged, trying to keep her voice casual. "It's fine. I'm glad it helped. Thank you for teaching me."

A smile crinkled the thin skin near his eyes. "Being with you helped too." His fingers deftly unclipped her vest, lingering on her shoulder as if he had something more to say. "You understand."

"I . . . I do." Adrienne nodded. Her eyes met Quinn's before darting to Lucas, who was peering intently their way.

"I hope you'll try to sneak over tonight to the party," Quinn added as they parted.

"I'll try, but Gran will never let me. It will be late." Adrienne gripped the dive gear to her chest, briefly creating a barrier before handing it back to Quinn.

"Summer is almost half over." Turning to her, his eyes were earnest, his voice tinged with a familiar yearning.

"Guys, really? I'm dying from heat exhaustion," Lucas whined from the shade.

With a reluctant backward glance, Adrienne moved toward the shore. The day was long past its prime and yet barely begun.

CHAPTER SIXTEEN

Once again, the Merritts' house transformed into a glittering oasis from her bedroom window. Sweat trickled down Adrienne's forehead as she peered out, the air inert and solid as if the heat index were a wall keeping the breeze at bay. Millions of tiny white lights were restrung up in the trees. When evening came, the whole yard would glow.

She ruminated on half-formed plans to make it to that party. There was no question that it would happen. The charged memory of being underwater with Quinn roiled inside her, making her reckless, daring her to think she could crash the party unnoticed. Every time she tried to focus, to steady her shaking hands, her thoughts slipped back to Quinn, leaving her in a state of restless disarray. In the span of an hour, she spilled the BBQ sauce, broke two plates, and cut deep into the flesh of her finger. Once Gran had had enough of her antics, she banished Adrienne to her room.

She twisted the shower knob to its coldest setting, but the cascade did nothing to cool her skin. The image of her legs coiled around Quinn's waist filled her with a heady sense of need she couldn't ignore. A need to know what it might be like to press even closer, to push that burning point between her legs against him. Her hand instinctively moved down, pressing at the ache. The pressure offered a reprieve for a fleeting second, only for the sharpness to return. She pressed harder as Quinn's face hovered in her mind's eye, until the pain reached a pure point of pleasure and release.

She slid down the cool tiles, panting. *How will I survive the rest of the summer?* As her breathing slowed, dread crawled through her. Being so affected by Quinn was exhilarating, but she couldn't help but wonder: *Are these feelings going to kill me?*

—

THE HARRISES' BACKYARD barbecue stood in sad contrast to Mr. Merritt's party. They had set up a few picnic tables with vinyl coverings depicting cartoonish scenes: a smiling charcoal grill, a dancing hot dog, and friendly mustard and ketchup bottles. Old, rusting lawn chairs they had collected over the years dotted the lawn. Christopher, who would never abandon them, stood at the grill, basting the whole suckling pig that Gran had specially ordered. Adrienne couldn't bring herself to look at its face. It seemed barbaric to cook something with a face. Sure, it was delicious, and Adrienne would eat it . . . once Gran took care of the head.

As Adrienne stepped into the kitchen, she caught Gran's lips moving in a bitter monologue, the giant meat cleaver in her hand emphasizing each silent syllable. "I've bought all this food and gone to all this trouble. I know he did this because he got wind of my party. That fool will do anything to get revenge."

Gran plunged the cleaver deep into the chicken's spine. The crunch of metal severing bone made Adrienne's whole body cringe.

"Well, he did plan his party first." As the words left her lips, she braced for Gran's ire. *But what does it matter?* She almost dared Gran to unleash her fury.

The older woman turned her head and eyed Adrienne. "These chickens need to go now," she said, pointing toward the grill. She was letting it go, this time. Adrienne carefully took up the tray beside Gran, avoiding her cleaver.

—

THE PARTIES ON both sides of the tree officially began at six o'clock. Adrienne stood on the front porch in a new dress and waited to welcome the guests. As the clock's hands inched forward, Adrienne's hopeful smile faded, replaced by a sinking feeling. Only three people from town had come. Cars began parking in the empty lot across the street. Shoes scuffed along the pavement, but the sounds moved past the hedge line toward Mr. Merritt's house. They were all going to his party. *And why wouldn't they?*

The front door slammed open, and Gran emerged, a tea towel hastily thrown over her shoulder as if she'd left the kitchen mid-crisis. Her bright-orange dress with its pink hibiscus pattern was too bright to stare at directly. She even had a matching fresh flower from her garden tucked into her hair.

"What the hell is going on? Where is everyone? The whole town surely cannot be over a half hour late?" Her dark eyes were like smoldering coals.

Adrienne pointed. "I think most of the people are going next door."

"Well, go out to the street and convince people to come to our party." Gran patted at the sweat along her hairline with her tea towel.

"I can't make people come to our party. They've made up their minds."

"Oh, for God's sake! Do I have to do everything?" She threw the towel at Adrienne and stormed down the porch steps, disappearing through the dense growth. Her posture ramrod straight and eyes like laser beams, Gran managed to intercept and reroute an impressive number of partygoers. Within thirty minutes, their backyard had filled with enough people to get Gran to stop hijacking guests.

Adrienne weaved through the party people, holding a tray of cocktail wieners and mini gherkin shish kebabs. Her eyes flickered compulsively toward the neighboring yard. Some party guests crossed enemy lines, going back and forth between the dueling events, bringing about equilibrium on both sides. Instead of taking satisfaction in the balanced turnout, Gran's face seemed to tighten.

That's when she pulled out the heavy artillery. With all the ceremony and pageantry of a royal wedding, Gran emerged with a pie in each hand. And like ladies in waiting, her collection of elderly women trailed behind, all in a row, carrying two pies each. They lined up at the long picnic table, setting the pies down with synchronized flair.

If the town had a heart, it was made of pie. Pies were expected at every holiday, festival, wedding, and funeral. And for all the pain and suffering Gran put the town through, her pies were her redemption. Adrienne noticed people she hadn't seen all evening converging on the double-crust apple and the lemon meringue. Even the mayor, who had chosen Mr. Merritt's party, was now stuffing a massive forkful of strawberry rhubarb into his fat face. Finally, when their yard had the most guests, the corners of Gran's lips curled up subtly, her eyes twinkling for just a moment as she surveyed the crowd. Whispers flitted from guest to guest, their faces animated as they savored each bite.

Adrienne ground her teeth while Gran basked in compliments meant for her. The old woman's deception was only forgiven when Adrienne overheard Ida Hoffman exclaim that the pies seemed to improve yearly. Adrienne smirked as she cleared the table, sure that remark had stung Gran. The omission was never a lie in Gran's book. So what if Adrienne had been up all night making the pies? So be it if the party guest wanted to assume it was Gran. With the woman lulled by accolades, Adrienne was finally able to escape the party.

Sneaking into the shadows on the side of the house, Adrienne crossed over to the Merritts'. She longed to tell Quinn and Lucas about Gran's party. The moment her foot crossed that unseen boundary, the atmosphere changed so dramatically that it was like stepping into Neverland.

Quinn stood near the edge of the dance floor, but he wasn't alone. Charity was on his arm and dressed in a skimpy white dress. Adrienne froze as the new girl batted her big doe eyes up at Quinn.

The world around her seemed to blur and tilt as if she were trapped on a nightmarish carousel. Finally, she found her legs and turned to leave, fearing she might throw up. Her fingers grazed her cheek and came away damp. She didn't even realize she'd started crying.

Lucas caught her as she stumbled into the shadows dividing the two houses under the banyacado tree. She desperately wanted to be alone but found letting go of his warm and comforting embrace impossible.

"Hey, why so glum, chum?" Lucas said soothingly. He patted her head as she loosened her grip on his button-down shirt.

"The party is stressing me out. I wanted to come over, but I was worried Gran might come for me and cause a scene." Adrienne backed away, quickly wiping the streaks from her face. "I just want this night to be over."

"I thought you saw Quinn with Charity, and it upset you," Lucas said. He clasped his hands behind his back and watched the partygoers. "He hasn't said anything to me, but I knew it would happen. They're a goddamn matching set."

His tone was amused and light, in stark opposition to her thoughts.

The anticipation she had built up for the summer disintegrated. She had lost Quinn before he was even hers. Under the veil of darkness, Lucas and Adrienne shared a loaded silence, their eyes locked on Quinn and Charity swaying to the music.

"I guess it's just you and me this summer." Adrienne's words came out in a shaky whisper.

His eyes sparkled. "Would that be so bad?" He pushed a lock of her hair behind her ear.

Before she could answer, a silvery bloom of fire exploded over their heads, and fiery tendrils spiraled over the banyacado tree. It was like standing under an umbrella of shooting stars. Automatically, they clasped hands.

"Dad hired a team to shoot off big ones for the party," Lucas said.

Her grip tightened. Lucas glanced over at her and smiled shyly. "You look beautiful tonight, Adrienne."

The odd little twinge returned. In the dappled shadows of the great banyacado tree, Lucas's dazzling blue eyes reflected her own internal battles. It would be so natural to simply reach up and . . .

Gran's voice pierced the night like a siren, and Adrienne dropped Lucas's hand. Her muscles seized, each echoing shout from Gran making her more rigid.

"My God, he'll burn down the tree before the night ends!" Gran appeared with her hands raised above her head.

Her rant halted when she spied Adrienne and Lucas in the shadows. "What the hell are you doing in the dark with that boy?" she demanded, every word edged with frost. "I told you to stay away from them. They're no good. Their father is trying to burn down my tree with those fireworks! He'll take out the whole neighborhood before he's done."

Her eyes narrowed as they flicked from Adrienne to Lucas.

Adrienne took all her frustration and angst and concentrated it into her first true act of rebellion. Her hands curled into balls.

"He's my friend. And we're going to be friends, like it or not."

"Oh really?" Gran's head oscillated slowly, her eyes widening as if she'd been slapped. "You think you can tell me what you're going to do? Well, you have another thing coming, missy. Until you're eighteen, you follow my rules."

Adrienne caught sight of silhouettes gathering around the tree, the murmur of voices rising in the dark air. Mr. Merritt appeared.

"What's going on here?"

"Your son was doing God knows what to my granddaughter, and I caught him." Gran crossed her arms, a human barricade.

"We were watching the fireworks," Lucas explained calmly.

Gran's voice soared. "And that's another thing. Your fireworks show is going to set my tree on fire. Do you see how close those molten hot pieces are getting? What if one catches my roof on fire?"

"I have the proper permits. I hired a professional company. They know what they're doing. Your precious tree is safe. Now, please stop accusing my son of such lies. The kids have all their clothes on. They weren't rolling in the dirt. I believe them if they say they were simply watching the fireworks. Sadly, they have to hide in the dark to avoid you. Their friendship shouldn't be a secret. And stop ruining a lovely night with your ranting. Frankly, I think the whole town is tired of your bullshit."

A smattering of applause broke out, the dark emboldening some to express their agreement with Mr. Merritt. A subtle change rippled through the crowd. Gran sensed it too, her eyes and sharp inhale belying her proud stance. Of course, no one expected her to go quietly into the night.

With few options left to recover her pride, Gran grabbed Adrienne by the arm and dragged her back toward the house.

"Go to your room. I don't want to see you until tomorrow." Her knobby fingers pounded the numbers on the phone, her voice hitting a pitch that made the windows vibrate.

"I'm seventeen. You can't send me to my room."

Gran's eyes shot daggers at Adrienne, compelling her to retreat. But she made sure to slam the bedroom door to convey her frustration.

She slid down the wall until she hit the floor, her spine pressing back. Gran yelled at the police over the phone about the dangerous fireworks threatening her house. A lone squad car arrived fifteen minutes later. Red-and-blue lights danced across the foliage outside, painting eerie shadows on her windowpane. Whispers rippled through the crowd, and the parties dissolved like sugar in water. Adrienne craned her neck out the window, straining to catch the fragments of escalating voices.

"It's over now. Nothing caught fire."

"He intentionally put my property in danger. You didn't see how close they got."

—

LATER, ADRIENNE SAT still, holding her breath until Gran's raspy snoring signaled the "all clear." She slipped down to the beach, where she willed Lucas to read her mind and meet her there. He seemed finely tuned to her, so it didn't seem out of the question. Thoughts of Lucas's potential suffering from the night's events twisted through her mind like vines.

A lone figure stood out on the beach, and Adrienne thanked the heavens. But it wasn't Lucas. It was Quinn. Adrienne's instincts told her to turn back, but Quinn's wave locked her in place.

"Another glorious battle between Merritt and Harris tonight?" His lips curved into that practiced, enchanting smile she knew all too well. In response, Adrienne's face twisted involuntarily as if she had tasted something sour.

"I was looking for Lucas," she said, her voice unsteady.

"Yeah, he sacked out pretty early. Don't worry about what your grandmother said. He didn't take it seriously."

"Okay. Good." Adrienne turned and started to head back to her house.

"Wait. Is something wrong? You're acting kind of funny. Lucas is too. Did something happen I don't know about?"

She paused and closed her eyes. *What the hell can I say that won't ruin everything?*

"You're with Charity." Ugh, she had opened Pandora's box.

"Would it matter?" he replied with an edge to his tone that made her turn around. His features remained unreadable, a chiseled mask, while his eyes searched the restless waves.

"Yes, it matters. I was surprised, that's all. After this morning." She pivoted, her shoulders slumping as she braced for the sting of rejection.

He abruptly gripped her arms, steering her to face him. Adrienne inhaled rapidly in surprise. Just as quickly, he released her and stepped back.

"What about Lucas?"

"What about him?" Adrienne shook her head, though that nagging twinge played a faint note within her.

"I was sold on you being into him. You two are so touchy-feely, always in your own little world. And then, I saw you two tonight, under the tree. It didn't look like two friends hanging out; that's for sure." Quinn raked an unsure hand through his hair. "I didn't think you . . . I only asked Charity to the party to be nice, so I'd have company. I feel left out sometimes when you and Lucas are together."

Adrienne's feet rooted in the sand as her own ragged breathing filled her ears. *Is this really happening? Is Quinn giving me the moon?*

"Christ, Adrienne. I'm falling apart here." Quinn put his hands on his hips.

"I'm not into Lucas," A flush swept over her cheeks, her pulse quickening in anticipation. Outside of friendship, thoughts about Lucas receded as quickly as they had arisen.

"Well, I'm not into Charity."

Adrienne blinked dumbly as she grappled with the dissonance between Quinn's words and her expectations. He reached out and hesitantly took her hand. "How could you think I would be interested in her? I thought you knew me."

Before Adrienne knew what was happening, Quinn's lips were on hers. She clutched at him with desperation. A new version of Adrienne was born into the world, one who did not hesitate to attempt to yank Quinn's shirt off, fumbling at the buttons.

"Not here." Quinn's eyes strayed toward the mansion, where caterers still scurried about, disassembling the remains of the night's festivities. "Come with me?"

Adrienne nodded, letting him pull her down the beach. They rounded the point and ended up on the dock where Mr. Merritt kept their boat. Quinn jumped on board, then helped Adrienne down.

The sense of perpetual surveillance in Harbor Point—the realization that scrutiny might reach them even here—hung over them. Quinn turned the engine over and backed the boat out of the slip. They glided slowly over the blackness, and as soon as the ship was free from the channel, Quinn took her hand, pulling her close. She wrapped her arms around him, and he threw the boat into full throttle. They sped through the moonless night on the calm ocean until the lights from the shore vanished. Once alone, Quinn cut the engine and let the boat drift. The stars hung bright overhead, and Adrienne clutched her hands together to quell the sudden rise of moths in her stomach.

His hand found the curve of her waist, his grip reassuring. "I promise we won't get lost."

"I'm not scared of getting lost." Her words wavered, barely escaping, betraying a vulnerability she hadn't intended to show.

Quinn pulled her to him, but it was awkward. Nervous laughter burst from both, crackling like static electricity before a storm. He unbuttoned his shirt and let it fall onto the deck. His bare chest and back emerged before her, uncharted territory etched with gash-like scars. A landscape as alluring as it was alien. She traced one of the thin, raised marks on his stomach. His body tensed, a fleeting grimace crossing his face. She pulled back.

"Sorry, it's okay," Quinn said. "It was a reflex. Scuba diving is dangerous. Got rolled across a reef. Nearly bled to death."

This terribly exciting, beautiful man wanted her. *Why? Why me?* His lips traced her jawline, sending molten lava through her veins, making everything inside her liquefy and pool.

"I've never done this," Adrienne confessed reluctantly.

"Adrienne, I'm a virgin too." Quinn smiled and laughed. "Another reason I wasn't into Charity. Everyone thinks I'm some kind of stud, but really, I'm just a dork who likes the ocean."

Every tendon in her body loosened at his confession. He had been plucked from an exotic garden of contradictions.

"And summer," he whispered as he pushed down the strap of her dress to place a warm kiss on her shoulder. "I love summer."

"Who's Summer?" Adrienne scrunched up her face and then giggled.

Quinn returned the laugh and began exploring her throat with his lips, making it impossible to continue any jokes.

"Me too," she breathed. A catalog of other things she loved swelled within her, this revelation tucked away for a distant someday.

They moved to the boat cabin, where there was a small bunk. The air was dense, nearly suffocating. Quinn led her through the dark to the bed. Her fingers quivered against the delicate straps of her dress as she lowered them, her skin emerging into view like the moon from behind clouds. As his fingers traced the landscape of her skin, her trembling stilled. Loving Quinn was like stepping into the summer sea.

When their naked flesh connected, she gasped with surprise. She coiled her hands in his hair. He kissed her gently, asking permission. She responded, hoping he understood he could have everything. His hand knotted into her hair as he pulled her closer. She was tumbling through an endless sky, ground and gravity nowhere in sight.

Charity had told her the first time would hurt and never was any good. As Quinn slid inside her, an exquisite ache sang through Adrienne's body, like the spice of a pepper on the tongue. Adrienne's body buzzed with a thousand bees as the burning grew, and the flames licked every molecule of her body until nothing of who she had been that morning remained. She called out to the deep night, declaring that death had come and she was reborn. The vortex opened and swallowed her whole.

WHEN ADRIENNE WOKE, she sat up and peered out the porthole for land but found none. The first smear of light oozed from the sky. The water outside lay still, a placid pool, much like the serenity that had settled within her. Her thoughts meandered back to the sultry confines of the cabin, to each caress. Beside her, Quinn shifted, his movements whispering through the sheets like a soft prelude to morning.

He yawned as he touched her hot cheek. "Are we lost yet?"

"Thoroughly." Adrienne traced the line of his hip to his lower abdomen.

Quinn got up and stretched his long, lean body. Adrienne's eyes lingered, caught in an internal tug-of-war between modesty and fascination. He was pure art. *Will I ever be able to face him and act normal?* No. In the tapestry of her thoughts, their bodies wove together in an unending pattern of sensation and heat. The sounds she had made. How they both had discovered the art of making love on that tiny bunk. His essence, a tang on her lips and a musky perfume on her skin, had marked her. *How will I ever function as an average human again? How does anyone have sex and then simply rejoin the mundane world?*

Quinn went up on deck, and a moment later, there was a loud splash.

"Come in. It's almost morning," he called to her. "The sea monsters have all gone to sleep."

She came out and stood above him on the deck. "I'm not afraid of sea monsters."

"I know." Quinn motioned for her to jump.

She dropped the sheet; his eyes trailed her naked body as she stood on the ledge. With a flawless front flip, she met the water's bracing surface. Her eyes darted around when she emerged, finding no sign of Quinn amid the shifting reflection. Then his hands were on her legs, moving up toward the sky.

"I thought you might scream," he said when he surfaced.

She splashed him. "I told you, I'm not scared."

He tugged her beneath the water, their limbs like strands of seaweed caught in a playful current. When she wrapped her legs around his waist this time, he was ready for her. In an ideal world, she would have stayed beneath the ocean with Quinn, forsaking the need for air.

THEY RACED BACK to Harbor Point, the sun rising behind them. The familiar vision of Gran clad in her worn housecoat and nervously conversing with police in the driveway flickered through Adrienne's thoughts. But it wasn't Gran who met them at the dock as they pulled in. It was Christopher. At first, Adrienne couldn't understand why he would be there or how he knew they were on Mr. Merritt's boat. The deep creases framing Christopher's downcast eyes made everything horribly clear.

"Adrienne, it's your grandfather," he said, taking the rope from Quinn and looping it around the dock post. "I told your grandmother I'd find you."

"Is he okay?" Her words barely came out, the swell of an impending sob making each syllable a struggle as Quinn's arms encircled her.

Christopher's words sank in her belly like stones. "I'm sorry, but he's gone."

CHAPTER SEVENTEEN

The void left in her grandfather's absence had a gravity all its own, dragging at her day by day.

A terrible cocktail of emotions boiled within her, enhanced by Quinn's frequent absences. He finally resurfaced after a week away, having left the day after the funeral, and Adrienne found herself laughing hysterically as he shimmied through her bedroom window. The laughter was quickly replaced by sobs that racked her body. Alarmed, Quinn went to her, hugging her close to him.

"How are you doing? I'm sorry my dad sent me away right after the funeral. What a shitshow, huh?"

"God, I'm a hot mess," Adrienne said. She wiped her tears on his shirt. "I'm sorry I cried on your shirt. Did he send you away because of me?"

The question had been burning inside her since he left.

He rested his chin on top of her head. "You let me deal with old Pops. He has bigger fish to fry than you."

A sob rose again, but she swallowed it, unwilling to taint their fleeting togetherness.

"What about Lucas? He hasn't said a word to me about that night." She grabbed a tissue and blew her nose in as ladylike a manner as she could muster.

"Lucas doesn't even know we were gone. As I said, he was passed out when I left that night. He may have had a drink or two. I tried to keep tabs on him, but it was a busy night."

Quinn flopped onto her bed, stretching out like a cat in the sun. His feet dangled off the end of the twin bed, and she marveled at his slender limbs and the side profile of his face. Her hand hovered above his chest, suspended in an invisible force field of uncertainty, waiting for a sign, a single word from him to dissolve it.

"I thought I'd never get home." He dipped his head, and his breath blazed against the sensitive skin of her inner thigh.

"Me too," she murmured.

Adrienne tugged at his shirt. Quinn pulled it over his head and flipped over onto his stomach. The marks on his back made her queasy when she thought of him hitting the coral, raked over it, pulled by the undertow of the receding wave. Her fingers gingerly traced the pattern of his scars, each curve and line a signpost to an uncharted world. Gradually, he melted under her fingertips.

"You'll make me fall asleep doing that," he purred, his face in the pillow.

"I didn't know Lucas drank at the party. He seemed so normal this time." The warmth radiating from his skin enveloped her hand as if he were a living flame.

"He has some impulse-control issues. What worries me is he is getting really good at hiding stuff from me." He eyed her. "Don't worry, it had nothing to do with the show your grandmother put on."

Adrienne turned out the light and lay next to him. Her pulse quickened, defying the very thought of sleep. She tugged at the rim of his shorts.

"I see. I'm just some booty call to you?" Quinn turned his head toward her and smirked.

"Hmm." She nodded.

He rolled over and took his pants off. Adrienne's fingers followed the trails of moonlight over his hip bone.

"Your turn." His voice dropped an octave, tinged with an unmistakable urgency.

His invitation swept away any hesitancy. As she crawled on top of him, the hunger in his eyes erased all other realities, narrowing the universe to an expanse of skin and breath.

UNDONE, THEY LAY in bed as the ceiling fan made lazy circles above them. Adrienne noticed the first curls of light creeping into the dark sky. Quinn played with a curl of her hair, rubbing it across his chin.

"I think we should be careful. We need to be smart," Quinn said, breaking the lull. "No one is going to be cheering for us."

"You want to stop?" She choked the words out.

"No!" he said a little too loud, then softening. "Not that. I'd like to keep things quiet."

"You mean sneak around?"

"That sounds shitty, but yeah." He turned to face her, resting his head on the palm of his hand. "Do you hate me?"

"No," she sighed. "You're right, I guess. We are a freaking modern-day Romeo and Juliet."

"Let's leave out the 'dying' part, okay?"

She imagined they were both envisioning the repercussions of being found out. *Death by poison would be the better choice,* Adrienne mused darkly. Foreboding traced her spine.

"Nothing stays quiet for long in a town like this."

CHAPTER EIGHTEEN

September rolled in with a sky drained of summer's glow. Severe clouds pulsated with rain as Lucas hurled his shirts and trousers into his school trunk, each item an exclamation point to his frustration. His eyes held the echo of fruitless arguments, failed pleadings to stay in Harbor Point.

She caught his eye, reading in it a question she dared not voice: Was she the reason Mr. Merritt insisted on his departure?

"I'll make sure we come home for Christmas," Lucas told himself more than her.

"Sure." She tried to play along. "We'll write like last year."

"The year is so long, so cold." He shook his head. "I lie in bed and think of you, standing on the shore, the sun in your hair. I swear, it's the only thing that gets me through."

"I think about you too. I count the days."

"At least you'll have a good year at the new school, cooking cool stuff." Lucas patted her on the shoulder as he walked by.

She tried in vain to lighten the room. "I'll send you cookies."

"I can't stand any more packing," Lucas announced, throwing a shirt on the floor. "Want to take a walk?"

Adrienne glanced out the window. "It's starting to rain."

"Not much. We'll go up to the lifeguard tower and back."

The rain started falling harder, forcing them to run for shelter. Lightning stabbed down close. Adrienne's skin prickled from the energy.

Lucas laughed breathlessly. "Okay, not one of my best ideas."

Huddled together under the lifeguard tower, they listened as raindrops tapped a relentless beat above, each drop a moment slipping away. Lucas started a sandcastle. They worked on it diligently, affixing broken shells to the sides for windows and carving out a door with their fingers. Once the castle was perfect, Lucas pulled out his Swiss Army knife and cut their initials into the leg of the lifeguard tower. Her eyes followed the graceful movement of his blade as he etched intricate patterns and flowers into the wood, each mark a quiet, deliberate gesture.

Lucas sank into the sand, propping himself up on his elbows and letting out a contented sigh. "I'm going to miss this."

"It's not the same when you guys are gone." She stared up at the wooden planks overhead, the sand beneath her a reminder that summer couldn't last, that autumn was waiting on the horizon.

"The only good thing about boarding school is eight months away from my dad." Lucas stared intently at where the sea met the sky, perhaps seeking answers in the merging shades of blue.

"Two years until we are free." She let her thoughts wander to a future where Gran's influence would no longer anchor her.

"I'll never be free, no matter how far I go."

"You can't think like that." She met his gaze, and an icy undercurrent there made her shudder.

"The night my mother died, he got out of the car and left her. The police found him hiding in the trees, like a coward, a few miles up the road. He had been drinking. But with his money and influence, he got off with a slap on the wrist. They even sealed his record."

"That is so sad," she said as she touched his arm.

"I hate him for leaving her to die alone. I hate him for everything."

Adrienne scooted closer to him.

"I'm so sorry."

Frozen in the moment, her eyes widened like a startled deer's as he turned and his lips met hers.

She pulled away. "Lucas . . ."

"I'm sorry. It seemed like good timing." Casting a sidelong glance her way, a hesitant smile crossed his lips as he dabbed at the corners of his eyes. "I've wanted to do it for some time now."

Adrienne stood quickly. "It's letting up. We should go before it gets worse again."

She should have told him right there about Quinn.

"Sure," Lucas said. Rising, a crease appeared between his eyebrows as he swiped wet sand off his pants.

"I should let you finish packing. You leave early." Her words dissolved into the sea's roar as if the ocean could better understand her sentiment.

He sighed as they began their journey back home. "It seems like all we do is say goodbye."

"Sounds like a good song. We're always saying goodbye."

Lucas's shoulders slumped, and his face seemed to age years in moments, a vivid portrait of defeat. "You write it and send it to me."

Lifting his chin, he was clearly forcing the corners of his mouth upward.

—

AT MIDNIGHT, AS if on cue, Quinn hopped into her room. His fingers grazed her keepsakes, lingering longer than necessary on each item. Every pause, every caress spoke of a farewell. The question hung in the air like a solid entity: *What will happen to us over the next year?*

Finally, Quinn crawled into the bed next to her. She kissed him, wanting him to know that words were unnecessary. He leaned into her, his hand sliding under her shirt.

—

ADRIENNE SQUEEZED HER eyes shut and willed the dawn away. Quinn seemed to move in slow motion as he dressed in the dark.

She recorded every inch of his body, tucking it away for the lonely nights ahead.

"Quinn, what happens next summer?" It bubbled out of her.

He hesitated, then sat on the bed.

"Summer is our time." He kissed her. "Can that be enough?"

She took in his words with a sense of melancholy. Summer was their home. Beyond that yellow wall of sea and sunlight, there were no answers.

"Yes," she finally answered.

—

HOURS LATER, ADRIENNE bolted upright in bed as her grandmother's shrill cry pierced the early-morning air. She rushed out to find Gran standing under the banyacado tree.

Confusion gave way to disbelief as she took in the missing half of the tree. It was as if God himself had come down and expertly dissected half from the whole, straight down the middle. The cut portion on Mr. Merritt's side of the property line lay in the grass, exposing the pulpy insides. The half that lived on Gran's side of the property line remained intact: branches, leaves, and even the summer crop of avocados.

Detective Adams glanced at his notepad, eyebrows raised. "It's strange. Nobody in your house heard anything last night. A tree this size, cut so cleanly, you'd expect some noise. In fact, you would expect a great racket. And it would take quite a long time to cut away such a large portion."

"Are you calling me a liar?" Gran barked at the rookie. "Are you insinuating that I did this simply because I didn't hear it happening? Is my granddaughter a liar too? She didn't hear anything as well."

The poor officer retreated to his cruiser to finish his report.

Mrs. Peterson from the next road over appeared and squinted at the tree. "How did nobody hear anything? Bringing down such a massive tree would make a ruckus!" Though she was late to the game, everyone agreed that a tree of that size could not have fallen without making a terrible sound.

Naturally, the number one suspect was Mr. Merritt. He was questioned at length by the police. With a strong alibi—he had taken his sons to the airport in Miami and stayed overnight in a hotel—the police had nothing to charge.

Hushed conversations filled the local diner.

"Had to be lightning," murmured one group, while another retorted, "Merritt's finally lost it, I tell ya!"

"Premeditated." Letty Jorgenson nodded.

Georgie Pickens disagreed. "Freak-of-nature accident. No one man could do this."

Everyone was convinced the tree would die. Local experts agreed that the shock would be too much. The town arborist, Jean Joyner, commented, "I've never seen a tree survive such trauma. It's not looking good."

Yet it did not die.

Day after day, Gran marched to the wounded tree with a bottle of her latest concoction. Sometimes murky, sometimes fizzing, always mysterious. Surrounded by her botanical books and chattering friends, Gran would stir her brews, each recipe inspired by myth and arcane lore. Coffee grounds mixed with black licorice, steeped in gin poultices. Bacon grease and grapefruit juice tonics. Gran even had Christopher get up on a ladder and swab thick layers of smelly tar on the exposed pulp, like a Band-Aid, to keep the moisture inside the tree. Leaves stayed green, and new branches began to bud, defying all expectations.

Nobody expected the steady stream of visitors stopping by to witness the miracle of the half tree and giving Gran the spotlight she had always craved but never admitted to wanting. Jean Joyner made it a ritual to pay homage to the half tree and its caretaker. He hung on Gran's every word as she regaled him with tales of her unconventional arbor care. Now cleared—rightly or wrongly—of any blame, Mr. Merritt seized the moment. The contentious stucco wall began to rise, obscuring the big white house bit by bit as fall crept into Harbor Point.

CHAPTER NINETEEN
Summer 2012

Laughter and chatter filled the atmosphere at the gala, mingling with the aroma of grilled meats and spices.

Adrienne's hands moved in a blur, scooping generous servings onto paper plates. Meanwhile, Christopher juggled the sizzling pans on the propane cooktop. They exchanged quick glances and nods, trying to keep up with the growing line of hungry festivalgoers. Next Adrienne skillfully stirred an exotic saffron risotto on the propane cooktop as Christopher flipped a skewer of marinated scallops on the grill. Various chafing dishes were set up beside them, each holding another experiment they'd developed for today's event.

White tents lined Ocean Ave along the marina walk. Various vendors sold watercolors, oils, seashell crafts, and woven baskets. In the green space, a vast green canvas pavilion sat like the finial of a circus tent, holding the entire gala together. The food stalls were arranged in a crescent around the bandstand, where the mayor talked animatedly with a group of people. Adrienne wiped the sweat from her forehead and found herself transfixed by the swoop and sway of the mayor's hands as he spoke.

A visiting rival restaurateur broke the pause, feigning casual glances at their cooktop but loitering just long enough to scope out the chalkboard menu hanging overhead. He wasn't the first. His eyes narrowed briefly before he sauntered away.

Adrienne shook her head and grunted. "You'd think if they came all the way over here, they'd at least taste the food."

"They will. They're just warming up to it." Christopher chuckled. "Maybe we should think of a new name for the place," he remarked as the owner of Lucile and Ottlie's—a fine-dining restaurant that stood as an anchor in Harbor Point—stumbled into their tent with all the grace of a bumblebee.

"Goodness, I heard through the grapevine that the market was taking a stab at the dinner scene. I see it was no joke." Mr. Schumer gave a wide-eyed grin. "And Adrienne, back at the helm."

His eyes met Adrienne's, and with her face in a plate of scallop risotto, she flashed back to the countless catering gigs where her youthful ambition had gone head-to-head with Lucile and Ottlie's banquet dominance. The rivalry had been unspoken but unmistakable.

"Any thought on expansion?" Mr. Schumer asked.

Adrienne winked at him. "Nah, Mr. Schumer, we plan to stay small. For now."

The gentleman beat a hasty exit.

"Have you ever seen a man more terrified of a bowl of risotto? One taste and he's already worried you'll steal all his business again."

"The town has changed," Adrienne acknowledged. "There's room for both of us. If Mr. Schumer goes under, it will be because he hasn't changed that menu in thirty years."

"Too right," Christopher said amid gulps of laughter. "Ah, this town has been so boring without you."

Adrienne pursed her lips and quickly turned toward the line of customers. Things were still awkward with him. She had not found an opportunity to bring up her terrible behavior during opening night. The gala monopolized every moment of her time.

"Will you be open for dinner tomorrow, dear?" Mrs. Miller asked, lingering after receiving her order. Her scratchy voice grated across Adrienne's nerves.

Adrienne eyed the growing line over the woman's shoulder.

"I want to book for twelve. My grandchildren are in town," Mrs.

Miller continued, dipping a chunk of bread into the Styrofoam bowl of cioppino.

"No, we open next Tuesday."

"Well, put me down for Tuesday." The woman floated away toward the big tent next door.

The market kiosk was next to the tent for the food competitions. From Adrienne's station at the flat grill, she could watch the demo station where local businesses showcased their culinary skills—and where she was slated to appear later. Her stomach clenched at the thought of juggling sauté pans while making small talk with an audience. She'd much prefer the quiet alchemy of her kitchen.

When the first "meet the chef" request came in on the opening night, Adrienne's bones went liquid as she put a clean apron over her stained shirt. She blindly shook hands out in the dining area, nodding at the compliments, while a part of her longed for the sanctuary of her kitchen.

It should be Christopher, Adrienne thought now. He would command the demo table, his British accent adding a touch of charm. He'd catch the eye of all the ladies in the crowd, sending them casual winks as he finessed his pan.

Then he pulled her aside and presented her with a new chef's jacket, her name embroidered on the breast pocket.

"I am but a fan. This is your show."

Warmth spread through her, an unexpected softening. She looked up to meet his eyes and, for the first time, truly understood the spell he cast on everyone around him.

As Kali stepped in to take over, Adrienne let out a relieved sigh and leaned against the counter, grateful for the brief respite before entering the spotlight. Adrienne noticed Tam hovering close to the tent. *He'll be a sophomore soon,* she thought, the looming milestone adding to her apprehension. Kali wasn't even in high school yet. She was just a child, playing.

Impulsively, Adrienne went up to him. "Would you like to work at the market? We need some help, and you did a great job last night."

Tam's brows shot up for a split second before he broke into an earnest smile.

"Really, Mrs. H? That would be great!"

"Come by at three on Tuesday, and I'll show you the ropes." Adrienne patted Tam's shoulder, slyly convinced that her daughter's virtue would remain intact between his lifeguard job and keeping him busy at the market. Plus, she wasn't lying. He did a great job.

Tessa's scowl as Adrienne approached the demo kitchen was priceless. Though it was ninety degrees and Adrienne was wrapped in her new chef's jacket, she couldn't help but flaunt a triumphant smile.

"Um, I spoke with Christopher a few days ago, and he said he would be hosting the market's demo?" Tessa flipped through some papers she had pinned on a clipboard. "No one notified me of a change."

"We decided I was the right choice. You know, the historical significance. We both felt it would be better publicity for the new dinner service if I got my face out there." Adrienne packed the "we" part with false innuendo.

Tessa leaned sideways and peered accusingly at the market tent, where Christopher was mid-flambé with spicy tequila shrimp.

"You've made yourself very comfortable here quite quickly." Tasse brushed nonexistent fluff from her tailored light-pink top.

Adrienne nodded serenely. "Almost as if it was meant to be."

IT WAS REMARKABLY easy to talk about something she loved.

Adrienne soaked in the attentive faces, her nerves giving way to exhilaration. A large crowd gathered as she explained the delicate line between too much garlic and not enough in a scampi. She only knew her time was up when the audience erupted in applause. Adrienne searched past the portable spotlight keeping her in a circular glow and found Kali and Christopher hooting and hollering for her.

What she saw next was entirely unexpected: Gran, sitting hunched over at a small round table set off from the crowd.

But Adrienne couldn't take time to wonder how the old lady had gotten to the gala, for as the applause died down, a swarm of enthusiastic faces closed in. "Is your restaurant taking reservations?" one asked, while another inquired, "Do you cater?"

Once the crowd thinned, Adrienne found Gran shuffling toward the street. She ran to catch up, more curious than anything.

"How did you get here?" Adrienne said, a bit out of breath.

"That boy Kali is always with gave me a ride." Gran paused, squinting. "Kali mentioned your cooking thing. I was curious."

"What did you think?" A mix of anticipation and wariness fluttered in her chest, and she braced herself for Gran's typical bluntness. She wasn't disappointed.

"They seem to like you and your food. At least you didn't faint." Gran flipped her hand and kept moving.

Adrienne sighed. "Come on. I'll drive you home."

She went to the tent to collect Kali and tell Christopher and found them in a huddle with Tam. Their heads snapped up in unison, their faces a shade too innocent.

"What's going on here?" Adrienne squinted suspiciously.

"All in due time," Christopher said with a wink. He turned to Kali, and they traded a knowing glance.

A pleasant fatigue settled over Adrienne, dulling her usually keen sense of curiosity. Prying into their secret plans seemed a Herculean effort she wasn't prepared to make. And seeing the exchange between Kali and Christopher, their eyes lighting up in a shared moment, left her with little room for objection.

CHAPTER TWENTY

The Fourth of July fell on the Wednesday of the gala, coinciding with the juried art awards ceremony. Adrienne and Christopher invited people to the market for a festive final meal with all the favorites. Adrienne's feet barely touched the ground as she extended an invitation to Tam. The town was festooned in crepe and bunting. The streets surged with people, art installations, and delicious smells from various tents.

Kali's mood had seemed to lighten since the food demo, and Adrienne sensed a truce had been called. As she bustled about the market's kitchen, the thought of Quinn was a distant star. Though she sometimes caught herself looking for him across the cottage lawn or on the sidewalk in front of the market, he had seemingly retreated back from whence he came.

Ever fascinated with American holidays, Christopher bought out the local firework stand and planned a grand show for all in the parking lot. Though the town would have its performance after the awards, he hoped to prolong the evening as long as possible. Adrienne found herself humming, his enthusiasm catching her in its wake. She chuckled as she eavesdropped on Christopher's conversation with Tam. The Brit was waxing poetic about blue crabs, his voice tinged with earnestness bordering on zeal.

Adrienne was sure the poor boy was already second-guessing his decision to work there.

She pulled out Gramps's old steel barrel smoker and filled it with various haunches of meat; then, in the kitchen's heat, she baked an ambitious array of pies: peach, apple, strawberry rhubarb, blueberry—and pecan, Gramps's favorite. The two inheritors of Gran's domain set up a royal post for her in the front room by the bay window, where she spent her time barking reminders and orders to Adrienne in the kitchen. Tempted to retort, the words caught in her throat. *This might be one of Gran's final performances.*

Kali rescued Tam around noon, and the two set up out front to watch the parade.

"You better make some progress with that girl, or she will turn out like you," hollered Gran from the dining area.

Adrienne exited the kitchen, relishing the cool blast of air from the front room. Kali and Tam sat in beach chairs outside the market, holding hands under the summer sun. Police cruisers, their sirens piercing the summer air, and fire engines strung with patriotic garlands roared down A1A, announcing the parade's jubilant commencement.

Gran eyed the two kids outside the window. "You'll be a grandparent before next summer."

"Kali is nothing like me. Thank God." Adrienne sat next to Gran. "I don't think she would repeat my past after seeing what came of it."

"There was a time when you were pretty confident you wouldn't repeat your mother's mistakes." The older woman nodded to her. "You didn't abandon your child, though; I'll give you that."

"Evolution, I guess," Adrienne teased Gran. "I made my own mistakes . . . and took care of my mess." She leaned back as the teens played the game of love.

Gran shrugged. "Have you heard from her, my daughter?"

"Not for months. I wrote and let her know we were here. I told her about the fire."

"Makes no difference. I could have burned the whole house to the ground. Your mother wouldn't come." Gran leaned back as well, her gaze still locked on the scene outside and her lips thin with resentment as she spoke of her daughter's absence.

Adrienne knew so little of what had happened, but it was safe to assume that Diana had not taken well to Gran's micromanagement and had fled.

Adrienne got up. "Well, let's eat."

They spread the food along a long table, and Adrienne stood like a ship captain at the helm, Christopher by her side, doling out dinners to faces familiar and new. She felt firm in her footing for the first time, as if roots now extended from her soles into the earth. The usual restlessness in her heart stilled on that hazy summer evening.

"Tam and I are going to go. We'll see you there," Kali called out as Adriene stuffed paper plates into a garbage bag out back by the live wells. The girl practically bounced on her toes as she spoke.

Adrienne stood in the gravel parking lot behind the market, staring after the two kids as they vanished into the tangle of mangroves, taking the shortcut to the marina. The cicadas rattled incessantly in the shadows of the last afternoon light. The sound could drive a person mad.

It was starting. Kali was making friends. The town tugged at Adrienne, coaxing her to give in and stay. But with Quinn around, she would never be free of her memories. The pain would be a constant companion, a reminder of her terrible choices. Just as Kali's eyes tormented her.

We should never have come here, she thought with a chill.

"Hey, walk with me to the bandstand?" Christopher's soothing voice slipped into her thoughts. Adrienne realized she was clutching the chain-link gate so hard that the metal had left crisscross indents in her hand.

Adrienne nodded, and they headed across the lot next door.

"I'm sorry about how I acted the other night. I really don't know what's wrong with me." Adrienne dug one hand into the pocket of her jean shorts.

"You owe me no reason or apology. I haven't been very good at giving you the space you need. I have a hard time with boundaries."

Adrienne laughed. "Well, at least you're aware of it."

Christopher stopped in the liminal space between the marina and the empty shops of the new condo tower. "Adrienne." He took her free hand into his. "I don't want you to leave. Stay. Stay forever."

A knot formed in her throat. "I'm not sure I can be what you want, Christopher. You might regret wanting me to stay. I might hate you if I do."

Christopher bowed slightly and nodded. "You can't blame a guy for asking."

"No." Adrienne brushed away a tear. "But I will think about it. I promise."

"Well, I can't ask for more than that." He smiled, tipping his head down until their noses nearly touched, tempting her to kiss him.

The band started to tune their instruments on the stage. Christopher took a deep breath and said, "We should get going."

Adrienne nodded and stepped back, her heart thrumming like a hummingbird.

The awards ceremony was about to begin when they arrived at the marina. The mayor stood onstage, his face intermittently washed out and then crisply defined as the spotlight danced over him. He wore one of his trademark short-sleeved, button-down Tommy Bahama Hawaiian shirts.

Adrienne searched the crowd for Kali, but it was dark, and clusters of people made searching difficult. Memories of stolen kisses and hushed laughter on humid summer nights came flooding back, each memory like a drop of rain on parched ground. *Don't I want Kali to have those kinds of memories too?*

"She is fine." Christopher glanced at her, his eyes knowing. "She's fine. We'll find her before the fireworks."

"Is this thing on?" The mayor tapped the microphone, making the crowd jump from the audible feedback. "Sorry about that," he said sheepishly.

Christopher chuckled and touched Adrienne's back, guiding her gently through the crowd.

She couldn't help the slow, triumphant smile that spread across her lips as she caught sight of Tessa's face, pinched and drained of color, at the corner of the juried artwork tent. She could only imagine what Tessa saw: Christopher—her prized catch—with his hands all over another woman.

Adrienne smiled and waved as she linked her arm through Christopher's. Guilt rushed through her. *I'm sending him mixed signals.* But when she looked up at him, he simply smiled and squeezed her arm before returning his attention to the mayor.

"Okay, let's get started with the teen-division ribbons." The mayor studied his note cards, sweat dripping down his face.

"Blue ribbon for charcoal, Kali Harris."

Everyone clapped. The name "Kali Harris" hung in the air for a split second, not quite registering. Then, it hit her like a tidal wave. Kali had won, and she'd done it without breathing a word to Adrienne. Astonishment mixed with maternal pride surged through her. Kali appeared on the stage and posed for a photo with the mayor. Once she left the stage, she approached Adrienne, holding her ribbon and grinning.

"I didn't know you entered!" Adrienne shook her head, hugging Kali. "I'm shocked. And so proud."

"Christopher made me." Kali allowed her mother to embrace her momentarily before pushing away. "I asked him to keep it a secret."

Christopher held his hands up in defense. "Sorry, but I promised."

"This is a great surprise. Can we see your work?" Adrienne beamed.

They followed Kali through the tent. Tam, radiant with pride, joined them. His eyes lit up as they followed Kali.

Adrienne found her guard dropping, bit by bit. Gran had maintained such a tight grip on her youth. Adrienne resolved not to bind Kali in the same stifling hold.

"It's over here," Kali called, then froze.

Quinn stood admiring Kali's winning portrait. He seemed like his old self, in light-beige slacks and a breezy white button-down shirt.

Adrienne's heart did that odd little flip it only did for Quinn. She clenched her teeth as if she could will herself into equilibrium.

"Quinn! You came!" Kali ran to him with a familiarity that could only come from secret meetups, their smiles interlocking like pieces of a puzzle.

"I knew you'd win, kiddo," Quinn said. He touched Kali lightly on the shoulder, full of adoration. "You have your uncle's hands."

Adrienne was an outsider. Watching Kali's eyes, so full of admiration, lock onto Quinn, she couldn't help lamenting, *How does he earn her love so easily?* Protectiveness and a fit of sharp, biting jealousy swirled inside her.

"Mom, did you see my work?" Kali waved her hand in front of Adrienne's face, snapping her out of her cocoon of self-loathing.

The massive portrait of Gran stood under a soft beam of light in the middle of the tent.

Gran sat in her wingback chair with the large bay window in the background, revealing the sea. In the painting, her eyes carried a gleam that looked like a mix of wisdom and unforgiving love. At the same time, the slight curve of her mouth suggested a lifetime of restrained smiles. Kali had even captured the age spots, transforming them into constellations as if her flesh were a celestial canvas. Adrienne's eyes brimmed with unshed tears as she traced the swirls and scrolls of Kali's work, each stroke evoking a haunting resonance of Lucas's talent. A breeze rushed through the tent, bringing the scent of low tide from the Back Bay.

"Kali, it's breathtaking," Adrienne stammered, trying hard to keep from ruining the moment. "I don't have any words for it."

"No one will forget her now. They're hanging it in the library at the Women's Club." Kali stood back and folded her arms as she inspected the piece. Ever the artist, Adrienne knew she was still considering improvements. The same furrowed brow she had witnessed so many times on Lucas now belonged to Kali.

"I had no idea you were working on this, given the tension

between you two the past weeks."

"Nah, we're good. Gran's a cranky old bat, but I like her." Kali smiled. Her smile seemed brighter, her posture more confident as she stood back in proud examination of her art. It was like watching a flower bloom in a garden Adrienne had not tended. She glanced at Christopher, his eyes meeting Kali's in a silent exchange. Unease twisted her stomach, forcing her to take measure of her contributions to Kali's journey.

Quinn's slightly tanned skin and casual posture told Adrienne that he hadn't left. Another glance between him and Kali felt like a shot in the gut.

"I didn't know you and . . . Quinn had been spending time together," Adrienne said, her voice strained. "Quinn, I came by to talk. But the house seemed . . . abandoned."

She bit her lower lip, regretting each fumbled syllable. And she wasn't the only one struggling. Quinn couldn't seem to make eye contact. His gaze kept darting around the room, seeking an escape route.

"I went with the flow. When Kali came to see me, I just let things happen naturally. I thought it was the best way forward."

Adrienne didn't want this conversation playing out in front of everyone, especially at the gala. The whole town was milling about. But something had loosened an invisible gag. Her words, once restrained, now cascaded recklessly. "I thought we decided to pause until I could speak with Quinn."

"It just happened. I didn't do it to spite you, honest," Kali groaned with frustration. "I just want to know my dad."

"I think I should have been part of this whole thing." Adrienne turned back to Quinn. "You are a stranger to us, even if you are her father. I should have been told. I should have been the one to say it was okay." Her words were halting, like hiccups as she struggled through her words. When Christopher's hand clasped her shoulder, she noticed Quinn's eyes widen for a fleeting moment.

"If it were up to you, I'd never know who he is." Kali's guilty demeanor quickly turned defensive.

"For good reason." Adrienne folded her arms across her chest.

"He wanted me," Kali said in a soft, rage-filled hush. Tam ran his hand through his mop of brown curls nervously. As Kali revealed the great secret, Quinn's eyes went wide.

"What?" Adrienne snapped.

"Quinn told me. He wanted me. He came back to get you, but Gran told him you had an abortion and had run away. Gran said you wanted him to know that and leave you alone."

Adrienne's eyes zipped from face to face, trying to find a foothold in a reality that seemed to spin around her. "No" escaped her lips like a hiss, shaking her head.

"Kali, I can assure you that is not true." Christopher stepped closer, his eyes meeting Adrienne's in support as the tension reached a breaking point.

"You might have always been hanging around, but that doesn't mean you know everything." The old Quinn glimmered behind his eyes, the one with fight and conviction.

Christopher's tone was resolute. "I don't claim to know everything. I know what Adrienne told me. She searched for you. You completely vanished. That disappearing act only happens when someone does not want to be found."

His unwavering voice was an anchor in the chaos.

Quinn looked right through Christopher as if he were not there. His eyes met Adrienne's, filled with a raw desperation that seemed to beg for understanding. "I came back. You were already gone. I went to your grandmother's. I wanted to find you. She told me you were pregnant. She said the child was Lucas's. That you had an abortion and fled. It made sense at the time. It felt like pieces that had nagged me for years had finally fallen into place. I didn't know what to think or do."

Bile rose in her throat. "You believed her? After all the insanity she brought to our lives?"

"I was in a bad place; you know that." Quinn's eyes scanned the people watching them, the nervous jitter returning to his hands.

"You seriously thought something was going on between Adrienne and Lucas?" Christopher probed Quinn's cryptic response, like any good journalist.

"Shut up!" Quinn's voice rose, and the festivalgoers in the tent went silent. "You played your part in all this. You are far from innocent. I am sure Elizabeth spilled the tea, and you never told Adrienne about it all these years. Or told me the truth."

Adrienne stepped back. Her heartbeat reverberated in her ears, and the tent seemed close in on her. Christopher's cheeks flushed a deep shade of red, his eyes avoiding Adrienne's as he looked down at his shoes.

A cold emptiness replaced the warmth she felt for him.

Once again, Christopher manipulated the situation, only thinking about what he thought was best rather than including me.

She was not a child. Why did everyone treat her like fine china—something delicate and easily broken—and go about doing what *they* thought best? Adrienne had made it on her own this far. As far as she was concerned, she would make it without any of them if they continued to behave like this.

"You promised me you wouldn't keep anything from me," Adrienne hissed.

"I hated him for leaving you." Christopher sighed. "I have done things I can't undo."

She glared at Quinn, catching a fleeting smirk that quickly vanished.

"It doesn't matter." Adrienne's words were sharp, each one a dagger aimed at Quinn. "Your first instinct was to abandon me. You lied to me. You said you would say goodbye. But I was left in the dark, watching you drive away. Maybe your conscience got the best of you after a while, but I always knew, deep down, that you and I were just a means to pass the time until you went to college and started your real life. Summers with me were a pause, an escape, and nothing more."

Quinn's eyes widened, his mouth slightly agape. *Have I been too harsh?* she wondered, seeing the agony in his expression.

The first fireworks exploded above the tent, making them all jump.

"Whatever, this is my night, and I'm not going to deal with this crap right now," Kali announced over the noise. She grabbed Tam's hand and headed for the lawn.

Her words snapped Adrienne out of her pity party for one. Feeling all the eyes in the tent on her, Adrienne wished she could shrink away and hide. She took a deep breath and called after her daughter, "I want you home by eleven!"

Adrienne caught Tam's eye, mouthing the words "Thank you," silently imploring him to bring Kali home safely.

She then looked from Quinn to Christopher, measuring the weight of their presence against her waning energy. With a last, fleeting glance at both men, she pivoted on her heel and walked away.

—

ADRIENNE'S MIND WENT to her mother, constantly slipping out the back door when arguments got too heated, vanishing until the storm passed. She had learned the same evasive maneuvers. Tacky restaurant closing? Leave before they can sack you. Daughter too inquisitive? Change the subject. Get knocked up? Leave town. But now, as Adrienne sat at her bedroom window, the big white house looming, unlike her mother, all Adrienne wanted was to stop.

The back door creaked downstairs, and Adrienne knew Kali was home. It was close to midnight. Adrienne's fingers clenched and unclenched as she whispered, "Someday, we'll find a way to each other."

The light was on in the kitchen, a triangle of gold spilling out from the hallway. She descended the stairs to investigate and found Gran at the kitchen table with a steaming cup of coffee. Adrienne's eyes locked onto the old family photo hanging in the hall—of a young Gran, her smile enigmatic. It struck her how deeply Gran was entwined in the web of family turmoil—a root of scheming and chaos as stubborn as her beloved banyacado tree that refused to surrender to death.

"Quinn told me what you did. You told him Kali was Lucas's child and that I had an abortion." Adrienne planted her feet in the entryway, shoulders squared and chin lifted as if bracing herself for an incoming wave.

"It made more sense that she belonged to that poor dead boy." Gran nodded with her eyes closed. "You were better off without him in your life. Look what happened with you two sneaking around."

"It is my life. Not yours. Not Christopher's. Not even Quinn's."

Gran scooped a dollop of jam onto her toast, her hands steady.

Adrienne knew it didn't matter what she said. Gran would never hear her. It was more for her to say it aloud and let the universe record it. "Your actions played a part in all of this. You didn't want me to ruin my life, but you helped ruin it."

That got Gran's attention, her watery brown eyes accusatory.

"You got away. Your mother did, too. But here I am in this town. I'll die here and soon. I know it's coming for me." Gran set down her toast and gazed beyond Adrienne to something invisible. "All I wanted was to leave, to be a dancer. I wanted to travel the world. All I got was this prison."

Adrienne envisioned Gran as a teen with big dreams too large for Harbor Point. *Does she also see South Road as the end of the world?*

"If you knew he was here, you would have come back," Gran muttered more to herself than to Adrienne.

The moment ended, and Gran returned to her toast. Adrienne went to the back door and ran out to the beach. The last summer she spent with Quinn and Lucas filled her every thought. There was no place to hide.

CHAPTER TWENTY-ONE
Summer 1998

It was past midnight by the time Adrienne and Cristopher had finished their work. She stood at the sink and watched the yellow moon hover over the mangroves, reflecting on the wedding they had just finished catering. Though food-stained and weary, she felt like bouncing around the kitchen.

It all began when Twyla breezed into the market one day and begged Adrienne to cook a meal for her and eight of her florist buddies, waving a handful of cash in the teenager's face. Her eyes locked onto the wad of money, and despite her reservations, she found herself nodding.

A week after that, the phone started to ring endlessly. There were baby showers and anniversary dinners, barbecues, and holiday parties. The year flew by.

"I'll wrap up the leftovers and put them away," Adrienne said, scooting Christopher out the back door. "Go home and pay attention to Rachel before she comes and hunts you down."

"Do not clean anything." He gave her a stern look before heading to the parking lot. "We can do that tomorrow. Go. Be a kid for once."

Adrienne squinted. "How did you know the Merritts were coming back today?"

"How easily you forget. I am a nosy journalist when I'm not here with you." Christopher gave her a salute and vanished into the night.

Since Gramps's passing, the once cluttered countertop between Adrienne and Christopher had morphed into an assembly line of seamless cooperation. At first, she dreaded spending hours in the kitchen with him. But now she found herself smiling when he handed her a spatula without her asking.

As Adrienne wrapped up the food, the back door opened, and she groaned.

What has Christopher forgotten now?

She peered around the fridge door, ready to tease him. But it was Quinn, standing in the kitchen under the harsh fluorescent light. His eyes were red and swollen from lack of sleep, and his hair was two days past due for a wash.

"I went to your window." Quinn put his hands in his pockets. She caught the cautious look in his eyes, and her step faltered, her arms halfway raised for an embrace she suddenly wasn't sure he wanted.

"We've been busy. I hardly ever get out of here before midnight most days." Adrienne leaned against the counter for support.

"I know I said I'd be here last week, but stuff came up. I had to go down to Costa Rica for my dad without notice. I'm not even sure what today is."

"Saturday," she said.

"Saturday," Quinn repeated, nodding.

"I'm always covered in food and sweat when you see me." Adrienne laughed, releasing some of her nerves.

"You look fine. You look different." He had finally let his eyes settle on her, and only then did he relax and touch her cheek.

When Quinn's fingers met her skin, every nerve ending sparked to life. He slid his hand into hers and pulled her to him. She was taller now, almost matching him in height. As Quinn buried his face in her hair, the muscles in her shoulders seemed to melt. For the first time since September, the world felt right.

"Is everything okay? You seem . . ." She reached for the right words.

"I'm just tired." The crimson lining of his eyes was unmistakable as he pulled away.

"Your letters were so short. I thought maybe you wanted to forget me."

"I know. I never know what to say. Words never seem . . ." He trailed off.

"Enough?" She shook off the gnawing doubts that kept her awake at night. His heartbeat against her seemed to confirm their connection.

"I suck at all of this." He pulled her in for a kiss, which grew needy. "If it helps, all I think about is being here," Quinn whispered once they parted.

"We can't stay here. Christopher and his fiancée are right above us in the apartment." The familiar slow burn began inside Adrienne. She might die if she had to wait one more second.

"I know where we can go." Quinn took her hand, and Adrienne followed.

—

QUINN PUSHED OPEN the empty maid's room just off the kitchen. "Trust me, this house becomes a ghost town after midnight. No one comes in here," he whispered. "I haven't been sleeping well." As he pulled off her shirt, his words hung, the unsaid understood. *I don't sleep well when I'm not next to you.*

"What if we wake up your dad or Lucas?" Adrienne turned toward the hallway, where a patch of light crept in from under the door.

"We won't." Quinn's voice, laced with urgency, pulled her back to him.

Her gaze locked with his as if daring the universe or the Coast Guard to interrupt them. He fell onto the bed, pulling her along with him. She abandoned her cares and concerns to the night.

As their limbs tangled, Adrienne closed her eyes, imprinting it all onto her memory. Everything. Summer—such potent lightning—would become like a spark in the dark, soon to be snuffed out. Adrienne could hear Yale calling Quinn through the small open window in the cramped room. She envisioned how the world would spread its welcoming arms and enfold him as he walked toward his shiny future and Adrienne faded like a dream upon waking.

"When do you leave?" Her voice quivered, barely a whisper, as she fought back tears.

"I'm trying to stay as long as I can." Quinn rubbed his rough chin back and forth on her stomach. "But, you know, we have to be careful."

"Yes, I know." Her lips pressed together. "How is Lucas?"

Adrienne only knew Lucas's side of the story. Quinn never mentioned the expulsion in his brief notes. She knew that Lucas was kicked out of school three weeks before the end of the year, but he hadn't gone into detail, saying he would tell her everything once he was home.

"He's had a rough year. My father has no choice now. Lucas does his senior year in Harbor Point or ends up in military school."

"Your father must be upset."

"You can't even imagine how upset." Quinn's voice was heavy with meaning. "What if I deferred college for a year? Waited for Lucas to graduate?"

Adrienne sat up abruptly.

"Dad told me I was nuts." Quinn propped himself on his elbows. "But I think it might be the only choice. He has no clue how to handle Lucas."

The thought of Quinn tethered to Harbor Point by his brother eased some of the pressure in her chest. Yale's gravitational pull seemed to have weakened a little.

"If I can't stay, I need you to keep your eyes on him. I'll come back as much as I can."

"Let's run away," Adrienne said suddenly.

"To Neverland, where we never grow up, and it's always summer." Quinn pressed his face into her stomach, wrapping his arms around her as if she were a life preserver.

"Neverland." She swallowed hard.

Adrienne played with Quinn's hair, knowing that running away always sounded like a solid plan to a kid, which they still kind of were, if only for a short time.

She rose and moved toward the window, captivated by the sky's pink blush. Each motion felt like a secret as she pulled her clothes on in the dim light.

"Where are you going?" Quinn said, his voice insistent.

"It's morning. I have to go." Adrienne pressed her lips against his back.

"It's not even light out." His every syllable seemed to wrap around her, tempting her to forget her reasons for leaving.

"I've heard the lark," Adrienne said with a sigh.

Quinn swallowed hard as he took her hand. "It's but the nightingale."

She mustered a smile before kissing his forehead. "It's nearly seven. I have to get to the market. Christopher is at the paper this morning."

"Can I send Lucas to the market? You two need to talk."

"You know." Inside, she tightened like a spring, awaiting Quinn's reply. "Don't you?"

"He told me." Quinn flipped over, his eyes reaching for answers in the blank ceiling above him. "I'm not happy he kissed you, but it's not like he knows about us."

"Did he get kicked out because of me? I worried that rejecting him might have messed him up."

"No, he has a smart mouth, you know that. He doesn't do well with authority. It was a string of small infractions that built up over time. He's made peace with the rejection."

Adrienne rose reluctantly. "I don't want to hurt him, Quinn."

"We won't."

She knew his words were castles in the air, but still, she wanted to live there.

"I'll see you tonight?" Quinn called to Adrienne as she opened the door.

LUCAS APPEARED AT the market the following day, bounding in like a puppy. Adrienne hardly recognized him. His features, once too big for his face, now fit. Long, dark hair brushed over his eyes. Long gone was the skinny kid with the moon face. Adrienne mused how fast a boy could change into a man as she admired his broad shoulders.

"You don't know how great it is to be home." As they hugged, Lucas pulled away just a second too soon, leaving a chill where warmth used to be.

"You look so different." Adrienne patted his shoulder a bit too hard. *Why did he have to kiss me?*

"Puberty finally arrived, if a little late," Lucas joked. "It smells good in here. Is it alright if I help out again?"

"Sure, Christopher always complains. I work him to the bone, and now we are doing all these catering jobs." Adrienne laughed.

Lucas smiled. "Sounds like your dream is coming true."

Adrienne nodded. A chapter that once defined her now felt like a story from another life. There were other dreams now. She bit her lip, locking away words that weren't ready to be set free.

"Great!" Lucas smiled and grabbed a fresh apron.

"So, tell me, what happened at school?" Her voice straddled a shaky laugh.

"I don't belong there." Lucas picked up a potato and began peeling it.

Her gaze darted to his lips and then away. The seconds stretched longer as she weighed her words against the potential sting. But he spoke first.

"I know I was kind of a dick last year. Sorry about that." Lucas averted his eyes as he spoke. "You're my best friend. I don't want to screw that up."

"You're my best friend too." Adrienne finally found the will to touch his hand. "So, we're good?"

"We're good." When Lucas smiled, the sparkle in his eyes brought instant ease. That light, unforced, washed away her lingering doubts.

—

THE NEXT DAY, Adrienne chauffeured Gran to her weekly appointments. The last stop, Wanda's New Do Salon, was across from the marina. Adrienne squinted at it through the storefront window, waiting for Gran to sit under the spaceship-like hairdryer. She noticed Quinn waving to her from the dock. Gran had twenty minutes to go, so Adrienne slipped out of the salon and raced across the street.

Quinn kissed her as soon as they were out of sight, tucked into the cabin of the Merritts' boat.

"How did it go with Lucas?" He leaned against the galley counter, keeping his arms around her.

"Lucas didn't tell you?" She was sure he would know more than she did.

Quinn's eyes seemed to search for something in the distance. He sighed. "He doesn't talk to me like he used to."

"He apologized for the kiss." Adrienne touched Quinn's shoulder and noticed something of Lucas in his smile. "He seemed okay."

"Good." Quinn relaxed. "I think being home is good for him."

But his fingers drummed nervously on Adrienne's arm.

"What is going on?" A trill of worry slithered across her skin.

"Don't hate me," Quinn finally blurted.

Adrienne swallowed hard, staring at his mouth as if she could stop the words before they escaped his lips. She recognized the fidgeting, the restless glance toward the door. It was a dance she saw each time Quinn's father pulled him away.

"How long will you be gone?" Adrienne went to the sliding glass door and scanned the marina.

"A week at the most. But there will be more trips."

She sank onto the banquette, her gaze unfocused. The news came with a heaviness she hadn't anticipated.

"The team found something trawling yesterday. We need to do a more in-depth sweep. Dad thinks this might be it." The undertones of disdain in Quinn's voice made her ache.

"You just got here." Adrienne winced at the plaintive edge in her voice.

"I know." Quinn leaned his head against her shoulder.

She contemplated the scene through Wanda's window, seeking signs of Gran, before saying again, "Let's run away."

"I wish," Quinn said, kissing her forehead. "Family duty is a bitch. I do it all for Lucas. Hate me, but know that's why."

Tears blurred Adrienne's vision, one drop breaking free and tracing a slow path down her cheek. Quinn pulled her onto his lap. The fences she'd built crumbled, exposing tender parts of herself she never wanted him to see.

CHAPTER TWENTY-TWO

August came as swift as a falling star, with long, thick days, and the streets of Harbor Point emptied. Hired workers erected a large white tent on the lawn of the white house, but this party held no interest for Adrienne. It was part graduation, part a "good luck at Yale" party for Quinn.

Adrienne gave the tent the finger from her yard before heading to work. Mr. Merritt had done a fantastic job of keeping Quinn away nearly all summer. Time with him consisted of fleeting moments—an hour on the boat, a night in the maid's quarters—stolen between their work schedules. Upon returning, Quinn would crawl through her bedroom window at all hours, falling into her bed and a dead sleep.

Adrienne couldn't help but imagine strolling arm-in-arm with Quinn, not hidden in the shadows but out in the open, her heart pounding but, for once, not in fear. A smile tugged at her lips as she pictured the stunned expressions of the townspeople.

Lucas shot her concerned glances in the kitchen at the market but seemed to sense her composure was resting on a thin sheet of ice. As the days blurred into a countdown, Adrienne became absentminded, ignoring the subtle tremors in his voice and the hesitations in his smile.

"It's pointless to keep the market open. Harbor Point is empty," Christopher reasoned with her.

Adrienne glanced at the empty tables, her spirit as vacant as the store, and nodded in defeat.

With the market closed, Gran hatched a plan. "Adrienne, pack a bag. We're going to visit Aunt Shirley up in Juno Beach."

Adrienne furrowed her brow. "What are you talking about?"

"I can't stand being in the house while the idiot next door has another one of his obnoxious parties." Gran waved her hand in a dismissive manner. "We are going to stay with Aunt Shirley for a few days. I need to get out of this town."

Adrienne cringed at the thought of Aunt Shirley's condo—the pungent smell of mothballs and gin, the air mattress that left her back aching. And she wasn't even a real aunt, just a longtime friend of Gran's. There would be nothing to do but listen to Gran and Shirley's endless conversations about all the dead people they once knew.

"I can't go. I have to cater the Tupelos' party on Sunday," Adrienne lied.

"Christopher said you had no jobs until September." Gran's eyes narrowed as if she could peer into Adrienne's soul and pluck out any lies.

"I booked it yesterday after he left." Adrienne tried to remain casual and relaxed. "You can call Darla and ask her if you want."

Danger threatened as she spoke the lie, but Gran's lip twitched at the mention of Darla Tupelo. Darla, the head of the Harbor Point Historical Society, had butted heads for over fifty years with Gran about various historical matters.

"Well, cancel it." Gran arched an eyebrow skyward, her gaze like a spotlight on Adrienne, searching for the tiniest flicker of doubt.

Adrienne folded her arms across her chest and smirked. "Really? You want me to flake out on Darla? She'll tell everyone how I ditched her party at the last moment."

—

A FEW HOURS later, Adrienne waved to Gran as her train rolled out of the station.

Three days alone with Quinn. It would be the perfect time to reveal her plan to him. As Adrienne thought of the CIA being just a train ride away from New Haven, a wave of clarity washed over her. She had found the answer she had sought since their first kiss. They could be together beyond the limits of Harbor Point, beyond the boundaries of the summer.

She tried to imagine Quinn wrapped in a wool coat and scarf, colorful leaves swirling around him, but all she could conjure was a hazy, watercolor version in her mind. *No matter*, she thought. The actual moment would be better than anything she could imagine.

An itch of apprehension wormed its way in. She couldn't help wondering whether he was ready to release her from the little summer prison she'd been trapped within.

Will Quinn want me so close to Yale? Does he want me?

—

AS SOON AS Quinn's bedroom light turned on, Adrienne slipped out of the cottage and ran toward the big white house. She pinged his window with gravel from the flower bed. The light turned off a few seconds later, and she went to the side door.

"Gran is gone for three whole days," she said breathlessly when Quinn opened the door.

"That's great." His words were a soft murmur, and he sagged against the doorjamb as if it were the only thing keeping him upright.

Adrienne stepped back from the door, regretting her impulsiveness. "I should've waited for you to come see me."

"Sorry, it's been a long day." Quinn stifled a yawn. "Wait a sec. I have something for you."

He disappeared into the dark house and returned with a flat, white box a moment later. When she reached for it, Quinn grabbed her hand and pulled her to him. The scent of salt and sea enveloped her as he pulled her closer, sending a shiver of pleasure from her nose to end at her tingling toes.

"I'm beat," Quinn whispered, his shoulders subtly easing even as a haunted look passed across his eyes. "The last few days have wrung me dry." His hand pressed into the small of her back.

"Did you find anything?" She rested her cheek on his chest. He had been back and forth from the secret dive spot so much that Adrienne sometimes lost track of whether he was leaving or returning.

"Nope."

She looked up at him, silently begging for reassurance. "It's over now, right? You're done for the summer?"

"Yeah," Quinn murmured. "It's over."

"Will you come over . . . tonight?" Adrienne knew he was dead tired, but the incessant clock ticked off the seconds in her mind.

"I'll be there soon. Open the box when you get home." Quinn's lips brushed against hers in a fleeting kiss.

Adrienne tore at the box's ribbon at home, her fingers trembling. Inside lay a shell necklace, each intricate piece shimmering in the lamplight.

CHAPTER TWENTY-THREE

Friday night at 5 p.m., Adrienne twirled before the mirror, the fabric of her new dress swishing around her legs. The water rat of three summers ago was gone. Her fingertips traced the carefully applied eyeliner, and she touched up her lipstick as she tried to recall the last time she had crept through the mangroves. The days of baitfish and blue crabs belonged to a girl she no longer knew.

Muffled laughter and the strumming of a guitar floated through her bedroom window, a prelude to the night's possibilities.

Unshackled, Adrienne wove through the sea of faces with new confidence. People took notice. She felt all eyes on her as she sought out Quinn. Above her, the sky held a million captive stars. She noticed several familiar faces in the crowd of expensive-looking Palm Beacher types from the market and catering jobs. Many stopped her and shook her hand. Murmurs of "delicious canapés" and "exquisite dessert" were bestowed upon her like a culinary laurel wreath, affirming her place among this elevated crowd.

This is my life now.

One day, the white house might be Quinn's—and hers. They would be the ones throwing lavish parties under the summer sky.

"You're here." Quinn's voice was low and deep.

Adrienne turned and smiled, fingering her new necklace.

"I'm glad you wore it."

"I love it." She yearned to leap into Quinn's arms, but she caught herself, aware of the gossip and stares it would unleash.

Quinn seemed to sense her frustration and led her to the dance floor. There, they could touch, and no one would be the wiser. The certainty of Quinn's grip on her sent tiny jolts through her spine. Her veins pulsed as if her bloodstream had been infused with sunlight as they spun around in the dreamy haze of light and music.

The sight of Mr. Merritt's inscrutable gaze was a dash of cold water, snapping her from her reverie. Adrienne sensed his displeasure from the dance floor. Alarm buzzed through her, but she endeavored to dismiss it.

"So, this is what normal feels like," she whispered.

"Well, as close as we've come." Quinn gave his best effort at a smile but seemed distracted.

Rather than pressing him about it, Adrienne rebelliously put her head on his shoulder. He leaned in. "I wish everyone would go home."

Lucas appeared and asked to cut in. Quinn bowed dramatically and handed Adrienne off.

"I'm so happy I get to stay. We'll be seniors together."

"It will be great," Adrienne agreed.

Lucas squeezed her hand as they headed to a table after the song ended. Quinn joined them, and workers began to serve the lavish meal. Mr. Merritt had food flown in from around the world for the multicourse fanfare. Prawns from the Mediterranean and lamb chops from New Zealand. Delicate pastries from Paris and fine cheeses from Spain. Adrienne now understood why people were hell-bent on being rich.

When the brothers left the table to replenish their drinks, Mr. Merritt made a beeline for Adrienne through the maze of tables.

"Adrienne, I'm glad you could come. May I sit?" He motioned to Quinn's empty seat.

She found herself nodding.

Words were scarce commodities for her when facing Mr. Merritt, but that didn't matter; he effortlessly commanded the conversation.

"I was hoping to get to talk with you. Many of my connections in town have reported only good things about your cooking skills."

Mr. Merritt rested his folded hands on his chest. He reclined, scrutinizing Adrienne as one might a thoroughbred about to race.

"So young and yet so accomplished. I don't doubt that you will succeed. I was the same as a young man, and look where I am now." He splayed out his hands to gesture to his large estate.

"Thank you . . . again, Mr. Merritt," she stammered, wishing he would stop his praise.

"Please call me Bob. I hope you understand what I mean by saying that now is not the time to do foolish things. One mistake now could ruin your bright future as a chef."

The levity in Mr. Merritt's face gave way to a stern, almost paternal look as he leaned in, his voice dropping to a near whisper. A curtain had been drawn back, revealing the real purpose of his visit.

"You sound like my grandmother." Adrienne tried to make it sound funny.

"She and I might not see eye to eye, but we can agree that we want what's best for our children." Bob rubbed his thumb around the rim of his brandy glass. "A well-respected culinary school could help you go far in this world. Lucas tells me you have your sights on the CIA. I want to offer to pay for your tuition."

Adrienne's jaw went slack in disbelief at Mr. Merritt's unexpected offer. "That is amazingly generous."

"You've been a good friend to Lucas. I've seen a change in him. I want to help the people my children care about. I want to ensure that all three of you make good choices. Lust is never a good choice, Adrienne." He raised his brow. "My pull to get you in only applies to the campus in California. I'm afraid New York is off the table. Do you understand?"

A cauldron suddenly boiled within Adrienne as his meaning became clear.

"Wouldn't it be easier to pay me off to leave Quinn alone?"

"I could give you cash, but that is so . . . unnecessary. Tuition is a win-win. I, the secret patron, give a lump sum to the school, which, in turn, provides you `with a scholarship. Even your grandmother would approve."

"Quinn is going to Yale. You don't need to do this. I can't change any of that."

"You underestimate your power over him. I've seen *this* coming for some time. He has changed. His focus is skewed, and that worries me."

"You must be seeing things I don't." A laugh erupted from Adrienne, louder and bolder than she would have managed before the champagne had worked its magic. Her cheeks, usually reserved and rosy only in discomfort, were now flushed at his audacity.

"Insurance, then." Mr. Merritt threw up his hands. "Simple as that. I need to know that Quinn's path stays on the right course. This is not the time for distractions. It's nothing against you. I understand you are a smart, bright girl, but you all are young and dumb. If you two still want this after college, I won't stand in your way."

"You underestimate your son. Both of them." Adrienne stood. "And me."

"You may want to make your goodbyes this evening. Quinn is heading up to Yale early. He has company duties Monday morning." Mr. Merritt paused, adjusting his bowtie and sweeping his hand across his dinner jacket as though ridding it of invisible imperfections. Then, he rose from the table. "Regardless, the money is there. St. Helena awaits you. All you have to do is apply."

"No," Adrienne said, shaking her head.

"Someday, my dear, you will look back on this and thank me."

"I have to go." Adrienne whirled away from the table with a sudden jerk, her hand clasped over her mouth as nausea rose within her.

Her vision clouded. Each step she took toward the beach was like walking through a mist. Quinn's hands seized her shoulders, pulling her into an abrupt spin that left her staring directly into his puzzled eyes.

"What's wrong? Where are you going?"

"Why didn't you tell me you were leaving?" Adrienne wiped away the tears, her mascara leaving black streaks across her hand.

"Shit," Quinn said. He let go of her. "Shit, I'm sorry. I wanted this night to be good. He couldn't even give me that." The words oozed with disgust.

Adrienne shook her head and pushed past Quinn. "I want to be alone."

—

OUT ON THE beach, Adrienne slumped into the sand. She let herself cry as long and as loud as she wanted. Mr. Merritt had clipped her wings before she could even fly. College would change Quinn. It was already happening. Gone was the liveliness of his summer eyes, replaced by a sober quietness, as if someone had snuffed out his inner fire.

After a while, Lucas's hand settled on her shoulder. "What happened?" he cooed like a dove.

Your father had me blacklisted from the Culinary Institute in New York because I've been sleeping with your brother.

She couldn't tell him. No portion of her woes wouldn't give away her secrets.

Lucas sat next to her in the sand. "Are you going to make this easy on me or hard?"

She noticed his shirt was unbuttoned, and he wore no shoes. A halo of alcohol hovered around him, the scent mingling with the sea. She had been with him most of the night and never noticed him drinking anything stiffer than club soda.

"It's the song, the last one the band played. It was Gramps's favorite," Adrienne said, her voice hitching as she formulated the half lie. "He used to sing it to me when we were out on the boat."

Lucas nodded. "It's funny what can mess you up. I walked by someone wearing my mom's perfume once, and my knees buckled. We can just hang out here until you're ready to go back to the party."

"I'm not sure I feel like going back."

"That's okay too. I hate parties."

"You've been drinking," Adrienne probed.

"Just one. Dad's been an ass with Quinn leaving and my . . . high jinks." Lucas sighed. "I promise, just a nip to take the edge off this pony parade." He gestured back to the party.

He wiped the tear caught on her cheek with his thumb and placed it in his mouth. It made her laugh.

"You are so weird." She pushed him playfully.

As moonlight danced over his features, it illuminated nuances she had never seen before, casting his familiar face in a mysterious, newfound beauty. In a just and fair world, she would love Lucas, not Quinn. His quirky grin could defuse any tension, and he always found the words that needed to be said, even when she couldn't find them herself. She could almost imagine Mr. Merritt nodding in approval, his stern features softening.

"You are so beautiful when you cry." He put his hand back on her cheek but with a new kind of firmness.

She leaned over and kissed him on the lips. It was far different from kissing Quinn. Here was reliable landfall, a presence she knew would never drift away. Maybe she could give up and give Lucas what he wanted, make him happy. Perhaps that was the key to solving all their problems.

Cruel clarity finally struck, sweeping away the fog of her lapse in judgment. Adrienne pushed away as delicately as she could. Lucas's eyes shone with unguarded jubilance, and she felt as if she were holding a fragile bird and feeling its heartbeat against her closed fist.

"Wow," he said, leaning back on his hands in the sand. "I wasn't expecting that."

Adrienne eyed the partygoers on the lawn. "I'm sorry, Lucas. I drank too much. I shouldn't have done that. I'm tired. I think I should go home." She stood and brushed the sand from her dress.

"Okay. I'll see you tomorrow?" He got up, and his eyes locked onto hers, expansive and hopeful.

"Sure, yes." She nodded.

Seemingly empowered by the electricity of their earlier kiss, he took her hand and pulled her to him, pressing his lips against hers. Instead of recoiling, she momentarily lost herself in the sensation.

I do love him. But not enough.

She teetered on the edge of a cliff. One last chance to confess and right the wrong of her actions. But she said nothing.

"I have to go." She pushed away from him and ran to the cottage.

There, Adrienne sat in Gran's old rocking chair by the bay window as the ocean waves crashed on the dark shore. An icy dread seeped into her bones, solidifying her regret into something tangible.

"What have I done?" she whispered, her words swallowed by the beach and its ceaseless thunder.

—

QUINN APPEARED AT her bedroom window. "Come out, little girl," he said in a menacing voice.

She was sure it was over. Twenty-four hours had passed since they parted. Adrienne wallowed in her room, convinced Lucas had spilled his guts to Quinn.

Yet Quinn's eyes held an amusement in them that she hadn't seen in weeks. A stay of execution was granted.

A devilish grin stretched across his lips as he leaned on the windowsill. He was giving her a last slice of summer, with every bite bittersweet.

Adrienne approached the window with a playful sigh, her fingers instinctively twining through the unruly strands of his hair. With Quinn by her side, the pill went down easily. She passed through the mirror, slipped into his world, and left everything behind.

"I wasn't sure if I'd see you," she said as they stood on the lawn. "We left things pretty awful."

"Let's pretend it's June. Just tonight? Please?" He raised her hand to his cheek. "Let's be Peter and Wendy."

"Okay," she said, her throat tight.

Their footsteps muffled by the sand, they nestled behind the dunes, hidden from unwanted observers. A languid yellow moon emerged from the ocean, casting a soft reflection over the water. Adrienne fixated on his long fingers as they deftly wove palm blades into a hat to keep from getting "moonburned." Her own fingers fumbled, unweaving what she had just woven. Whenever she thought she had made progress, her creation would uncoil, defiantly reverting to its original form.

"You must be using glue," she teased. "Where are you hiding it? Mine keep falling apart."

"You accuse me of cheating, miss?" Quinn demanded as he got into a crouching position. "You better run, or I'll catch you."

Adrienne shot toward the cottage, Quinn right behind her. He was fast, but she managed to stay out of his reach. White bedsheets drying on the line gleamed in the moonlight as Adrienne weaved in and out, staying just out of reach. She clamped her mouth shut to stifle her giggles, but Quinn found her as if guided by some invisible connection.

His fingers caught her wrist, and with a playful yank, he prompted a guided tumble onto the moonlit grass. His face floated above her, the moon like a halo behind him. The hanging sheets made a makeshift room for them to hide in. Her eyes met his and lingered, their bare skin painted in shades of silver and desire. Quinn's face turned serious as she pushed down the top of her nightgown. Her fingers froze on the fabric momentarily, caught in a web of hesitation. Then Quinn's expression melted, his hands gently gliding her dress off, letting it flutter to the grass.

"We'll get all itchy," he murmured.

"I don't care." She pulled his face down to hers.

—

ADRIENNE LAY ON his chest, her skin tingling with a grassy itch she chose to ignore. Her eyes flicked toward the beach at the movement of a fleeting shadow near the edge of the lawn. Then, it was gone. *A heron*, she reasoned, trying to dismiss the disquiet within her. A shiver remained despite her efforts to shake it off.

"Wham, bam, thank you, ma'am," Quinn sat up, laughing as Adrienne quickly dressed.

"I got a weird feeling," she said, and the cold crept into her stomach. "Let's go inside."

In her bathroom, she slipped into the old iron tub, nesting between his legs. The warm water somewhat soothed the external itch, but something within still scratched at her.

She reclined against his chest. "We could go to Africa. They have great waves there." With her CIA plans dashed, it was the only scenario, wild as it was, that she could offer now.

"I could build a hut out of palm fronds. You could cook the fish I catch."

"You're making fun of me." She turned. His face held only amusement. "Maybe I'm serious."

With a sigh, Quinn reclined his head against the tub's edge, his eyes half closed in contemplative surrender. "How about we run away all day tomorrow?"

"Really? Where?" Adrienne sat up.

"Does it matter?" He laughed, shaking his head.

"We could take the boat," she suggested as the memories of last summer tickled at her.

"Sounds perfect." He kissed her forehead and pulled her back into him.

A sour realization settled over her. Tomorrow was a fixed point they couldn't move. The last page in a chapter they both wished had no end.

Quinn's soft snoring filled the small bedroom later. Adrienne lay beside him, eyes wide open. The sky outside gradually traded its black cloak for a shroud of gray. Quinn woke, pulling on his clothes in the half-light. For a moment, he hesitated on the windowsill.

"Peter, always at the window," Adrienne murmured.

—

DRAPED IN THE predawn light, Adrienne settled onto the front porch, her restlessness giving her no other option. The morning birdsong comforted her, as if Gramps himself were there, spinning old stories in her ear. It was the perfect place to wait for Quinn to prep the boat before leaving for their last day together.

"Am I interrupting you?" Lucas's voice startled her daydreams. She hadn't even heard the familiar crunch of the shell rock under his feet as he came up through the jungle.

Noticing that Lucas wore the same outfit from last night's party, a siren blared inside her head.

"Hi," she managed, her voice quivering from the anxiety she typically felt when dark clouds gathered on the horizon.

"Hey," he said, kicking at some ancient, bleached shells by the base of the steps, making no move to come up to where she sat on the porch. His eyes dodged hers.

The birds halted their racket. Lucas's fingers idly scraped away flakes of peeling paint from the newel post of the railing as if trying to unmask an uncomfortable truth. "I thought it would be romantic to show up at your window in the middle of the night. I guess Quinn beat me to the punch, huh?"

Her throat constricted as bile threatened to escape, urging her to swallow hard.

"What did you see?"

"Enough." Lucas wrapped his arms around himself. "I wasn't trying to be a pervert, but you two were out . . . in the grass." His eyes pierced hers, making her feel as insubstantial as mist.

A long silence grew. Adrienne struggled desperately to find the right words to shrink the canyon her betrayal had created.

"How long have you been fucking my brother?" Lucas's words flowed smoothly, a calm river that caught her off guard with its turmoil.

"I never wanted to hurt you. Neither of us did. That's part of why we hid it."

Lucas glared at the ground. "What about the kiss? I thought . . . I thought it meant something." He lifted his gaze. "I know it meant something."

"I'm sorry."

"Why did you kiss me?"

"I was hurting. I know Quinn is leaving tomorrow. I know he will go to Yale and forget me, and I will lose him." Adrienne hated having to say the truth out loud. "It was wrong to get you mixed up in my pain."

"You are lying." Lucas shook his head. "Maybe that's part of it. But people hurt all the time and don't kiss their best friends like that."

"Okay. I do feel something for you." The words were alien, as if they had come from another person, yet the truth rang through her like a bell. She rose and placed her hand on the rail, intending to go to him. But her courage dissolved, compelling her to take a hesitant step back. "But I love him more, Lucas. It's a shitty thing to say, but it's true."

Now she forced herself to descend the steps. Lucas yanked away when she tried to touch his arm. Her hands snapped to her chest, fingers folded inward.

"Quinn always wins." Lucas's eyes narrowed on Adrienne. "And I get to watch."

Quinn's wealthy and terrible friends' warning about Lucas replayed in her head. Something unsettling entered his eyes—something she'd never seen before.

"Can we fix this?" Adrienne started to tremble again.

"I don't know. I'm too tired to think."

"Quinn leaves tomorrow. We'll have the whole year to work this out." Adrienne wiped the tears away that now freely spilled. "Just you and me, remember?"

"Sure." He nodded, but his eyes darted away.

—

QUINN'S CELL RANG five times and then went to his voicemail. Adrienne left a short message, asking him to call her, trying to sound ordinary. Her eyes remained glued to the silent phone on the kitchen table, each tick of the clock amplifying her anxiety.

It was two o'clock when Quinn called.

"Sorry, I was at the marina working on the boat. My phone was in the cabin." His words tumbled out in a jumble, propelled by his heavy breathing. "I won't be able to get away for another hour."

She hesitated before asking, "Is Lucas home?"

"Um, yeah, he just went into the bathroom."

"Lucas knows about us," she managed to get out, hearing Mr. Merritt's voice in the background.

"Meet me at the boat in an hour," Quinn said softly.

"Okay."

—

ADRIENNE PACED THE dock until Quinn appeared.

"Did you speak to Lucas?"

"I told him everything." He sat on the rim of the boat. "We haven't talked like that in a long time. He is hurt, but I think he understands why we kept it hidden."

"Maybe we shouldn't go out. Maybe we should stay." Adrienne picked a wet leaf off her flip-flop. "I don't feel right leaving him. I've never seen him like that before."

"I have. I know him. It's part of the package. You only know the summer version of Lucas. The rest of the year, he's a different person. We're so close in age. A girl was bound to come between us at some point." Quinn flashed a smile, but Adrienne wouldn't be assuaged.

"I'm sure he was drunk when he came over this morning. You said he shouldn't mix his meds with alcohol."

But Quinn was the expert on Lucas, not her. Adrienne glanced over her shoulder, her stomach still a tangle of worry. He got up and put his arms around her.

"He told me what you said, that you love him too. I get it."

Adrienne pulled away. "He told you that?"

"Everything after today is whatever it will be. All I know is I only have this one day left with you. Give me that, Adrienne. Then we can figure out the rest." Quinn's voice wavered, the words catching in his throat as his arms constricted around her, pulling her closer yet somehow feeling miles away.

Adrienne took a deep breath and let it out slowly. "Okay, let's go."

—

A BREWING STORM cut their trip short. Ships frequently sank off South Florida's coast in bad weather. Some blamed the Bermuda Triangle, that mythical patch of sea between Florida, the Bahamas, and Bermuda. Locals understood it better. It was no supernatural phenomenon, merely the depth of the water, the Gulf Stream's proximity, and the unfortunate Bermuda High that determined a craft's destiny. Two teen boys had been lost to a storm trying to make the seventy-mile run to Grand Bahama the summer before. Their bodies and the boat were never recovered.

Without words, Quinn steered the cruiser toward the mainland as Adrienne stowed loose gear. Each wave was a mountain, the boat heaving and pitching as they wrestled their way home.

Quinn's eyes were heavy-lidded by the time he flopped onto Adrienne's bed, each muscle visibly strained.

"I could sleep for a week." He gave a showy yawn so loud that Adrienne was glad Gran was not home.

"Gran will be home by the afternoon." Adrienne's shoulders

tensed at the thought, her eyes darting toward the clock.

"At this point, I don't care about anything."

"Quinn, can we talk?" she said softly, finding more courage in the dark where half sleep was settling in.

"Can we talk later?" he said, his face already buried in the pillow.

She pressed closer to him, her form aligning with his. In that silent embrace, awareness hovered. The sands of their time together had slipped away. There would be no later.

"Sure," she said.

There would be hundreds of pretty, petite blonds lined up at Yale. Rich, young, and knowing.

"Stop it, Adrienne." Quinn's hand found her chest, his featherlight touch a whispered reassurance. "I know you. Stop overthinking everything."

She turned to him. "Do I only know the summer version of you, Quinn?"

He lifted his head from the pillow and frowned as if wrestling with thoughts too complex to articulate in a single glance. "I didn't say that to make you worry, just that Lucas is good at hiding things."

She wanted to ask if he was good at hiding too. But she bit her lip.

"Everything is going to be okay." Quinn rubbed a coil of her hair between his fingers.

She almost believed him.

CHAPTER TWENTY-FOUR

Adrienne bolted up in the bed, struggling to place her surroundings. Breaths came in sharp gasps as if invisible hands had been clamped over her mouth while she slept. Quinn lay beside her, his face in the pillow with an arm slack over her waist. The clock said five in the morning. A low boom of thunder shuddered far out on the water.

Fully awake now, nausea twisted in her stomach.

Did someone tap at the window?

Phantom noises gnawed at her nerves, blurring the line dividing sleep and wakefulness.

Could it be Lucas?

Her heartbeat pounded in her ears.

Trusting the uneasy prickle crawling through her, Adrienne leaned out the window, her eyes straining to make sense of shapes in the gloom.

The backyard was empty.

She pulled away from the window. Goose bumps rolled over her arms in waves. The stillness was smothering, the impending storm lending an extra layer.

Even the crickets paused when the thunder bellowed. Adrienne dressed and headed for the front door, unable to shake the feeling that someone had been there. Another rumble of thunder, closer now.

Adrienne peered out the kitchen window. The overhead light revealed an empty porch. It was then she wished she'd woken Quinn, but she didn't want to go back to bed until the agitation subsided. She craved the peace of knowing she was alone. A troubling change tickled at her nerves, as palpable as the humidity before rain.

The vacant porch seemed somehow crowded. The birds, restless in the trees, rose to a fevered pitch. Adrienne stood on the landing and tried to penetrate the dark mess of branches for signs of movement. She grabbed the old rusty shovel Gran had propped against the rooting table. Yet aside from the agitated song of the waking birds, the world remained eerily empty.

Convinced her fears had been woven from the fabric of a dream, she spun, ready to wake Quinn, but a single sheet of drawing paper, folded in half on the daybed cushion, caught her eye.

Lucas was here.

Her hands fumbled as she reached for the paper, struggling to unfold it. With a final effort, she coaxed it open, eyes widening as the image spread before her. An ominous storm churned the sea, its fury captured in swirling lines and frenetic shades. The clouds were sketched in furious, jagged strokes as if slashed by a knife.

And in the far background, a small figure stood, watching her.

The paper floated from her numb fingers, back to the daybed. The usual warmth of Lucas's artwork had been replaced by something wild and cold.

Adrienne sprinted down the path, jagged shell fragments slicing into her bare soles, barely feeling the pain as she hit the road. The street lay abandoned as if holding its breath. A hesitant light stained the sky. *What am I even looking for? What is Lucas luring me toward?*

Gusts from the west whipped her face, and inky storm clouds swelled above the Everglade like dark omens stitched into the sky.

She noticed something across the street.

Another breadcrumb.

Lucas's sketch pad lay in the dirt by the side of the road. The cardboard cover was flipped open, and a few empty pages ruffled in the growing breeze. A peal of thunder resonated from the sea behind her, urging her to hurry. Caught between the face-off of storms from east and west, the air grew dense, its pressure intensifying with a disturbing urgency.

Adrienne sank to her knees, the prickly beach daisy burs biting into her flesh. She flipped through the sketch pad and found nothing but ripped pages, void of any sketches. As she touched the torn edges, she peered down the path to where the mangroves hid the Back Bay.

Does he want me to follow? Is he waiting for me?

Beneath the shadowed canopy, Adrienne moved carefully, clutching the book to her chest like a shield. A hair-thin blood trail drew a line of red from her knee to her ankle.

The dock was empty.

Realizing her fears had been a conjuring of her imagination, her muscles slackened. The sun broke through the cloud cover, rolling long shadows over the mangroves and turning the clouds into towering titans. Adrienne held on to a branch. The birds had hushed, and the sound of moving water as the tide turned filled her ears.

Her foot met the first plank of the dock hesitantly, eliciting a low groan from the weathered wood. A warning.

Her eyes shot to the boat moored at the end of the dock.

As she crept up to *The Dolly,* something at the end of the dock caught her eye. Against her will, she drifted toward a lone splash of color, a discordant note in a somber symphony of grays and browns. A beach daisy, its petals bruised and wilted, lay abandoned on the final plank.

Something flickered in the water.

That's when her gaze landed on Lucas. His body was suspended like an underwater statue, his arms raised toward the surface but not quite able to break the tension of the water. That beautiful face, his dark hair moving with the water. Now vacant yet imploring, his blue eyes punctuated the ebbing tide's sorrowful refrain.

Adrienne's limbs turned to stone.

There was a strange, incomprehensible beauty in how he seemed to be trying to surface, his body nudged by the current ever so slightly, yet something kept him tethered to the muck of the Back Bay. His pallid skin radiated an ethereal glow against the water's dark canvas, capturing Adrienne in a trance. Without thought, she bent down, reaching out to his outstretched hand, just below the surface. A fish darted across Lucas's face, jolting her from her spell as if someone had snapped their fingers before her eyes. With a guttural cry, Adrienne's legs found their function, propelling her away from the nightmare.

As fast as she ever had run, she hurtled up the dock and through the mangroves, bursting into the field before taking a breath. She reached the edge of the grass before bewilderment set in, and she couldn't take another step.

A scream clawed its way out of her throat, raw and shattering, filling the predawn with its terrible truth. Time stretched into an agonizing eternity as she screamed, only snapping back when Quinn, shirtless and wild-eyed, erupted from the trees and into her field of vision. He seized her shoulders with a shake before slapping her, his palm stinging her cheek in a desperate bid to halt her screams.

Struggling through racking sobs, she choked out the words "He's dead"—her voice a broken whisper—"in the water."

As if watching from a distant vantage point, trapped outside her own form, she saw Quinn's hands fall away from her as he pivoted toward the Back Bay. The knowing look in his eyes: She was an omen—the harbinger of doom.

He disappeared into the groves. Nausea surged and broke like a wave, expelling its contents as her mind reeled with the awful certainty of what Quinn would discover.

A numb longing settled in her, a desire to dissolve into the ether, to escape the grind of existence. Her body betrayed her. The earth tilted sharply, and the edges of her vision narrowed, consumed by encroaching darkness until nothing remained.

ADRIENNE BLINKED AGAINST the soft light of her desk lamp. She stretched, extending her limbs as far as possible while a thin veil of comfort from the long sleep still covered her.

The weight of the room shifted; the serenity frayed at the edges, unraveling fast. *No.* Lucas was dead. Her mind flashed the reminder like the red-blue pulse of a police cruiser's lights. She folded inward to shield her broken heart, sobs pouring from her. When she closed her eyes, the image of Lucas in the water greeted her, burning into the darkness like a negative. Her ragged gasp pulled hot tears across her cheeks to form a salty trail down her neck.

After a while, her bedroom door opened. Through her tear-soaked hair, she spied Gran with a small tray in hand containing a bowl of something steaming and a glass of water. Adrienne wiped at the tears.

"You've been out a long time. The paramedics had to use a powerful tranquilizer to calm you." Gran carefully placed the tray amid the clutter on the desk. "You need to eat, or you'll end up in the hospital."

"How did I get here?" Adrienne pulled a hand through her hair, feeling the knotted clumps and clods of dirt trapped from when she had passed out in the field.

"That boy. He carried you." Gran busied herself by picking up the dirty clothes on the floor. "When you weren't at the train station, I knew something had happened."

"He's dead." The words strangled in her throat, her voice tinged with a finality that made the room colder.

Gran righted a pile of scattered books. "Ms. Pilchard said that the poor boy used a weighted belt they use for diving. He tied it around his waist before he jumped in. I guess he wanted to make sure he didn't come up." She paused her manic cleaning, the look in her eyes calming for the first time, replacing what Adrienne feared might be judgment with unmistakable pity.

"Lucas would've never set foot in the water willingly, not even to dip his toes," Adrienne murmured. Her stomach convulsed at the smell of the chicken noodle soup.

"I don't want you going over there. There's been police in and out all day and a whole bunch of madness. The TV station was even out there, parked on our property. I had to make them move." Gran's silhouette eclipsed the oval of light from the desk lamp, her arms folded tightly over her chest. "They almost took out my prized oleander."

Adrienne rose, towering over Gran. "My friend is dead. All you can think about is your stupid bush? I'm going over to Quinn's. I love him."

Gran's grip closed around her wrist, unyielding as a steel vise. "Don't go and do something stupid."

Adrienne wrestled her wrist away with a forceful jerk. "I need to see him. He needs me."

Her feet found the sandy path leading to Quinn's house, instinctively avoiding the Back Bay.

Quinn sat on the stoop, a cigarette hanging loosely from his lips, its embers pulsating like a dying star. He nodded as she approached. Adrienne sat next to him on the step. He should be gone by now. Headed to Yale, to his bright future. Laying eyes on Quinn now, beyond the deadline of their summer, unsettled her almost as much as the gutting reality of Lucas's death.

"I tried to come and check on you. Your grandmother wouldn't let me in." He flicked the butt of the cigarette out onto the grass.

"I didn't know you smoked." She leaned into him, the salt mingled with suntan oil wrapping around her like a comforting embrace.

Quinn stood, taking his warmth with him. "I only smoke socially."

She rose with him and put an unsure hand on his shoulder, coaxing him to face her. With eyes glued to the ground, Quinn finally surrendered, allowing his forehead to rest against hers.

"Did we do this, Quinn?" she managed to ask.

"He's been fighting demons his whole life," he said, his arm curling around her, each word emerging with great strain.

In the darkness, they remained entangled, two souls bound together by a labyrinth of questions with no answers. After a while, Quinn dipped his face and kissed her.

"We are leaving tomorrow to take Lucas back to Ohio to be buried in the family plot. Next to my mom."

She wanted to escape the agony in his voice, but her feet were anchored to the spot.

"Tomorrow night was the only flight we could get"—his voice fractured mid-sentence—"the coffin on."

Adrienne pulled away. Quinn's face seemed to hold every shade of gray.

"Take me with you," she said.

"I don't want to go."

"I loved him too." Her words quivered with an aching tenderness.

Instead of answering her, Quinn captured her lips again, his fervor speaking of a desperation words couldn't convey. Adrienne relented, letting the moment's intensity guide them as they clumsily ascended the steps to their secret hideaway, the unused maid's quarters by the back door.

IN THE FIRST wisps of morning light, Adrienne knelt beside the bed, entranced by the movement of Quinn's eyelids as he journeyed through his dreams. Her desire to stay and her discomfort in the imposing white mansion played tug-of-war within her, and her resolve wavered.

She tenderly brushed back his wayward bangs, and his soft groan sent a ripple through her gut. Her lips brushed his in a whisper of a kiss, prompting his eyes to meet hers.

Quinn lightly grazed her wrist with his fingers as he spoke. "I'll make sure to say goodbye before we go."

The world seemed to hold its breath. Adrienne finally asked, "Meet at the beach?"

"Okay," he agreed, his words laden with an ambiguity that almost allowed her to believe him.

—

AS DARKNESS UNFURLED across the sky, Adrienne planted herself on the cool sand, each wave that broke on the shore muttering doubts in her ear.

She fought against the doubtful sea. *He always comes.*

Pulling her arms close to her chest to protect her brittle hopes, she cast a gaze toward the looming white house. It was nine o'clock, and the flight was set to take off at midnight. The haunting vision of porters consigning Lucas to the dark belly of an airplane, entombed in a coffin, sent a nauseating spasm through her stomach.

The minutes stretched into an agonizing hour, each second a mocking reminder of what she already knew.

The lights in the mansion went out. No Quinn. Adrienne got to the house just as the red brake lights on Mr. Merritt's car blinked and turned out onto the street. Adrienne sprinted down the gravel drive, skidding through the gate, only to find herself a desperate step behind.

Betrayed by the promise she had clung to, she stood alone with the knowledge that Quinn had abandoned her. Adrienne replayed the previous night's conversations, each evasion a thorn in her mind. Nausea now drove her to the grass, where she retched as if her body sought to expel the taste of betrayal.

It was almost morning when she left the street and went home. The tufts of pink in the sky made the truth all too clear. With each weighted step toward home, a gut-wrenching certainty settled deep within her. Quinton Merritt had vanished from her life, perhaps forever.

CHAPTER TWENTY-FIVE
Summer 2012

Adrienne knocked timidly at the front door, almost hoping Quinn wouldn't hear her and she could retreat. But that was the old Adrienne; she couldn't be a coward.

He must have been waiting for her because the door opened before she stopped knocking. The quick reaction startled her, making her stumble back over her own feet and fall on her butt.

"Sorry." He reached out, taking her hand to help her up. "I saw you coming across the yard."

She followed Quinn's guiding hand into the kitchen. He filled a kettle with water and set it on the stove. Her eyes traced his movements—the way he reached for the tea bags, the half smile as he poured the water—each action an echo of the boy she once knew, now layered with the mystery of the man before her. He set a cup of tea next to her. They faced each other across the island, the steam from their cups creating a curtain. Adrienne had rehearsed what she would say, but it was all forgotten.

"I have to confess something. I was home the day you came to the house. I heard you knock, and I panicked." A sheepish grin crossed Quinn's face as he looked down. "I was holed up in the downstairs bathroom, crouched behind the shower curtain like a child. Brave, right?"

"It's a good thing I didn't have to pee," she said dully, twirling the mug in her hands.

"Yeah." His gaze settled on the shadowed outlines of the room behind her as if searching for something he couldn't put into words.

"I found one shirt in your closet."

"I use my dad's bedroom now. If you had gone in there, you would have found me out."

Each sip of tea became a measured effort to fill the silence. The door to the maid's quarters seemed to vibrate just feet from where they sat.

Quinn got up and moved to the chair next to her. "Do you hate me?" He hunched over the counter with his hands folded.

"No." That damn gravitational force was drawing her closer to him. She tightened her grip on her mug as if it were an anchor.

Quinn's stare bore into her, stripping away years and armor, making her feel exposed in a way that bare skin never could. *What does he see? Does he see the lines at the corners of my eyes, the strands of gray in my hair?*

"Did you know you were pregnant that last night?" He reached out and placed his hand on top of hers. "After Lucas . . ." His voice faltered.

The moment his skin met hers, memories of salty skin, warm lips, and all the gut-wrenching goodbyes swamped her, commingled into some kind of terrible soup.

Adrienne pulled away. "I didn't know for sure, but I had a feeling." She wiped the wetness from under her eyes.

"I knew you hated me for disappearing. I hated myself for all of it." His features twisted. "I knew what your grandmother said was untrue. I took the coward's way out."

The night Quinn disappeared without even a goodbye plagued her thoughts. "I was sure you hated me. That you blamed me for Lucas's death."

His brow furrowed. "God, Adrienne. You really think that?"

"Lucas went into the water because of me. I fucked it all up." Adrienne buried her head into her hands.

The image she had suppressed—Lucas, lifeless in the Back Bay—

surfaced mercilessly, bringing the knowledge that she had been the catalyst. She could almost see her own hands pushing Lucas into the dark, unforgiving water, a place he had always feared. Lucas had plunged into his nightmare, choosing an end as terrifying as it was final.

Quinn stood and held out his hand. "Come with me?"

His touch felt like that of a stranger. The flesh of his palm was soft and smooth, a far cry from the rough texture they once bore from endless days on the sea. But the pain they shared was a strong magnet. Adrienne clutched his foreign fingers.

He led her up the stairs to Lucas's bedroom, and Adrienne hesitated to enter. When she had broken into the house, she avoided going in.

Inside, Lucas's drawings, paintings, and sketches—his life's work—covered the walls. Many projects stood in various stages of completion, some mere pencil outlines on paper. Others were finished and full of vivid swaths of colors. Every brushstroke and pencil line seemed to whisper of their summers, turning the room into a silent museum of captured moments.

Adrienne meandered the room, lingering on each picture to absorb the essence locked within the canvas and paper. But the one that made her stop was a sketch of the point. It was barely outlined, but she knew instantly what it was. It captured that ephemeral night on the beach, a birthday celebrated under the stars and kept alive through the strokes of Lucas's pencil.

There she was, sketched at the very tip of the point, toes flirting with the gentle sea. Stars mirrored themselves on the water's surface, merging sky and ocean into a singular canvas of twinkling infinity. Adrienne traced the cloud line, her fingertips smudging the sky. She rubbed the pencil dust between her thumb and finger.

"Could I have this one?"

"You can have them all if you want. I still can't bring myself to take any down." Quinn sat in the chair at the draft table.

Jars of cerulean blues, burnt-umber brushes with frayed bristles, and pencil stubs crowned with chewed erasers lined the wall, a dormant arsenal of Lucas's creative spirit. Christopher had been right. Quinn took on the role of Mrs. Havisham after Lucas's death, each of Lucas's things preserved since the moment he died.

"I never told you what I said to Lucas that day. I laid my cards bare, Adrienne. I told him I loved you."

She turned to find his head bowed over the desk.

"When I left to meet you, he was at peace. He understood that you were not just some summer fling to me. It was hard because you were those things to him too, but he knew. He got why we fit."

His words sliced through her, leaving her legs wobbly as if all the ligaments had been severed. "You were the boy I should never have had a chance with. I could never understand it."

"I should have told you how I felt. Maybe it would have kept you from developing feelings for Lucas. I don't know. I guess we can't obsess over what we should have done long ago."

"No," Adrienne said, her eyes tracing the patterns in the worn carpet beneath her.

"Did Lucas ever tell you why he was afraid of the water?"

She settled on the floor by Lucas's bed. "I never did ask."

"My father decided when Lucas was four years old that it was time for him to learn how to swim. It was summer. I was older and knew Father's method. Luckily, I always seemed natural at anything to do with the water. But Lucas was smaller and weaker. He was sick a lot as a kid. He always had ear infections, bronchitis, or asthma. I used to call him the walking medicine cabinet."

Quinn settled next to Adrienne. They both leaned back against the bed frame.

"I remember my father throwing Lucas into the water. We were at our house in Bimini. He tossed Lucas into the ocean from the end of the dock. It wasn't too deep, but Lucas was so small. I remember him trying to stay above the surface of the water. I can still hear him screaming every time his head broke the surface. I tried to dive in after him, but my father held me back. He struck me across the face, and I fell. He told me I better not interfere."

His voice trembled, each word barely escaping his lips. Adrienne felt herself gasping for air alongside a young, panicked Lucas. Before she knew it, tears—hot and unrestrained—trickled down her cheeks,

"Lucas stopped coming up. My father finally jumped in and pulled him out. He had to pump on Lucas's chest to get him to breathe, to cough out the water."

Quinn closed his eyes.

"I lay there, my face pressed to the hot wood, and my eyes never left Lucas's face. I waited for his eyes to open. I reached out, took his limp hand, and prayed that he would live. It's the only time I prayed. All the time at church, I only faked it. Then Lucas coughed, the seawater dribbled out of his mouth, and he opened his eyes."

Their hands found each other's, fingers intertwining with a silent understanding.

"My father left us on the dock under the sun, and we stayed there for I don't know how long, my hand still holding his. Lucas never went back into the water after that day. Dad never spoke about it. Lucas and I never spoke about it either."

The image of Lucas, weighted down by the dive belt, sinking further away from the light, hovered in her thoughts.

"I wasn't surprised when I found him in the water like that." Quinn's eyes shifted away as if his confession could be avoided as easily as eye contact. "I never told you any of this. It was hard for us growing up. It was always harder for Lucas, though.

"Lucas lied to you about why he left Oakhurst. He took some pills he bought from one of the guys in our dorm and OD'd. He said he didn't mean to overdose, but I had a gut feeling he was trying to kill himself." Quinn's fingers went to work on his cuticles, tearing at the tender skin. "We put him back in the hospital for a month, but he fooled them all into letting him out. He was a master at deception."

"I wish I had known."

"I shouldn't have kept it from you. Lucas was afraid it would scare you."

"Tell me now. Tell me what happened when you got to Lucas in the water," Adrienne said, touching his face. She made him face her. "I want to know."

"I jumped in, pulled him out, and laid him on the dock. I tried to do CPR, but it was too late. Even before I put my hands on his chest, my mind said he was gone, but my heart screamed for me to try anyway. His skin was ice." Quinn took a deep breath. "I lay there like we did that day in Bimini. I lay there on my stomach, waiting for his eyes to open, though I knew they never would. I guess I went a little crazy."

"We all did." Tears blurred her vision once again.

He rested his head in the palms of his hands. "Dad wasn't going to let Lucas finish school here in Harbor Point. It was all a lie. He was going to stick Lucas in a hospital somewhere in Costa Rica. A place where Lucas wouldn't be able to fool anyone as long as my father's money kept coming in. My father told me Lucas found the papers when you and I went on the boat. They had a terrible fight, and Lucas took off."

"No," Adrienne whispered.

"Lucas would choose death over another hospital. He pretty much told me that when he got out of the last one." Quinn exhaled deeply, as if releasing his burden. "When my father finally told me, months later, that's when I came looking for you."

At Quinn's words of absolution, it was as if someone had flung open a door to unexpected freedom. He trailed his thumb down the side of her cheek to wipe a tear away.

"I was so broken, I thought I'd go mad without you." His voice cracked. "But I knew it was my own doing. I did everything wrong. I ruined your life. It made sense you wanted nothing to do with me. That you would get rid of the baby."

"You were?" She zeroed in on the first part of his speech, her heart thumping in disbelief. All these years, she had convinced herself she was an afterthought to him.

Quinn shook his head with a grunt. "Of course I was. I was ready to chuck my whole planned-out life for you. I was sure Dad told you as much when he tried to pay you off. I started coming down and staying in the house to be close to your ghost. Then, I just never left. I slipped in and out when no one was watching."

"You really did Havisham yourself," Adrienne marveled.

"Havisham?" Quinn asked, puzzled.

"The jilted bride in *Great Expectations* who hid away."

"Oh. Yeah, I really did." He chuckled. "I had it all planned, you know. I planned to pretend to leave and then show up at your door the next day and tell you I decided not to go to Yale."

Adrienne's teeth sank into her lower lip, the bite a physical tether as she grappled with the near miss of their past. A mix of regret and revelation washed over her. All this time, she had been orbiting so closely to the life she'd dreamed of, entirely unaware.

"We were so close," she couldn't help saying aloud.

"No, Adrienne. We would never have made it." Quinn turned his gaze to the window. "I shouldn't have told you that."

He abruptly stood and took off his shirt, dropping it to the floor. Heat blossomed despite herself. Quinn bowed and turned slowly, showing his back to her. His shoulders rounded forward, each muscle tensing before slowly relaxing.

Adrienne stood and touched one of the marks with the tip of her finger, recalling how she had once traced the lines like the roads on a map.

"They aren't from a reef accident. My father favored an old bamboo fishing pole. He liked to tell us how his father had used it on him and how well he turned out. That's why you never saw Lucas without a shirt on. He was intimately acquainted with my father's cane. I could always tell the reef accident story."

Adrienne traced the longest line from his left shoulder blade to the dimple at the base of his back. He quivered at her touch.

"Lucas wanted to die long before we met you. There were days I wanted to die too, but I never had the guts."

"All these years, I've been walking around like the Grim Reaper." She leaned into him, her arms finding their familiar place around his waist.

"Me too."

Quinn turned to her, and they held each other, crying in the middle of Lucas's room. For a fleeting moment, they could breathe again.

"God, I've missed so much." He buried his face in her hair.

He pulled away, his face red and speckled with red blotches from crying. It was a new look. Even when Lucas died, Quinn had been stoic, never shedding a tear in front of her.

His head lowered, their foreheads touching. Adrienne recalled that day in the Back Bay when Quinn taught her how to scuba dive and how they had locked eyes under the water. Time seemed to pause, the world around them suspended like water droplets in the air, every sound and movement stilled. It was the first time she had a glimmer of hope. And now the yearning returned. A shiver of recognition raced down her spine, rekindling a hope she thought had died. She found traces of the Quinn she knew in his eyes, hidden beneath layers of time and hardship. Their faces inched closer, the space between their lips closing until barely there.

Memories of her last day in Harbor Point rushed back—from the salty breeze off the bay to the last goodbye.

But that goodbye had not been with Quinn.

CHAPTER TWENTY-SIX
Summer 1998

For weeks, Adrienne rushed daily to an empty mailbox, her heart pounding in vain. Every ring of her silent phone became a cruel joke, adding to the gnawing feeling of abandonment. She dialed the house number only to hear a cold, impersonal message about a disconnected line. When she tried the Ohio number, it rang endlessly. She wrote a heartfelt letter addressed to the Ohio residence. Days later, it returned, stamped RETURN TO SENDER. She would walk by the house each evening, peering through the overgrown hedges. But the windows remained dark.

Whispers spread through the town's grapevine. The Merritts were not returning. Their empty castle loomed on the corner as a silent sentinel. One morning, the grating sound of hammers and saws intruded on the quiet hour. A work crew was boarding up the windows. Each thud hammered another nail into the coffin.

—

ON THE DAY that marked three weeks since Quinn's disappearing act, Adrienne gripped the edges of the bathroom sink, her knuckles whitening as the room wobbled around her. Her eyes fixated on the two blue lines on the EPT test, a logical explanation for the nausea that had taken up residence in her stomach. Her future constricted with each passing second.

The reality settled over her, punctuated by the strange but

undeniable sensation of new life stirring within her. In her half-crazed state, all she could think about was that the little tadpole was Quinn's, and so that tadpole became a life raft rather than a ball and chain.

The first order was to throw out the sleeping pills the doctor had prescribed. Her hands hesitated over the bottle of antidepressants before tossing it into the trash. She would have to call a doctor immediately and get an appointment.

Then, she took a shower. Her first one in a week or more. The hot water woke her from her fog. She couldn't stop touching her belly. A seismic shift happened within her as water droplets cascaded down her back, washing away her selfish self-pity. Nothing else mattered but keeping this budding human inside her alive and healthy. When Adrienne stepped out of the shower, her reflection seemed to stare back with new, unyielding eyes—a woman hardened and reshaped by destiny.

―

GRAN SAT ON the porch, her hands nimbly maneuvering a needle through the fabric, weaving patterns as intricate as the thoughts swirling through Adrienne's mind.

"I'm pregnant," Adrienne announced. Just an hour ago, those two blue lines had redrawn the map of her life. The path was irrevocable.

She stood at the door, waiting for Gran to respond. The woman's eyes narrowed, her gaze turning icy.

"How could you do this to me?" she finally said, throwing down her supplies. "How could you make the same stupid mistake your mother did?"

The rage built as Gran stood. Adrienne backed into the house a step, her mind returning to her younger years—to the swift sound of Gran's footsteps and the whistling wooden spoon that always seemed to find its mark. It had been many years since such an episode, but Adrienne wasn't convinced it couldn't happen now. And even though

Gran was starting to show the common signs of old age, Adrienne didn't think for one moment that the old woman wouldn't catch her.

"I sacrificed much of my life to ensure you wouldn't fuck up like your mother. And what do you do? You fuck up your life just like she did." Gran's hands shot up, rigid with incredulity as her voice scaled the octaves. "We are cursed! You hear me!"

Then her voice turned chillingly calm. "I want you out of this house. Today. You should not be here when I come back." She then went down the steps and left Adrienne alone on the porch.

Christopher showed up at dusk, just as Adrienne finished packing the back of her grandfather's old Ford truck. Adrienne glared at the truck, silently bargaining with it to last long enough to reach Seaside.

"This is a surprise. I'm glad to see you're back in the world," Christopher said, leaning against the rusty red bed. "Where are you going?"

"I'm knocked up, and Gran kicked me out, so I'm getting the hell out of here." Adrienne slammed shut the tailgate, hooking a bungee cord across it for extra insurance.

His eyes widened, the corners of his mouth pulling down. "Where will you go?"

"My mom has a condo up in Seaside. She never uses it unless she has some layover till her next sailing gig." Adrienne glanced down the driveway. "I'm going to get a job cooking up there. It's a big touristy spot. I'll get my GED, and when the baby comes . . ."

She stopped and wiped the sweat from her brow. She felt like an actor reciting someone else's lines.

Christopher said nothing, his face a canvas of helplessness.

"Well, I'll figure out what to do next when the time comes," she finished. Her hands trembled against the truck bed. It was easy to act tough, but her body threatened to give her away. Inside, she was mush.

Every day since Lucas's death and Quinn's disappearance, Christopher's footsteps had echoed across her porch, breaking up the endless stretch of hours. He would chat with Gran and bring them things from the market since Adrienne spent most of her time in bed and Gran couldn't drive well. He had even cooked them dinner a few times. It was safe to say he was her only friend left.

It was easy to be around him. He would sit with her on the porch sometimes, never prodding her to talk. He didn't seem to mind her silence or that she wore the same clothes for several days. He would put Gramps's old records on and read while she stared out at the yard. When he was around, she felt lighter. His visits had evolved into lifelines that she clung to as the days rolled on.

"You should stay, Adrienne." He put his hand on top of hers. Her eyes widened briefly at the contact. "You can't run away. There's the little apartment above the fish market. I'm buying a house, so I'll be out of there. It could be all yours. You could stay there and finish school, and I'll help you however I can. I'm sure your Gran will come around. This will blow over eventually."

She hesitated. "I . . . can't." She couldn't stay. Every mention of Lucas, every sympathetic or judgmental glance her way, would feel like a stone cast. Each visit from the society ladies would be an interrogation, their barbed questions wrapped in silk. "I don't belong here. I'm done."

She pulled her hand away and went to the driver-side door. Trailing behind her, the lines on his forehead deepening, Christopher moved awkwardly and hesitantly.

"Will you come back?" he said. In the dim light, the green in his eyes was more vivid than she remembered. "This is your home. Your Gran is the only family you have."

"No." She shook her head. "I can't waddle around here as big as a whale and have the whole town talking about me behind my back. I can't do it anymore. I can't be here where Lucas died. I can't be next to that fucking house."

"Stay, Adrienne. Stay, and we will figure this out. I will take care of you." He sank lower as if gravity were pulling him there, and his hands enveloped hers in a desperate grip.

As his voice wavered, a sudden shift unsettled her, a tectonic movement in her core that she couldn't yet name. And her body reacted with an unspoken knowing she'd later attribute to the capricious whims of pregnancy hormones.

Adrienne grabbed Christopher's head, curling her hands into his black hair, and kissed him. Their lips clashed with violence, almost bruising, yet there was an undertow of something more. Then, she pushed him aside—he didn't protest, probably too shocked by the kiss—and got in the truck. She couldn't face him, or she might stay.

It doesn't matter. No one wins whether I stay or go.

She turned the ignition, and the old Ford roared to life. Through the side mirror, she watched Christopher retreat, backing away from a war he could never win.

"Don't come after me," she said as she eased the truck back down the driveway.

Now he trailed behind her, his silhouette coming to a standstill in the middle of the road. Some force kept her eyes locked onto his dwindling figure, and even as distance and darkness swallowed him whole, the afterimage of him haunted her rearview mirror as if etched into the glass.

CHAPTER TWENTY-SEVEN
Summer 2012

Adrienne drew back from Quinn. "We can't do this."

"I know." He took a step away. His voice was firm.

Written in the stars from the day we met, as Quinn had said, we would never win.

"No more Neverland," Quinn said.

"Peter and Wendy grew up," she said, feeling lost.

Adrienne wanted to reach for that lost summer as if it were a tangible thing, something she could reshape. But it was impossible. Their relationship would live forever in childhood, but childhood was behind them.

"How did your dad die?" Her question seemed to vacuum the room of its lingering sentiment.

"I'm sure you heard all about it already." Quinn plopped onto the bed and tucked his hands under his head, contemplating the ceiling. "He was diving a new spot for the damn wreck. He came up too fast. People don't understand how all that nitrogen affects the brain. He must have gotten confused, and he drowned."

"Were you with him?"

He turned and studied Adrienne's face for a moment. "Yes."

"He was a great diver. It's hard to believe that he would die that way."

Quinn's eyes drifted away. "The sea can be unforgiving. It can take an expert. It can take a fool. It takes what it wants." His shoulders slumped wearily. "Don't ask me. That is a story I'm not willing to tell."

Adrienne tried to put herself in his place. She knew that Quinn would never do anything outright. *But could he have allowed such a thing to happen? Something easily remedied?* She recalled the time Quinn taught her how to dive. How quickly she had become disoriented. If he hadn't been there to help, she might have drowned.

It would have been easy to simply watch . . . and wait.

"What now?" Quinn tested the thin line of loyalty that would forever bind them.

"I'm glad he's dead," Adrienne said with absolute finality.

His shoulders eased.

With a shake of her head, she folded the unpleasant thoughts away, tucking them into a dark corner of her mind. "We need to think about how we go from here. We have Kali now."

"She terrifies me." A laugh escaped Quinn's lips. "She dazzles me."

"She's a teenager. They're supposed to be terrifying . . . and dazzling." Adrienne touched his shoulder. "She's a great kid. She's worth it."

"She has Lucas's eye. The same moon face." Quinn's jaw tensed, as if fighting to keep certain words from escaping.

"Yes, I've let that be a barrier between us for too long. It's a gift, not a curse. We both need to see it that way."

"I can't believe she's mine." He lifted his face, his eyes shimmering with unshed tears, the red rims revealing a vulnerability he rarely showed. There was the face of her Peter, the boy who never grew up.

She couldn't help but wonder whether each day would oscillate between such extreme feelings, leaving her like a ship tossed from cresting waves to low troughs. Time alone would weave this emotional tapestry, thread by uncertain thread.

"She is and will love you forever," Adrienne said. Each syllable came from a tender place within her.

CHAPTER TWENTY-EIGHT

The cicadas filled the last moments of darkness before morning with their buzzing and clicking as Adrienne tiptoed through the brush toward the cottage. The lush smell of salt and heat rode the breeze. It was the first time since returning to Harbor Point that Adrienne no longer felt like an outsider. The fears that had clung to her evaporated, surrendering to the advancing sun. The big white house at her back was absent of ghosts.

Instead of heading inside, Adrienne wandered to the front of the cottage. She found herself contemplating the line of mangroves guarding the Back Bay across the street. Each twisted root and leafy bough hanging over the path seemed to whisper an invitation. The dappled sunlight flickered on the mulch trail like fireflies.

Kicking off her flip-flops and leaving them in the dirt, Adrienne headed for the faint path that led deeper into the tangle of green. She navigated effortlessly, instinctively dipping her head, swaying her hips, and twisting her body to accommodate the trees.

The sun barely penetrated the crossed limbs of green above her. The tidal waters sucked out as if the sea were exhaling decades of mire to inhale afresh with the next high tide. A distant, guttural cry of a gull reached her ears, prompting her to clutch a low-hanging branch for a brief, steadying moment.

A sudden explosion of white caught her eye, stark against the green and brown. With a majestic sweep of its wings, the bird disrupted the tranquil pool, scattering droplets like stars as it ascended to the sky. A great white heron. The giant bird disappeared into the sky, its strange honking call slowly fading.

Adrenaline coursed through her veins. The urge to run came over her. The sucking sand tried to hold her feet, but she wouldn't let it. Her feet pounded a tattoo on the earth, each step a declaration of intent until she burst through the final veil of leaves, arriving at the barricade at the end of the peninsula. A jubilant laugh escaped her lips. The seething, swirling ocean pulsed in and out of the Back Bay through the cut in the land.

As a child, she stood with her feet at the waterline. It had been the edge of the world—but not its end. In that crystalline moment, as the sea roiled before her, she understood that Harbor Point wasn't just a place but a part of her.

Imagine that.

ADRIENNE GOT IN her car and let the Malibu slide down the driveway in neutral before turning the engine over, not wanting to wake Kali or Gran.

She wasn't sure exactly where Christopher's house was, but she knew it was on the street that ran alongside the market. She wandered down the sidewalk, scanning for his old Jeep until the familiar vehicle caught her eye, parked in front of a cottage painted in cheerful yellow. The house butted up against the bay, though an impenetrable wall of mangroves hid the water.

Adrienne paused her march when Christopher passed by the front picture window. Worst of all, he noticed her and waved.

There is no turning back now.

She commanded her feet to move.

He was wearing a white towel wrapped around his waist when he opened the door. Water glistened like dew against the dark strands of his hair. It was the first time she'd seen him without clothes on, and a wild vibration ran through her. His chest was smooth and tanned with fine, lean lines from all his work under the sun.

"I'm sorry I walked off last night." Her fingers curled into fists in her pockets. "It's been a roller coaster."

"Adrienne, you don't have to apologize. I'm the only one who should be begging you for forgiveness." He ran his hand through his wet hair. "I wasn't sure if I'd see you again."

Adrienne flashed him a tight smile. "Well, here I am."

"Come in for some tea?" He moved aside so she could enter, their bodies nearly touching. A briny scent clung to him despite his recent shower, mingling with his unique smell. Adrienne inhaled deeply, an unexpected thrill tingling through her. She'd never found anything more alluring.

His cozy little house matched her expectations. Bookcases stuffed with books lined the walls. Books even made up the side tables. A lone yellow couch was the only place to sit.

He led her to the kitchen. "Tea's on the stove. I'll put some clothes on and meet you in a jiff."

The kitchen, though small, was laid out with such efficiency that Adrienne could immediately see Christopher's careful hand in its design. Every surface was well maintained, and every tool was thoughtfully placed. She pulled the screaming teakettle off the flame and poured the water into the teapot, ready with loose tea.

Peering out the back door to the yard, she spied his impressive garden: spiraling heirloom tomato vines and topiaries of rosemary and thyme; lush beds of field greens providing the backdrop to a patchwork of flowers in every color imaginable. Adrienne's eyes widened in admiration. This was not something she had expected from Christopher—yet another surprise in a day that seemed full of them.

Everything he touches seems to flourish.

But the biggest surprise awaited her when she stepped outside: *The Dolly,* her grandfather's boat, up on a boat trailer. The wood gleamed in the late morning, fresh navy paint on the hull, all barnacles scraped off, chrome shining. Memories rushed back with a sting of tears.

"Pet project. I've been working on her for a few years in my spare time." Christopher stood close behind her, the warmth of his body seeping pleasantly into her despite the hot summer air. "She's been a rather royal pain in the butt. I found her sunk right to the bottom of the Back Bay, still tied to the dock. Your Gran sold her to me for a few bucks. It cost me a mint to raise and haul her, but I couldn't let her go."

"She'll last a hundred years, I think. I should have taken her when your gramps offered, but I didn't have the heart to take her away from you."

"She's beautiful. I always loved that boat." Adrienne's voice hitched.

As they returned to the cottage, her eyes were drawn to a photograph hanging on the wall by the small dinette. Recognition dawned. She traced her fingers over the cool glass, absorbing the beauty of the image that held her silhouette frozen in time. The image captured a moment of pure serenity, an outline embraced by the rising sun, filled with promise and beauty.

"Now I'm embarrassed," Christopher said behind her.

She turned to him.

"When did you take this?"

"I didn't. Your grandfather did. I found a roll of film at the market a few years after you left. I had it developed. This was on it." Christopher sat at the small table and motioned for her to do the same. "I close my eyes. I see you facing the sea, ready to tackle any wave. I hope you don't think I'm a lunatic for having it. It brings back fond memories."

Adrienne settled at his side and reached up, touching his face.

"Last night, I was thinking about the last day before I left and how you were there. You were always there for me. I see now. I think I understand."

"I remember," he said as gray colored his face. "Did you and Quinn talk?"

"Yes."

"Do you want to talk about it?"

Her stomach somersaulted. "You need to know that I think I might be in love with you."

He smiled and bowed his head a bit. "That's an excellent thing because I was going mad. I didn't want to be the first one to say it. Last night, I thought it was all over and done with."

Adrienne took a deep breath. "I nearly kissed him. I don't want to keep anything from you. Secrets got me into this mess in the first place."

Christopher regarded her then, his face full of contemplation. Methodically, he removed his glasses and wiped them with a cloth as though using the action to collect his thoughts.

"It was difficult but worth it," she pressed on, the vault now unsealed. "I think I can forgive myself—let go of the blame I've held about Lucas's death all these years. Just talking and saying everything out loud was overwhelming. We both got caught up in it for a moment. But that part of our lives is over, and we can never reclaim it. We are not those kids anymore."

By the time she finished, her breath was an uneven staccato, and her heart seemed lodged in her throat. Secrets had always been her silent guardians, protecting her from immediate fallout. The truth, meanwhile, was a ruthless judge, delivering its verdict and punishment in quick succession without granting the luxury of bracing for the impact.

"Adrienne." Christopher held out his hand for her. "You must know that nothing you could say or do would change how I feel for you."

She let out the breath she had been holding and sat on his lap, pushed his glasses up on his nose, and kissed him softly. She pressed into him, feeling the chasm between them close. And she allowed herself to be swept away.

Christopher pulled her up with him. A breeze came in through the window above the sink. She could smell the herbs in his garden and the faint exhaust from a boat on the hidden bay. The old tin clock clattered the seconds off above the back door. A cricket chirped somewhere behind the fridge.

She was amused by how she dug her fingers into the meaty parts of his back, surprised by how she hoisted herself upon him, wrapping her legs around his waist. He wrapped his arms around her and carried her to his tiny bedroom.

Adrienne didn't overthink it. Christopher's mouth left little hot patches along her neck that cooled as he moved to her shoulder. His lips touch the base of her throat. She inhaled deeply and let it out slowly. The heat built in her toes and rose through her body, curling and blistering, awakening primal, reckless instincts within her.

She stepped into the unknown with no hesitation.

—

A FEW HOURS later, she lay drained, loose, her body taken apart and reassembled, her essence altered. Even the light filtering through the small window seemed that of a different sun, casting a new hue across the room, on them, on everything. He lay beside her, his eyes closed, and she contemplated leaving. *What am I supposed to say to him now?* It would be impossible to look him in the eye without Christopher knowing he had unglued her and then reshaped the pieces in some strange new form. She knew not who she was now.

With a tremor of uncertainty, she attempted to slip from the bed, her movements careful and clandestine.

Too late. Christopher turned to her and smiled. He cupped her face, his hands roughened by years of fishing and cooking. As he pulled her closer, excitement flushed through her.

But the falling night demanded her attention. There was so much to do for the final evening of the gala. As she tried to leave again, his hand on her arm was firm. Confident.

"Stay. Just stay," Christopher urged.
"We have work to finish. Two hours till the tent opens."
"Fuck the work. Stay forever." He tightened his grip on her hand. And she stayed.

CHAPTER TWENTY-NINE

The gala was over. The final dinner went off without a hitch, and Adrienne savored the applause from the guests. She also allowed herself to appreciate how red Tessa's face got when Christopher kissed her full on the lips during her standing ovation.

Now Harbor Point would slow and return to its sleepy summer pace. Adrienne flung open all the cabinets in the kitchen and went to work. When Kali entered the kitchen, the shelves were bare, stark white, and smelling of pine and bleach.

"What's going on here?" Kali paused at the kitchen threshold, her arms crossed, eyebrows arching up.

Adrienne's eyes flicked to the sponge in her hand. "Tidying up the place. Dinner's next on the list." She tossed Kali a damp kitchen towel. "I wanted to tell you I spoke with your father. We decided to focus on ensuring you get what you need from both of us."

"Well, well, seems someone found the adulting manual," Kali quipped, her voice tinged with playful sarcasm.

"I'm sorry, Kali. What it comes down to is this: I was really messed up by what happened back then. It's affected my whole life and made me a shitty parent. But things are going to get better now. So can you give me a chance to fix things? It's hard for me to talk about, but I want you to know everything."

They locked eyes like gunslingers waiting for the other to draw. Finally, the hard edge in Kali's eyes dissolved.

"Alright," she finally said. "So, does that mean we're going to stay?"

"Hmm. Do you want to stay?"

Kali shrugged. "It would be cool to go to the same school as Tam. But if we stay, we stay until I finish high school. I don't want to be moving around and starting over again."

"It won't be easy." Adrienne's thoughts bounced from Christopher's smile to her complicated history with Quinn, Gran's presence, and the quaint market chaos. "But I think it will be worth it."

"Weird." Kali smirked. "I'll be going to your old high school."

"Totally weird."

For an hour, the room whispered with the scrape of scouring pads against pans and the swish of water swirling down the drain. A rhythm developed between them, like a well-oiled machine preparing to shift into its next gear: dinner. Adrienne piled the damp, clean dishes in fearless stacks wherever there was a clear spot on the counter.

There was as much history here as in the closets: Tupperware from Tupperware's inception in once cheerful colors with lids that never did what they claimed to do. There were rusted ricers and hand-cranked whisks with gears that sang hoarse, creaky songs as they beat eggs into omelets. The yellowed pastry cloth was bready and full of the sweet wheat of a thousand pie crusts. Gran's favorite knife had come to this country with her father. The steel, now black and tired, spoke of generations of tomatoes, cabbages, chickens, and watermelons. The cookware also murmured their stories as they clanged, banged, and clinked in the wash pan.

Kali's towel glided over the contours of each utensil, and she marveled aloud at the craftsmanship, the way even the tiniest screw or spring seemed to hold a purpose, like brushstrokes in a masterpiece. It became clear to Adrienne why Gran had kept it all. Why Gran had been so resistant to throwing out a single thing.

Gran slipped quietly into the kitchen. Adrienne turned from the sink and found her sitting in her assigned chair at the table. Her weathered hands rested in her lap. They had not spoken since their late-night encounter. Still, it didn't seem to concern Gran as she sat in the pose from Kali's portrait.

A mere handful of Gran's words had been the turning tide, an implied permission to let go, transforming the landscape like the first rays of dawn. She too had been trapped but, unlike Adrienne and Diana, had never escaped.

"We're going to make paprikash, Gran," Adrienne said, pulling items out of the fridge and putting them on the counter.

The air lightened. Adrienne moved with a renewed fluidity, no longer dragging the chains of yesterday's anger.

They got to work on dinner. Adrienne poached the chicken thighs until the meat was soft and silky and fell off the bone. She stood behind Kali and showed her how to pick out the gristle and fat and shred the meat to drink the cream sauce. Adrienne took out the unglazed beige mortar, stuck her face into the bowl, and inhaled the memory of a hundred years of spices crushed into the soul of the pottery. Adrienne showed Kali how to grind the sweet dried red peppers, holding her hand to show her how to gently move the pestle around the bowl. The peppers turned into a cloud of fine dust, releasing the sweet, earthy scents that bit at the back of her tongue.

They added the chicken and paprika to the pan of golden chicken broth. They slowly added the sour cream, making sure it didn't scald. Adrienne hesitated, her eyes darting to Gran. *Is it time to add the bay leaves or the ginger?*

She began to push the stiff yellow dough down through the small holes of the ricer, pausing before the first spaetzle fell. Gran nodded once, letting Adrienne know she was on the right track.

"I changed the recipe," Gran said, almost dreamlike. "Spaetzle is from Germany. You should use Hungarian dumplings. They are heavier than the spaetzle, but your grandfather's mother was from Germany, and he preferred them, so I made it that way."

"Cool," Kali said.

Adrienne's eyes strayed to Gran every so often after that, finding her in tranquil repose, eyes sealed shut, her breaths long as if she were absorbing every scent, every sound of the culinary ritual.

A noticeable change had washed over Gran since the night before. Perhaps Adrienne's words had finally landed, settling into Gran's fortified resolve. It would mark a milestone.

It wasn't that. A familiar intuition prickled her skin, an acute awareness that wove into her nerves, murmuring of transformations only she could sense.

She paused and looked out the window. "Storm's coming."

"You could always tell," Gran replied, and Adrienne was surprised the old lady had heard her. "You inherited the gift of perception from my mother. It passed me by, but you always could tell when a change was coming. In Hungary, they called her *boszorkány*. Witch. But it was not an evil thing. People knew that she was sensitive."

"I never knew this," Adrienne said.

"You never asked."

And Gran was right about that.

You always remember the bad stuff, Adrienne: Her mother's well-worn refrain whenever Adrienne listed the trials she had to endure living with Gran. Adrienne begged Diana to come and get her. Crinkled letters tucked away in a drawer and sparse phone calls were all her mother had to offer.

But Diana was right for the most part.

The kitchen became an alchemist's lab, each ingredient subtly transforming the atmosphere, unlocking a vault of childhood memories. Now Adrienne looked back and saw only the moments of light and warmth in the kitchen, the womb of the cottage. It was here that Gran's demeanor would shift. Her voice would soften, her hands moving deliberately as she guided Adrienne's youthful fingers. When Gran stood by her side, instructing her on the precise moment to turn the roast, the older woman's patience draped around Adrienne like a shawl, reassuring her that here, at least, mistakes were merely stepping stones.

The image of Gran working a lump of dough on the counter, her sleeves rolled up to show the powerful muscles in her arms, a bright-red bandanna tied around her head to keep the sweat out of her eyes, came to Adrienne. She realized the beauty she had overlooked all those years ago. A wistful ache settled into her chest. Each moment since then seemed like a missed chance, a door once open that had swung silently closed over time.

—

THEY SAT IN front of their plates at the table. After a long pause, Gran's eyes slipped shut, her lips parting for a soft murmur as if each bite were a verse in an old love song known only to her taste buds.

Kali smiled at Adrienne. "This is so good."

Adrienne brushed her fingers against Kali's cheek and returned the smile.

"So, what happened today?" Adrienne asked as she tore a chunk of bread from the loaf.

"They hung my portrait of Gran."

Kali prattled on between bites. Adrienne rested her chin on her hand and listened to her daughter's animated words.

Has there ever been such a night?

CHAPTER THIRTY

Only Adrienne knew the recipe for her grandfather's fisherman's stew. It had never been written down, instead getting passed on to her through the daily creation of the mesmerizing dish. Even her grandmother wasn't privy to the recipe. Gramps was not what anyone would call a cook, but his stew brought the market some notoriety as more than a place to buy fish. When Adrienne asked where he got the recipe, he told her a wild tale.

In his youth, Adrienne's grandfather had been a driver and companion for a wealthy widow residing in Palm Beach. The widow seemed to brighten even the dimmest room, her kindness leaving an indelible impression on those around her.

Every winter, the woman went on holiday to her great house on the tip of a peninsula in Haiti. There the woman employed a cook from the local village. The cook had mastered harnessing the sea's flavors using the abundant local ingredients. Every evening, Adrienne's grandfather found himself at a dining table set for two, breaking bread with the lonely widow and savoring culinary masterpieces that seemed to defy description.

A tantalizing aroma wafted from the kitchen one evening, so irresistible that Gramps found himself drawn as if by an invisible string. The cook hovered over a large pot. When he asked her what she was making, she replied, "This isn't just a stew; it's an heirloom," stirring the pot gently. "A liquid love spell passed down through the women in my family for generations."

Of course, Gramps wasn't buying it. The real magic was the taste. He begged the cook to teach him how to make it, and she agreed. He brought the recipe back with him. The recipe lay in a drawer for years, decades, gathering dust while life took precedence, until Gramps found himself staring at retirement papers and an empty calendar. That's when Adrienne arrived, like a burst of color in a monochrome world.

"I took one look at you, and everything fell into place," Gramps had told her. "I know it sounds silly, but that's what happened. I figured I would buy a little market, sell fish, and cook the stew for hungry fishermen. I knew we'd be okay."

The stew became a local legend, its rich flavors permeating the kitchen so often that the air seemed to be composed of its scent. Adrienne had not made a pot since her grandfather's death.

Its aroma now permeated the cozy kitchen, the simmering pot a love letter inked in spices and sealed with steam. Soon, Kali appeared, lured by the heady stew.

"What is that?" She stood on her tiptoes, trying to peer into the tall pot.

"Magic," Adrienne said as she chopped up an onion. She put Kali to work and shared the story of the fish stew.

Christopher appeared next, clad in worn fisherman overalls and black galoshes that had seen their share of ocean spray. He looked like a man ready to wrestle the sea for its treasures. "What is going on here? I could smell it all the way from the bridge."

Adrienne leaned over the pot, inhaling deeply, hoping to catch the subtle note that signaled the stew's readiness. He came to the stove and stood close to her. "God, that is a pot of memories. You haven't made it since he passed."

Adrienne continued with her story. "He made it for Gran on their first date. He was convinced it made the stubborn old coot fall in love with him."

Christopher's gaze lingered on the stew for a heartbeat before he reached for a spoon. Holding it aloft, he turned toward Adrienne, eyes questioning. "Taste test?"

Adrienne nodded, dipped a spoon into the yellow, brackish elixir, and gently blew on it to cool it off. The flavors hadn't peaked; the fish bones still had more to offer the simmering broth, and the pot needed more time to marry. Nevertheless, she carefully brought the spoon to his lips.

He savored the mouthful, then met her eyes. "It is certainly magic." He took the spoon from her hand and placed it on the counter. "I can understand why your Gran was helpless to its spell."

"Give it a few more hours, and it will transcend to a full-blown spell," she said, leaning closer.

"Geeze, you two. There's a child here, remember?" Kali's tone was sarcastic, but she spoke with a smile.

"Quite right." Christopher straightened up. "I will return for dinner."

He gave Kali a little bow and shot a wink at Adrienne before heading to the marina.

"Is he always so . . . shiny?" Kali asked after they heard the front door shut.

"Yep," Adrienne said, laughing.

GRAN WAS SILENT through dinner. She ate the stew without remark or criticism, though she had not tasted the stew for fifteen years.

Once everyone finished and Christopher kissed Adrienne goodbye and headed home, Gran rose from the table and disappeared into the great room. When she returned, she set an old shoebox at the table. Kali lifted the lid to find black-and-white photos inside. Adrienne's eyes widened as she peered into the box, taking in the stacks of old images. Gran never threw anything out. Around them, the cottage walls bore testament to Gran's obsession, a jumble of frames and faces from eras long gone. Adrienne recalled countless hours poring over thick photo albums as a child, each page a glimpse into an unfathomable family history. But she had never seen these photos.

Adrienne picked up a few images from the top of a stack. They showed Gran as a young girl. Adrienne had seen very few pictures of Gran before she married Gramps. This was a vital, beautiful young woman dressed in a sequined outfit and an outrageous hat. Sorrow twinged in Adrienne's chest as she studied the joyful young woman in the photo, trying to reconcile this distant happiness with the Gran she knew.

"I was such a good dancer. I was going to be a star." Gran bent between them, touching the girl in the photo with the tips of her fingers. "I was never going to be married or have children. I was going to know the world. I was going to make men want me."

Gran eased into her chair, a wistful smile playing at the corners of her mouth. "I was in love. Not with your grandfather. Another man. He was my dance partner. We had such plans. We dreamed of New York and leaving this terrible little town."

"You never did get to New York, did you?" As Kali spoke, her fingers delicately touched a gold filigree clip holding her hair in place. Adrienne recognized it immediately. It was one of Gran's, a relic now finding new life.

"No, I would never have returned if I had the chance to leave." Gran's gaze wandered to the window, her eyes seemingly sifting through years as they settled on the fading horizon. "If you think this town has nothing now, you should have seen it when I was young."

As Gran's voice waned like a distant radio signal, Adrienne unconsciously leaned closer. "What happened to the man you loved?"

"I couldn't go. I realized I was all that remained of the Harris family, and we would be erased if I left. I felt a duty to my father to stay and preserve our family's history. This gossip-riddled town had its theories on my father's lost fortune. Many believed he had stolen the money that made him a rich man. I heard the whispers. Sometimes, depending on the day, he was a bank robber, swindler, or bootlegger." A wry chuckle escaped Gran's lips, a sound caught somewhere between amusement and regret. "Some thought he had buried the money somewhere or pissed it all away on the horses. They were all wrong, of course. If I left, there would be no one to make sure the correct history was told. So my beau left with another girl from our dance studio, and they headed to New York."

Adrienne and Kali exchanged glances.

"Where did the money come from then?" Kali finally asked when Gran had lost her train of thought.

"I have no clue, nor did I ever ask him. Children back then did not question adults. If they did, they got the strap." Gran's brow arched upward, returning a trace of severity to her wistful expression. "A lost practice that could benefit today's youth."

"No theories? I always thought rich men liked to boast about their skill at making money. Mr. Merritt was never shy about talking about his expedition company," Adrienne commented, intrigued.

"It was always known that it came from Hungary with him. Family money from the old country. My father did not talk much but occasionally would mention we came from a royal lineage, Hungarian royalty." On cue, Gran removed an ancient tintype photo from the box. It was faded, and the woman in the image was disappearing from time and wear, but an ornate dress that flowed out around her and a crown on her head could still be made out. "The royal family ended rule in 1918, and Hungary became a republic. We were not allowed to tell people because my father was in exile, and he never told us why."

Kali's eyebrows knit together, her lips pressing into a thin line as she processed Gran's tale. "I'm going to go to the library tomorrow and try to figure this all out."

A soft chuckle escaped Adrienne's lips, tinged with disbelief; yet she was reluctant to dismiss Gran's vivid storytelling. "It certainly is a wild story."

Gran's face tightened into a scowl. "Believe it or not. But I couldn't allow my father's name to be tarnished. Then your grandfather came into town for the season. He was handsome. All the girls thought he was something special, and he liked me. I was so heartbroken over my decision to stay that I went wild. And then I was pregnant with your mother. Back then, there was no choice but to get married. And though I had chosen to stay, I had no hope of ever leaving after that."

Kali insisted on clearing the dishes on her own.

Gran's eyes drifted back to the window. "I'm tired," she murmured, the words sagging under the weight of regrets. The animation with which she had shared her recollections had vanished.

She rose gracefully from her chair, melting into the hallway's darkness. Kali and Adrienne followed her up the stairs to her room and perched on the edge of the bed as Gran settled before her vanity, its gilded frame gleaming softly, and began her nightly ritual.

Adrienne thought of how, as a little girl, she would sit on the bed as Gran readied for a party. Gran would sit at her dressing table and take up the paddle brush, pulling it through her wispy hair. Lightly touching her cheek, she would spy Adrienne in the mirror, her eyes twinkling. "You're lucky, my girl. This skin of mine is your inheritance. It's the kind that women my age dreaming they'd have."

Once she had removed all her jewelry and applied the silky cream to her face and the backs of her hands, Gran picked up a framed photo of her with Gramps on their wedding day. Her eyes lingered on the photograph, tracing the younger contours of her face and the man beside her. A moment passed before she gently set the frame back in its place.

"Maybe your father buried the money somewhere in the yard. Many did that back in the day because they distrusted the banks after the Depression."

"I did try to find it, but I never found a cent. If money is out there, my father took its location to his grave."

Images of Mr. Merritt armed with a metal detector and wading through muddy fields in his endless quest for buried treasure flitted through Adrienne's mind. She felt a spectral hand tracing down her back. So, this was the genesis of what Gran had coined the Harris curse.

"Do you hear something? I swore I heard..." Gran's hand extended toward the windowpane as if to catch a whisper from beyond it. "Is someone passing by on the street? It sounded like humming."

Adrienne went to the window, but no one was on the road. "There's no one there."

"Close the window, child. I don't think I could sleep if I heard it again." Gran eased onto the edge of the bed, her posture stooped.

Adrienne went to the walk-in closet next to the master bathroom. The teak shutter doors let out a reluctant screech as Adrienne pushed them back. She removed one of Gran's filmy movie-star nightgowns. Even when she slept, Gran had to look her best.

"You are a good cook." Gran's eyelids drooped shut. "You should add more recipes to the Harris box. They have a place in our histories. We may not get much right in this world, but the Harris women know how to cook." She swayed gently on her perch, to some internal tune only she could hear.

Adrienne slipped the chiffon sheath over her grandmother's head.

"No, there is nothing there. These ears are playing such tricks on me." Gran laid her head on the pillow, letting out a great sigh. "Ah, yes, that is nice," she said, her eyes closed, hands folded on her chest.

Adrienne touched Gran's hands. The skin was warm, silky, and flimsy like gold leaf.

"You could have left this place, Gran. You could have been happy," she said softly. "Like I did. Like Diana did. You could have escaped."

"A baby and a husband were the life I was given." Gran's eyes began to flutter, and her breathing deepened.

Kali and Adrienne stayed until she was asleep.

—

DOWNSTAIRS, KALI GRAVITATED to the sink and began washing up the dinner dishes. The window was open, letting the breeze in. The rays of the evening sun enveloped Adrienne as she stood next to her daughter, automatically reaching for the wet plates.

"I was thinking, maybe I can add a recipe to the box?" Kali scrubbed a plate. "Maybe I could make dinner tomorrow night if you help me."

"I'd love to help you." Adrienne leaned in, her nose brushing the soft strands of Kali's hair, and she kissed the top of her daughter's head, sealing a promise.

"Maybe Christopher could come over again for dinner?" Adrienne said casually.

"You like him." Kali nodded to herself. "He's a little old but seems kind of cool."

"I like Tam. He seems like a good kid."

"He is. He wants me to join the debate club in the fall. I'm not sure about that." With a skeptical shake of her head, Kali passed another plate to Adrienne, water droplets skittering across its surface.

"Well, you might like it. One thing is for sure: The Harris women know how to argue."

Laughter bubbled between them, filling the room. Adrienne settled into the moment's comfort, light and airy as the breeze through the window.

―

LATER THAT NIGHT, Adrienne stood at the bay window in the dark living room. The old grandfather clock groaned a metallic midnight alert.

Gran's confessions remained trapped in the house with them. *Are we all serving time for the choices Elizabeth Harris made? Do we all suffer a genetic flaw passed from mother to daughter?* Whatever afflicted the Harris line of women, the cure seemed clear to Adrienne now. For Gran, the perceived remedy had always been sacrifice in the face of unyielding circumstances. Diana chased her vision of the fix by running away and never returning. Neither had worked. They blamed something external that was out of their control to fix. No Harris woman had ever turned their eye on themselves. None of them sought the antidote within.

Adrienne spied her faint reflection in the panes of glass, her image superimposed on the dark sea—a watermark etched into the town's fabric, her spirit intertwined with it, as inseparable as the roots of the banyacado tree that twisted absurdly outside the cottage. She was as much a part of this place as it was a part of her; like Quinn, she had never really left.

CHAPTER THIRTY-ONE

Gran was gone by the morning. Adrienne woke early, though she'd fallen asleep well after midnight, and found the house eerily still. Her stomach knotted. It soon became clear that the stillness stemmed from the absence of Gran's house-rattling snores.

Her footsteps hesitant, Adrienne entered Gran's room, her mind a battleground of dread and disbelief. And when she leaned over Gran's body, still and frozen, the room seemed to close around her, making real what she had feared. Adrienne shook her grandmother's arm more out of instinct than alarm. Her fingertips met a lifeless chill, reminding her of meat hanging in a butcher's window. Gran must have died not long after Adrienne and Kali helped her to bed.

Adrienne stood transfixed. She didn't experience any of the emotions she expected. She had always considered Gran an indestructible force, a constant like the North Star. After an argument with Gran, Adrienne would lie in bed and think of what the world might be like if Gran suddenly keeled over dead. It became a morbid coping mechanism to get her through her most challenging times with the old lady.

Adrienne assumed there would be a great sense of relief. The weight pressing down on her would suddenly lift, and she would have freedom. In the reality of the moment that Gran was truly gone from the world and would never again open her eyes, a lump lodged in Adrienne's throat. A heightened sense of the world filled her. The birds chattered in the trees outside the window as a strong wind blew from the east. On the street, a garbage truck rumbled by, and the slow, aching whine of the rusted fan blades from the porch whined below.

Outside, life hummed its indifferent tune. Elizabeth Harris lay motionless, her own song silenced.

The abruptness of Gran's passing left Adrienne spinning. She'd made her exit not with a bang or wild death throes but with a whisper.

Elizabeth Harris would show them all and go quietly.

Adrienne recalled Gran's penchant for wearing flamboyant hats to club and arguing politics at family dinners—a contrarian to the very end. There had never been a world without Gran, without the unwavering scrutiny in her eyes dissecting Adrienne's choices like an unforgiving Jiminy Cricket, and Adrienne tried to grasp what tomorrow would hold.

She sighed and sat at the edge of the bed. Without thought, she clipped Gran's favorite brass barrettes into the thin mat of the fearsome woman's hair. She touched a bit of Gran's favorite orange lipstick to her lips and smudged rosy-pink rouge on each cheek. Then Adrienne slipped on Gran's beloved silver lamé ballet house slippers. When she was sure Gran was perfect, she went downstairs to make the call. She couldn't allow Gran to make her final departure in anything less than her full regalia.

When she called Christopher, he didn't answer. She checked the clock and found it was six in the morning. There was a good chance he was at the marina to meet the fishing fleet. A moment after she hung up, the phone rang.

"Is something wrong?" Christopher asked.

"Gran's gone. She died sometime last night. I found her," Adrienne said, her voice hitching in her throat.

Breath escaped him like a leaky balloon.

"I'm on my way," he said.

Adrienne realized she didn't technically need him to be there. Yet, somehow, she knew he would come, as dependable as the tide.

Adrienne found Kali in the kitchen eating a bowl of cornflakes and hesitated. Kali was so young, even though she'd start high school in a few weeks. Gran had only been part of her life for a handful of moments. Adrienne didn't know what to expect when she broke the news.

"Gran is gone." Adrienne kneeled beside her at the table and put her hand on her daughter's. "She died last night."

Kali turned to the window, trying to hide that she was crying.

"I was starting to get used to her, you know." She wiped the tears from her cheeks.

"I know," Adrienne said as she regarded Gran's empty seat at the kitchen table. The world seemed to hesitate, unsure of its next move.

—

THEY WENT INTO the garden and collected clippings of Gran's favorite flowers. Once they had amassed a proper bouquet, they climbed the stairs side by side and went to Gran's room. Kali tucked the flowers Gran loved so dearly into her clasped hands. Adrienne slid a favorite orchid into her hair. They stood there for a while. Adrienne studied Gran's face, finding an unfamiliar tranquility.

"What happens now? To us?" Kali asked as they descended the stairs and went back outside. They sat on the porch steps, waiting for Christopher.

Adrienne shook her head. "I really don't know."

"Can we still stay here?" Kali's voice trembled, and Adrienne heard a fleeting echo of her daughter at four years old.

"Whatever happens, Kali"—she wrapped her arm around her, and this time, her daughter leaned into the embrace instead of pulling away—"I promise you; Harbor Point is our home."

CHAPTER THIRTY-TWO

A tropical storm unleashed its fury on the day of Gran's funeral. Rain flooded the roads, and debris scattered across the driveway. Adrienne wrestled with fallen branches for twenty minutes, her wet clothes clinging to her skin before they could even leave the house.

A low moan of wind wormed inside the funeral parlor as the squall lines came through. Adrienne sat in the first row with Kali, and Christopher stood at the door, greeting the guests and helping them situate their wet umbrellas. Surprisingly, most of the town had braved the storm to attend. The room was jammed with faces from her childhood and new faces she didn't know. Among the mourners, Adrienne spotted a few with whom Gran had long-standing feuds. She couldn't help but think that Gran would relish the irony of them paying their respects.

Quinn appeared in the reception area, and Christopher tensed. His nod was polite but strained as he gestured for Quinn to take a seat. Adrienne pondered the two men from her vantage point. Two circles in a Venn diagram, connected by a tiny sliver of overlapping space. Could they all inhabit that small, elusive space? Adrienne rounded her shoulders and took a deep breath. *We will find out soon enough, won't we?*

Quinn slipped into the row right behind them. Both Adrienne and Kali turned in their seats to chat.

"Kali, I am so sorry you must go through this. It's unfair to lose someone, especially since you only met her a few months ago." Quinn's voice cracked as he spoke.

"Thanks, Dad," Kali said. They all paused, letting the idea and the word acclimate to their little circle. "She was a tough old lady."

"That she was," Quinn said, smiling. "I hope you will come over later. I want to show you some of my mom's things you might like. She was a painter too, though she never showed her work."

Kali was clearly fighting to keep her return smile restrained. "Sure."

Adrienne kept quiet as the two navigated the conversation, but inside, she was reeling.

"I'm sure you must be thinking a million things right now." Quinn turned his attention to Adrienne, placing an unsure hand on her shoulder.

There was the weight but not the spark. It was just a touch. Yet her arm quivered at her side, begging to place her hand on his. Adrienne willed the instinct to lie down and nodded in agreement.

"I'm sure it will take many years of unpacking to sort through it all."

Christopher settled next to Adrienne in the front row. Like a lighthouse guiding ships in the fog, he had an uncanny ability to show up when she was most adrift. He rested his arm along the back of the bench behind her. The touch of his hand on the nape of her neck sent warm currents through her. As she turned to look at Christopher, his eyes met hers.

Kali's portrait of the great Elizabeth Harris sat on an easel beside the casket. Adrienne couldn't help but think of all the little brass plaques scattered around town, bearing her grandmother's name, and snickered under her breath as the reverend read a passage from the Bible about the sins of vanity. The reverend's voice rose, and Adrienne pictured Gran rolling her eyes. It was a peculiar sight. Gran, who never uttered a prayer, had arranged for a minister to bless her farewell. Adrienne figured it was an insurance policy just in case God proved real.

Before she knew it, the sermon was over. A seemingly endless stream of people from town lined up to speak. Laughter broke out as one man recalled how Gran had tried to organize a "moonlight raccoon hunt" one summer in search of the varmint she was sure was eating her amaryllis. Another teary-eyed woman described how Gran's apple pie could mend hearts. The room was a mosaic of Gran's oddities and endearing qualities, and she enveloped the mourners like ocean mist. She might have departed the world, but she had left her mark all over Harbor Point. And Adrienne was glad for it.

Christopher was the last to take the pulpit.

"She was a grand old dame. This town will never be the same now that she has made her exit. All we can do is keep telling her stories, keep her spirit alive."

Then, it was over.

SHE FOUND CHRISTOPHER on the steps, holding a black umbrella. He waved for Adrienne and Kali to join him. Adrienne smiled, and she and Kali ducked under the umbrella. They all moved quickly through the rain to the car.

Adrienne had anticipated . . . more. It was hard to explain. Amid the chatter and memories, she found a stillness within herself, a serene pool that surprised her. Considering their turbulent history, she'd braced for a tempest. Even as calm settled over her, she stood on the edge of a cliff, waiting for the wind to shift, for some final act of Gran's to surprise her again. For the proverbial shoe to drop.

THE RAIN PAUSED as they arrived home, as if to remove all distraction from the astonishing scene that awaited.

The banyacado had been felled at last.

The surviving half was uprooted and on its side.

Adrienne gaped. "All the things this tree has been through, and a tropical storm took it down?"

"Will it die?" Kali said as she laid a hand on a branch.

"I don't know. I'm no expert like Gran."

Quinn emerged on the other end of the banyacado, his face framed by the wreckage of the wall the tree had toppled. He took it in as if regarding a fallen titan.

"I'm glad your grandmother and my father are not here to see this." Quinn ran a hand through his hair.

"How prophetic." Christopher smiled as they stood at the hole's edge, gazing at the giant root system.

A strange patch of yellow glimmered among creepy crawlies frantically trying to conceal their nakedness.

"What the hell?" Adrienne said. She scooted into the hole without thinking of her dress and began digging with her bare hands to expose what she had seen.

"Holy shit," Quinn said from behind her. Soon, he and Kali were at her side in the mud, digging. Mud-caked and panting, they finally straightened. In their hands, glinting against the black earth, lay flat gold bars, each no bigger than the palm of Adrienne's hand but heavy.

"Holy crap, Mom!"

"My God, do you think it's the treasure from the wreck your father was seeking?" Adrienne gasped.

Christopher slid down into the pit with them.

"He was right," Quinn's voice cracked as he cleared mud off the gold bar. "All these years, he was right. The treasure was right under his nose."

Adrienne's eyes widened as recollections of Gran's stories about her father and the tree merged into a coherent whole.

"Could it be? My great-grandfather didn't just plant this tree. He marked a treasure," Adrienne mumbled, almost to herself, hearing Gran recount her father's peculiar obsession with the tree for the first time in a new light. She regarded Quinn with wonder. "If your father had his way back then, he would have found it."

Christopher looked at the mud-covered trio, gold bars in hand, and then at the uprooted tree. He put his hands on his hips, an amused smirk crossing his face. "Can you imagine the row Bob and Elizabeth would have created then!"

Adrienne's laughter erupted, uncontrollable and liberating.

EPILOGUE

The whole town congregated on the lawn of the Harris cottage, spilling into the Merritts' yard now that the terrible concrete wall had been entirely demolished. They were there to celebrate the dedication of the new Harris-Merritt South Florida History Museum. News vans with satellite dishes had started showing up within days of the gold discovery, their reporters buzzing like flies, eager to tell the world about Harbor Point's new claim to fame.

No event in Harbor Point could exist without a succession of lovingly crafted casseroles, baked hams, fruit salads, and sheet cakes. Adrienne walked among her guests, a genuine smile on her face that belied her past reluctance for such social gatherings. She eagerly sampled the five-bean salads, a dish she had once avoided.

Christopher and Kali conspired about their new joint venture, a children's book about the treasure. Kali was going to illustrate it. Their heads touched while Kali sketched something on a paper napkin. As Adrienne watched Quinn blend into the conversation effortlessly, it struck her that different chapters of one's life could coexist.

On the sea-spice-laced breeze, she heard a group of kids as they ran by on the beach, screaming with sparklers trailing behind them like a comet's tail. For a moment, the whole world was alight.

Later that evening, Adrienne stood at the point and beheld the swirling sea. For a moment, the shiver of unseen eyes twisted through her belly. But Adrienne no longer feared the spirits that roamed the mangroves.

Gran's absence, on the other hand, was like an unexpected cold spot in the ocean. They had just been learning the map of each other's minds. Adrienne fingered Gran's old brass hair clip, now threaded into her dark locks.

What could have been?

As the sea ebbed and flowed before her, Adrienne let the salt air polish her memories, wash away the years of bitterness, and leave behind only the sweet ones.

She felt Christopher's presence behind her, and she turned. For a moment, they were alone in the world. He smiled a shy smile. As his lips met the back of her hand, a thrill spiraled through her.

She closed her eyes, letting Christopher pull her into his arms, and imagined a piece of herself floating out of her body, hovering higher and higher above South Road and the whole town. Beyond the barricade with the dull blinking lights at the end of South Road—warning you to go no further—there was another peninsula just out of sight. Reaching out.

It was then that Adrienne Elizabeth Harris realized that Harbor Point was, in fact, not the end of the world.

It was only the beginning.

ACKNOWLEDGMENTS

I WISH TO THANK my professors for their overwhelming support, encouragement, and guidance during my years at Florida International University. I would not be the writer I am today without you. Thank you for never allowing me to give up. I want to give a special thank-you to Lynne Barrett for always being the firm hand steering me down the right path. Finally, I would like to thank Les Standiford for his unwavering confidence in my writing and teaching abilities and all the wisdom he shared. Your words have shaped my whole life, and I would not be here without you. My life has been altered profoundly by my time spent in the creative writing program. All that you have taught me, I will carry with me. I can only hope to be as great a teacher, writer, and friend as all of you have been to me.

I also want to thank my family and friends. My mother, Bonnie Shepard, my husband, Dan Pearsall, and my sons, Hayden and Merrick Pearsall, for always supporting me, giving me time to write, and believing in me. A gal could not ask for a better family. Thank you as well to all my friends who read my work and gave me incredible feedback that shaped my stories. And to my workshop mentors, Meg Wolitzer at the Southampton Writers Workshop and Laura Lippman at the Writers in Paradise Workshop at Eckerd College, for their feedback and guidance in writing this book.

Last but never least, to my grandfather, Vernon D. Morningstar, the original storyteller, who raised me in a world full of stories and songs: Your unwavering love and devotion were and will always be my life raft. I miss you and love you every hour of every day.

www.ingramcontent.com/pod-product-compliance
Lightning Source LLC
LaVergne TN
LVHW091719070526
838199LV00050B/2468